THE BOY
IN THE
SUITCASE

**Center Point
Large Print**

**This Large Print Book carries the
Seal of Approval of N.A.V.H.**

THE BOY IN THE SUITCASE

LENE KAABERBØL
and
AGNETE FRIIS

Translated from the Danish by
Lene Kaaberbøl

CENTER POINT LARGE PRINT
THORNDIKE, MAINE

The text of this Large Print edition is unabridged.
In other aspects, this book may
vary from the original edition.
Printed in the United States of America
on permanent paper.
Set in 16-point Times New Roman type.

ISBN: 978-1-61173-352-5

Library of Congress Cataloging-in-Publication Data

Kaaberbøl, Lene.
[Drengen i kufferten. English]
The boy in the suitcase / Lene Kaaberbøl and Agnete Friis.
p. cm.
ISBN 978-1-61173-352-5 (library binding : alk. paper)
1. Crime—Fiction. 2. Denmark—Fiction. 3. Large type books.
I. Friis, Agnete. II. Title.
PT8177.21.A24D7413 2012
839.81'38—dc23
2011046593

Acknowledgments

Our sincere and deepfelt gratitude to

Anders Trolle
Daiva Povilavičienė
Henrik Friis
Henrik Laier
Inger Laier
Joana Mikalauskaitė Nørskov
Juozas Mikalauskas
Justina Mikalauskienė
Kirstine Friis
Liudvika Strakauskienė and Žemyna
    Day Care Center
Lone Emilie Rasmussen
Pranas Povilavičius

and the many others whose help and
    support made this book possible

Lene and Agnete, August 2008

THE BOY
IN THE
SUITCASE

Holding the glass door open with her hip, she dragged the suitcase into the stairwell leading down to the underground parking lot. Sweat trickled down her chest and back beneath her T-shirt; it was only slightly cooler here than outside in the shimmering heat of the airless streets. The strong smell of decaying fast food from a jettisoned burger bag did nothing to improve the flavor of the place.

There was no elevator. Step by step she manhandled the heavy suitcase down to the level where she was parked, then realized that she didn't really want it in her car until she knew what was in it. She found a relatively private spot behind some dumpsters, sheltered from security cameras and the curious gazes of passersby. The case wasn't locked, just held closed by two clasps and a heavy-duty strap. Her hands were shaking, and one of them was numb and bloodless from carrying the ungainly weight for such a distance. But she managed to unbuckle the strap and unsnap the locks.

In the suitcase was a boy: naked, fair-haired, rather thin, about three years old. The shock rocked her back on her heels so that she fell against the rough plastic surface of the dumpster. His knees rested against his chest, as if someone had folded him up like a shirt. Otherwise he would not have fit, she supposed. His eyes were closed, and his skin shone palely in the bluish glare of the fluorescent ceiling lights. Not until she saw his lips part slightly did she realize he was alive.

August

The house sat on the brink of a cliff, with an unhindered view of the bay. Jan knew perfectly well what the locals called it: the Fortress. But that was not why he looked at the white walls with a vague sense of dissatisfaction. The locals could think what they liked; they weren't the ones who mattered.

The house was of course designed by a well-known architect, and modern, in a functional-classical way, a modern take on the Swedish "funkis" trend. Neo-funkis. That's what Anne called it, and she had shown him pictures and other houses until he understood, or understood some of it, at least. Straight lines, no decoration. The view was meant to speak for itself, through the huge windows that drew the light and the surrounding beauty into the room. That was how the architect had put it, and Jan could see his point, everything new and pure and right. Jan had bought the grounds and had the old summer cottage torn down; he had battled the municipal committee until they realized that they most certainly did want him as a taxpayer here and gave the necessary permissions; he had even conquered the representative of the local Nature Society with a donation that nearly made her choke on her herbal tea. But why should he not establish a wildlife preserve? He had no interest in other people's building here, or tramping all over the place in annoying picnic herds. So there it was, his house, protected by white walls, airy and bright, and with clean uncluttered neo-funkis lines. Just the way he had wanted it.

And yet, it was *not* what he wanted. This was not how it was supposed to be. He still thought of the other place with a strange, unfocused longing. A big old pile, an unappealing mix of decaying 1912 nouveau-riche and appallingly ugly sixties additions, and snobbily expensive because it was on Strandvejen, the coast-hugging residences of the Copenhagen financial elite. But that was not why he had wanted it—zip codes meant nothing to him. Its attraction was its nearness to Anne's childhood home, just on the other side of the tall unkempt whitethorn hedge. He couldn't help but imagine it all: The large family gathered for barbecues under the apple trees, he and Anne's father in a cloud of Virginia tobacco, holding chunky tumblers of a very good Scotch. Anne's siblings by the long white patio table, with their children. Anne's mother in the swing seat, a beautiful Indian shawl around her shoulders. His and Anne's children, four or five, he had imagined, with the youngest asleep in Anne's lap. Most of all, Anne happy, relaxed, and smiling. Gathered for the Midsummer festival, perhaps, with a bonfire of their own, and yet enough of them there so that the singing sounded right. Or just some ordinary Thursday, because they felt like it, and there had been fresh shrimp on the pier that day.

He drew hungrily at his cigarette, looking out across the bay. The water was a sullen dark blue, streaked with foam, and the wind tore at his hair and made his eyes water. He had even persuaded the owner to sell. The papers were there, ready for his signature. But she had said no.

He didn't get it. It was her family, damn it. Weren't women supposed to care about such things? The nearness, the roots, the close-knit relations? All that stuff. And with a family like Anne's, so . . . right. Healthy. Loving. Strong. Keld and Inger, still obviously in love after nearly forty years. Anne's brothers, who came to the house regularly, sometimes with their own wives and children, other times alone, just dropping in because they both still played tennis at the old club. To become part of that, in such an easy, everyday manner, just next door, on the other side of the hedge . . . how could she turn that down? But she did. Quietly, stubbornly, in true Anne-fashion, without arguments or reasons why. Just no.

So now here they were. This was where they lived, he and she and Aleksander, on the edge of a cliff. The wind howled around the white walls whenever the direction was northwesterly, and they were alone. Much too far away to just drop in, not part of things, with no share in that easy, warm family communion except by special arrangement now and then, four or five times a year.

He took a last drag and tossed the cigarette away, stepping on the butt to make sure the dry grass didn't catch fire. He stood for a few minutes, letting the wind whip away the smell from his clothes and hair. Anne didn't know that he had started smoking again.

He took the photo from his wallet. He kept it there because he knew Anne was much too well raised to go snooping through his pockets. He probably should have gotten rid of it, but he just needed to look at it sometimes, needed to feel the mixture of hope and terror it inspired.

The boy was looking straight into the camera. His bare shoulders were drawn forward, as if he hunched himself against some unseen danger. There were no real clues to where the photo had been taken; the details were lost in the darkness behind him. At the corner of his mouth, one could see traces of something he had just eaten. It might be chocolate.

Jan touched the picture with one forefinger, very gently. Then he carefully put the photo away again. They had sent him a mobile phone, an old Nokia, which he would never himself have bought. Probably stolen, he thought. He dialed the number, and waited for the reply.

"Mr. Marquart." The voice was polite, but accented. "Hello. Have you decided?"

In spite of having made his decision, he hesitated. Finally the voice had to prod him on.

"Mr. Marquart?"

He cleared his throat.

"Yes. I accept."

"Good. Here are your instructions."

He listened to the brief, precise sentences, wrote down numbers and figures. He was polite, like the man on the phone. It was only after the conversation had ended that he could no longer contain his disgust and defiance. Furiously, he flung the phone away; it arced over the fence to bounce and disappear on the heathered slope beneath him.

He got back into his car and drove the rest of the way up to the house.

Less than an hour later, he was crawling about on the slope, looking for the damn thing. Anne came out onto the terrace in front of the house and leaned over the railing.

"What are you doing?" she shouted.

"I dropped something," he called back.

"Do you want me to come down and help?"

"No."

She stayed out there for a while. The wind tore at her peach-colored linen dress, and the updraft blew her fair shoulder-length hair up around her face, so that it looked as if she were falling. In free fall without a parachute, he thought, only to check that chain of thought before it could continue. It would be all right. Anne would never need to know.

It took him nearly an hour and a half to find the stupid phone. And then he had to call the airline. This was one trip he had no wish to let his secretary book for him.

"Where are you going?" asked Anne.

"Just a quick trip to Zürich."

"Is something wrong?"

"No," he said hastily. Fear had flooded into her eyes instantly, and trying to calm it was a knee-jerk reaction. "It's just a business thing. Some funds I need to arrange. I'll be back by Monday."

How had they ended up like this? He suddenly recalled with great intensity that Saturday in May more than ten years ago when he had watched

Keld walk her up the aisle. She had been fairytale pretty, in a stunningly simple white dress, pink and white rosebuds in her hair. He knew at once that the bouquet he had chosen was much too big and garish, but it hadn't mattered. He was just a few minutes away from hearing her say "I do." For an instant, his gaze caught Keld's, and he thought he saw a welcome and an appreciation there. *Father-in-law.* I'll take care of her, he silently promised the tall, smiling man. And in his mind added two promises that weren't in the marriage vows: he would give her anything she wanted, and he would protect her against everything that was evil in the world.

That is still what I want, he thought, tossing his passport into the Zürich case. Whatever the price.

Sometimes, Jučas had a dream about a family. There was a mother and a father and two children, a boy and a girl. Usually, they would be at the dinner table, eating a meal the mother had cooked for them. They lived in a house with a garden, and in the garden there were apple trees and raspberries. The people were smiling, so that one could tell they were happy.

He himself was outside the house, looking in.

But there was always the feeling that any minute now they would catch sight of him, and the father would open the door, smiling even wider, and say: "There you are! Come in, come in."

Jučas had no idea who they were. Nor could he always remember what they looked like. But when he woke, it would be with a feeling of muddled nostalgia and expectation that would stay with him all day like a tightness in his chest.

Lately he had dreamed the dream a lot. He blamed it on Barbara. She always wanted to talk about how it was going to be—him and her, and the little house just outside Krakow, close enough that her mother would need to take only one bus, and yet far enough away for them to have a bit of privacy. And there would be children. Of course. Because that was what Barbara wanted: children.

The day before it was to happen, they had celebrated. Everything was done, everything ready. The car was packed, all preparations were in place. The only thing that could stop them now was if the bitch suddenly changed her pattern. And even if she did, all they had to do was wait another week.

"Let's go to the country," said Barbara. "Let's go find someplace where we can lie in the grass and be alone together."

At first he refused on the grounds that it was best not to alter one's own pattern. People

17

remembered. Only as long as one did what one always did would one remain relatively invisible. But then he realized this might be his last day in Lithuania ever, if everything went according to plan. And he didn't really feel like spending that day selling security systems to middle-range businessmen in Vilnius.

He called the client he was due to see and canceled, telling them the company would be sending someone Monday or Tuesday instead. Barbara called in sick with "the flu." It would be Monday before anyone at Klimka's realized they had been playing hooky at the same time, and by then it wouldn't matter.

They drove out to Lake Didžiulis. Once, this had been a holiday camp for Pioneer children. Now it was a scout camp instead, and on an ordinary school day at the end of August, the whole place was completely deserted. Jučas parked the Mitsubishi in the shade beneath some pines, hoping the car wouldn't be an oven when they returned. Barbara got out, stretching so that her white shirt slid up to reveal a bit of tanned stomach. That was enough to make his cock twitch. He had never known a woman who could arouse him as quickly as Barbara. He had never known anyone like her, period. He still wondered why on earth she had picked someone like him.

They stayed clear of the wooden huts, which in any case looked rather sad and dilapidated.

Instead they followed the path past the flag hill and into the woods. He inhaled the smell of resin and sun-parched trees, and for a moment was back with Granny Edita on the farm near Visaginas. He had spent the first seven years of his life there. Freezing cold and lonely in the winter, but in the summer Rimantas moved in with *his* Gran on the neighboring farm, and then the thicket of pines between the two smallholdings became Tarzan's African Jungle, or the endless Mohican woods of Hawkeye.

"Looks like we can swim here." Barbara pointed at the lakeshore further ahead. An old swimming platform stuck into the waters of the lake like a slightly crooked finger.

Jučas stuffed Visaginas back into the box where it belonged, the one labeled "The Past." He didn't often open that box, and there was certainly no reason to mess with it now.

"There are probably leeches," he said, to tease her.

She grimaced. "Of course there aren't. Or they wouldn't let the children swim here."

Belatedly, he realized he didn't really want to stop her from taking her clothes off.

"You're probably right," he said, hastily.

She flashed him a quick smile, as though she knew exactly what he was thinking. And as he watched, she slowly unbuttoned her shirt and stepped out of her sand-colored skirt and string

19

sandals, until she stood barefoot on the beach, wearing only white panties and a plain white bra.

"Do we have to swim first?" he asked.

"No," she said, stepping close. "We can do that afterwards."

He wanted her so badly it sometimes made him clumsy like a teenager. But today he forced himself to wait. Playing with her. Kissing her. Making sure she was just as aroused as he was. He fumbled for the condom he always kept in his wallet, at her insistence. But this time she stopped him.

"It's such a beautiful day," she said. "And such a beautiful place. Surely, we can make a beautiful child, don't you think?"

He was beyond speech. But he let go of the wallet and held her for several long minutes before he pushed her down onto the grass and tried to give her what she so badly wanted.

Afterwards, they did swim in the deep, cool waters of the lake. She was not a strong swimmer, had never really learned how, so mostly she doggy-paddled, splashing and kicking. Finally she linked her hands behind his neck and let herself be towed along as he backstroked to keep them both afloat. She looked into his eyes.

"Do you love me?" she asked.

"Yes."

"Even though I'm an old, old woman?" She was

nine years older than him, and it bothered her. He didn't care.

"Insanely," he said. "And you're not old."

"Take care of me," she said, settling her head on his chest. He was surprised at the strength of the tenderness he felt.

"Always at your service," he murmured. And he thought that perhaps the family in the dream was him and Barbara, perhaps that was the point of it all—him and Barbara, in the house just outside Krakow. Soon.

Just one little thing to be done first.

S aturdays were Sigita's loneliest days.

The week went by quite quickly; there was work, and there was Mikas, and from the time she picked him up at kindergarten shortly before six, everything was done in a strict routine—cook, eat, bathe the child, tuck him in, lay out his clothes for the morning, tidy up, do the dishes, watch a little television. Sometimes she fell asleep to the drone of the news.

But Saturdays. Saturday belonged to the grandparents. From early morning the parking lot in front of their building was busy as cars were packed full of children and bags and empty wooden crates. They would return Sunday evening laden with potatoes, lettuce, and cabbage, and sometimes fresh eggs and new honey. Everyone was going "up to the country," whether the country was a simple allotment or a grandparental farm.

Sigita was going nowhere. She bought all her vegetables at the supermarket now. And when she saw little four-year-old Sofija from number 32 dash across the pavement and throw herself into the bosom of her hennaed, sun-tanned grandmother, it sometimes hurt so badly that it felt as if she had lost a limb.

This Saturday, her solution was the same as it always was—to make a thermos full of coffee and pack a small lunch, and then take Mikas to the kindergarten playground. The birch trees by the fence shimmered green and white in the sun. There had been rain during the night, and a couple of starlings were bathing themselves in the brown puddles underneath the seesaw.

"Lookmama thebirdis takingabath!" said Mikas, pointing enthusiastically. Lately, he had begun to talk rapidly and almost incessantly, but not yet very clearly. It wasn't always easy to understand what he was saying.

"Yes. I suppose he wants to be nice and clean. Do you think he knows it's Sunday tomorrow?"

She had hoped that there might be a child or two in the playground, but this Saturday they were alone, which was usually the case. She gave Mikas his truck and his little red plastic bucket and shovel. He still loved the sandbox and would play for hours, laying out ambitious projects involving moats and roads, twigs standing in for trees, or possibly fortifications. She sat on the edge of the box, closing her eyes for a minute.

She was so tired.

A shower of wet sand caught her in the face. She opened her eyes.

"Mikas!"

He had done it on purpose. She could see the suppressed laughter in his face. His eyes were alight.

"Mikas, don't do that!"

He pushed the tip of his shovel into the sand and twitched it, so that another volley of sand hit her square in the chest. She felt some of it trickle down inside her blouse.

"Mikas!"

He could no longer hold back his giggle. It bubbled out of him, contagious and irresistible. She leaped up.

"I'll get you for this!"

He screamed with delight and took off at his best three-year-old speed. She slowed her steps a bit to let him get a head start, then went after him, catching him and swinging him up in the air, then into a tight embrace. At first he wriggled a little, then he threw his arms around her neck, and burrowed his head under her chin. His light, fair hair smelled of shampoo and boy. She kissed the top of his head, loudly and smackingly, making him squirm and giggle again.

"Mamadon't!"

Only later, after they had settled by the sandbox again and she had poured herself the first cup of coffee, did the tiredness return.

She held the plastic cup to her face and sniffed as though it were cocaine. But this was not a tiredness that coffee could cure.

Would it always be like this? she thought. Just me and Mikas. Alone in the world. That wasn't how it was supposed to be. Or was it?

Suddenly Mikas jumped up and ran to the fence. A woman was standing there, a tall young woman in a pale summer coat, with a flowery scarf around her head as though she were on her way to Mass. Mikas was heading for her with determination. Was it one of the kindergarten teachers? No, she didn't think so. Sigita got hesitantly to her feet.

Then she saw that the woman had something in her hand. The shiny wrapper glittered in the sunshine, and Mikas had hauled himself halfway up the fence with eagerness and desire. Chocolate.

Sigita was taken aback by the heat of her anger. In ten or twelve very long paces, she was at the fence herself. She grabbed Mikas a little too harshly, and he gave her an offended look.

24

He already had chocolate smears on his face.

"What are you giving him!"

The unfamiliar woman looked at her in surprise.

"It's just a little chocolate. . . ."

She had a slight accent, Russian, perhaps, and this did not lessen Sigita's rancor.

"My son is not allowed to take candy from strangers," she said.

"I'm sorry. It's just that . . . he's such a sweet boy."

"Was it you yesterday? And the other day, before that?" There had been traces of chocolate on Mikas's jersey, and Sigita had had a nasty argument with the staff about it. They had steadfastly denied giving the children any sweets. Once a month, that was the agreed policy, and they wouldn't dream of diverging from it, they had said. Now it appeared it was true.

"I pass by here quite often. I live over there," said the woman, indicating one of the concrete apartment blocks surrounding the playground. "I bring the children sweets all the time."

"Why?"

The woman in the pale coat looked at Mikas for a long moment. She seemed nervous now, as though she had been caught doing something she shouldn't.

"I don't have any of my own," she finally said.

A pang of sympathy caught Sigita amidst her anger.

"That'll come soon enough," she heard herself say. "You're still young."

The woman shook her head.

"Thirty-six," she said, as though the figure itself were a tragedy.

It wasn't until now that Sigita really noticed the careful makeup designed to eradicate the slight signs of aging around her eyes and her mouth. Automatically, she clutched her son a little tighter. At least I have Mikas, she told herself. At least I have that.

"Please don't do it again," she said, less strictly than she had meant to. "It's not good for him."

The woman's eyes flickered.

"I'm sorry," she said. "It won't happen again." Then she spun suddenly and walked away with rapid steps.

Poor woman, thought Sigita. I guess I'm not the only one whose life turned out quite different from expected.

She wiped away the chocolate smears with a moistened handkerchief. Mikas wriggled like a worm and was unhappy.

"Morechoclate," he said. "More!"

"No," said Sigita. "There is no more."

She could see that he was considering a tantrum, and looked around quickly for a diversion.

"Hey," she said, grabbing the red bucket. "Why don't you and I build a castle?"

She played with him until he was caught up in the game again, the endless fascination of water and sand and sticks and the things one could do with them. The coffee had gone cold, but she drank it anyway. Sharp little grains of sand dug into her skin beneath the edge of her bra, and she tried discretely to dislodge them. Leafy shadows from the birches shimmered across the gray sand, and Mikas crawled about on all fours with his truck clutched in one hand, making quite realistic engine noises.

Afterwards, that was the last thing she remembered.

A seagull, thought Jan. A damned seagull!

He should have been back home in Denmark more than an hour ago. Instead he sat on what should have been the 7:45 to Copenhagen Airport, frying inside an overheated aluminum tube along with 122 other unfortunates. No matter how many cooling drinks he was offered by the flight attendants, nothing could ease his desperation.

The plane had arrived on schedule from Copenhagen. But boarding had been postponed, first by fifteen minutes, then by another fifteen minutes, and finally by an additional half hour. Jan had begun to sweat. He was on a tight schedule. But the desk staff kept saying it was a temporary problem, and the passengers were asked to stay by the gate. When they suddenly postponed boarding again, this time by a full hour, without any explanation, he lost his temper and demanded to have his case unloaded so that he could find some other flight to Copenhagen. This met with polite refusal. Luggage that had been checked in was already aboard the plane, and there was apparently no willingness to find his bag among the other 122. When he said to hell with the bag, then, and wanted to leave the gate without it, there were suddenly two security officers flanking him, telling him that if his bag was flying out on that plane, so was he. Was that a problem?

No, he demurred hastily, having absolutely no desire to spend further hours in some windowless room with a lock on the door. He was no terrorist, just a frustrated businessman with very important business to attend to, he explained. Airline security was very important business, too, they said. Sir. He nodded obediently and sat himself down on one of the blue plastic chairs, silently cursing 9/11 and everything that awful day had wrought in the world.

At long last they were told to begin boarding. Now everything suddenly had to be accomplished at breakneck speed. Two extra desks were opened, and staff in pale blue uniforms raced around snapping at passenger heels if anyone strayed or loitered. Jan sank gratefully into his wide business-class seat and checked his watch. He could still make it.

The engines warmed up, flight attendants began explaining about emergency exits *here* and *here,* and the plane began to roll forward on the pavement.

And then it stopped. And stayed stopped for so long that Jan became uneasy and checked his watch again. Move your arses, he cursed silently. Get this stupid aircraft off the ground!

Instead the voice of the captain was heard over the PA system.

"I'm sorry to inform you that we have yet another hitch in our schedule. On departure from Copenhagen airport on the way down here, we were hit by a bird. The aircraft suffered no damage, but of course we have to have a mechanical overhaul of the plane before we are allowed to fly it again, which is the reason for the delay we have already suffered. The aircraft has been checked and declared fully operational."

Then why aren't we flying? thought Jan, grinding his teeth.

"The airline has a quality-control program, in compliance with which the documentation for our check-up has to be faxed to Copenhagen for signature before we are given our final permission to take off. At this time, there is only one person on duty in Copenhagen qualified to give us that permission. And for some reason, he is not to be found at his desk. . . ."

The pilot's own frustration came through quite clearly, but that was nothing to the despair that Jan was feeling. His heart was pounding so hard it physically hurt his chest. If I have a heart attack, will they let me off the damn plane? he wondered, and thought about the advisability of faking one. But even if they let him out, it would still take time to get on some other flight, even if he forked out the cash it would cost to arrange a private one. He had to face the fact that he wouldn't make it.

What the hell was he going to do? He feverishly tried to think of anyone he might call on for help. Who would be loyal and competent enough to do what needed doing? And should he call Anne?

No. Not Anne. Karin would have to do what was necessary. She was already involved to some extent, and the fewer people the better. He took his private mobile phone from his briefcase and tapped her number.

The flight attendant descended on him like a hawk on a chicken.

"Please don't use your mobile, sir."

"We're stationary," he pointed out. "And unless the airline wants to be sued for a six-figure sum, I suggest you back off and let me call my company *now*."

The flight attendant noted the no doubt

exceedingly tense set of his jaw and decided that diplomacy was the better part of valor.

"A short call, then," she said. "After which I must ask you to switch it off again."

She remained by his seat while he made the call. He considered asking her to give him his privacy, but there were passengers all around him, and he wouldn't be able to speak freely in any case.

Tersely, he instructed Karin to go to his Copenhagen bank for the sum he had just had transferred from Zürich.

"There is a code you have to supply. I'll text you. And bring one of my document cases, one that has a decent lock. It's a sizeable sum."

His awareness of the listening flight attendant was acute, and he had no idea how to say the rest without sounding like something out of a pulp-fiction thriller.

"In fact, I'll text you everything else," he said quickly. "There are a number of figures involved. Text me back when you have read my message."

Though the show was over for now, the flight attendant still stayed demonstratively next to his seat while he texted his message and waited for the reply. It took a worryingly long time to arrive.

OK. But you owe me big-time.

Yes, he wrote to her. *I realize that.*

He wondered what it would cost him— particularly her compliant silence. Karin had acquired a taste for the finer things in life. But at heart she was a good and loyal person, he told himself soothingly, and she had several compelling reasons to stay on his good side. He had after all been very generous as an employer, and in certain other ways as well.

At that moment, the plane jerked forward and began to move, and he wondered whether he had after all been premature in involving her. But it turned out they were being taxied off the runway to a parking area. The captain explained that they had lost their slot in the busy departure schedule of the airport and were now put on indefinite hold while waiting first for their permission to take off to arrive from Copenhagen, and secondly for a new slot to be assigned to them. He was very sorry, but he was unfortunately forced to switch off the air conditioning while they waited.

Jan closed his eyes and cursed in three languages. *Fandens. Scheisse. Fucking hell.*

Nina looked the man right in the eyes.
"I think you had better leave," she said.

It had no effect. He stepped even closer, deliberately looming over her. She could smell his aftershave. In a different situation it might have been a pleasant scent.

"I know she is here," he said. "And I demand to see my fiancée right away."

It was a hot August day, and there were white roses from the garden in the blue vase on her desk. Outside Ellen's Place the sun was shining on dusty lawns and white benches. Some of the children from the A Block were playing soccer. One team was yelling in Urdu and the other mostly in Romanian, but they seemed to understand each other all the same. Recess, thought Nina with a small, detached part of her brain. Her colleagues Magnus and Pernille had deserted her in favor of the cafeteria ages ago, and she could see the psychologist Susanne Marcussen having lunch with the new district nurse in the outside picnic area. It was 11:55, and except for the soccer game, a heavy siesta-like tranquility had descended on Danish Red Cross Center Furesø, a.k.a. the Coal-House Camp. Or at least, things had been tranquil until the man in front of her had marched into the clinic four minutes ago. She threw a quick look at the telephone on her desk, but whom would she call? The police? So far, he had done nothing illegal.

He was in his late forties, with medium brown hair swept back from his temples, tanned and immaculate in a short-sleeved Hugo Boss shirt and matching tie. Apparently no one had thought to stop him at the gate.

"Get out of my way," he told her. "I'll find her myself."

Nina stood her ground. If he hits me, I can press charges, she thought. It would be worth it.

"This is not a public area," she said. "I'm going to have to ask you to leave."

This had even less effect than it had the first time. He looked straight through her to the corridor beyond.

"Natasha," he called. "Come on. Rina is already waiting in the car."

What? Nina tried to catch his eyes.

"She's at school," she blurted.

He looked down at her, and the smile that curled his lips was so smug that it physically sickened her.

"Not anymore," he said.

A door clicked open softly. Without turning around, Nina knew that Natasha had come into the corridor.

"Don't hurt her," she said.

"Darling, as if I would," said the man in the Boss shirt. "Shall we go home now? I bought pastries from that bakery you like."

Natasha nodded briefly.

Nina involuntarily reached out to stop her, but the small, blond Ukrainian girl walked right past her without looking at her. Nina knew the girl was twenty-four, but right now she looked like a lost and terrified teenager.

"I go now," she said.

"Natasha! You can report him!"

Natasha just shook her head. "For what?" she said.

The man put his hands around her slender neck and drew her close for a provocatively deep kiss. Nina could *see* the girl stiffen. He let his hands move down her back and slid them inside the tight waistline of her denim jeans until he was clutching both her buttocks. His hands bulged under the fabric. With an abrupt jerk, he forced her pelvis against his own.

Nina could taste the acid of her own stomach. She felt like taking the blue vase and smashing it against the head of that *vicious* bastard, but she didn't. She knew that this was a show put on for her benefit, to sneer and parade his victory. The more reaction she gave him, the longer it would continue.

Nina still remembered the brilliant happiness of the Ukrainian girl when she showed off her engagement ring. "I stay in Denmark now," she had said with a dazzling smile. "My husband is Danish citizen."

Four months later she showed up at the center with one hastily packed bag and her six-year-old daughter, Rina. She looked as if she had dragged herself out of a war zone. There were no outer signs of violence except for a few minor bruises. Hitting her was not his thing, it seemed. Natasha wouldn't tell them exactly what he did, she just sat there with tears she could not control rolling down her cheeks in a steady, unstoppable flow. At length, severe abdominal pains had forced her to agree to being examined by Magnus.

Nina had rarely seen Magnus so angry. "*Jävla skitstöfel,*" he hissed. "*Fy fan,* I wish I knew someone with a baseball bat." When Magnus was particularly upset, his native Swedish tended to come through in his swearing.

"What did he do?" said Nina. "What's wrong with her?"

"If the bastard would only stick to using his miserable little prick," said Magnus. "But you should see the lesions she has, in her vagina and in her rectum. I've never seen anything like it."

And now the Bastard was standing right in front of her, kneading Natasha's buttocks with his greedy hands, while his eyes, gazing across Natasha's shoulder, never left Nina's. She had to look away. I could kill him, she thought to herself. Kill, castrate, and dismember. If I thought it would do any good.

But there were thousands like him. Not exactly like him, but thousands of others who circled like sharks, waiting to exploit the desperation of the refugees and take their chunk of the vulnerable flesh.

Eventually, he pulled his hands out of Natasha's jeans.

"Have a nice day," he said, and left. Natasha followed him as if he had her on a leash.

Nina jerked the receiver off the phone and dialed an internal number.

"Teacher's room, this is Ulla speaking."

"Is it true that the bastard who is to marry Natasha has picked up Rina?" asked Nina.

There was a silence at the other end. "I'll look," said the English teacher. Nina waited for six minutes. Then Ulla Svenningsen came back on the line. "I'm sorry," she said. "He turned up just as the bell went for the recess. He had brought her a popsicle, the children say, and she ran right up to him."

"Bloody hell, Ulla!"

"Sorry. But this is not a prison, is it? Openness is part of the concept."

Nina hung up without saying goodbye. She was shaking with fury. Right now she was in no mood to listen to excuses or politically correct sermons on the importance of opening up to the commun-ity.

Magnus appeared in the doorway, out of breath and glasses askew, and big beads of sweat everywhere in his large, kind dog-face.

"Natasha," he gasped out. "I just saw her getting into a car."

"Yes," said Nina. "She went back to the Bastard."

"*For helvete da!*"

"He took Rina first. And then Natasha just followed."

Magnus sank into his office chair.

"And of course she won't report him."

"No. Can't we do it?"

Magnus took off his glasses and polished them absentmindedly on the lapel of his white coat.

"All he has to say is that it's nobody's business if he and his fiancée like rough sex," he said dejectedly. "If she won't contradict him . . . there's nothing we can do. He doesn't hit her. There are no X-rays of broken arms or ribs that we can beat him over the head with."

"And he doesn't abuse the child," sighed Nina.

Magnus shook his head.

"No. We could report him for that, at least. But he is too smart for that." He looked at the clock on the wall. It was 12:05. "Aren't you going to lunch?"

"I seem to have lost my appetite," said Nina.

At that moment, her private phone vibrated in the pocket of her uniform. She took it.

"Nina."

The voice at the other end did not introduce herself, and at first she wasn't sure who it was.

"You have to help me."

"Err . . . with what?"

"You have to pick it up. You know about such things."

It was Karin, she realized. Last seen at a somewhat inebriated Old Students Christmas Lunch, which had ended in a furious shouting match.

"Karin, what's wrong? You sound weird."

"I'm in the cafeteria at Magasin," said Karin, naming the oldest department store in Copenhagen. "It was the only place I could think of to go. Will you come?"

"I'm working."

"Yes. But will you come?"

Nina hesitated. Suddenly, all kinds of things were in the air. Old favors. Unsettled accounts. And Nina knew full well she owed Karin at least this much.

"Okay. I'll be there in twenty minutes."

Magnus raised his eyebrows.

"I'm having lunch after all," said Nina. "And, err . . . I'll probably be at least an hour."

He nodded distractedly. "Oh, all right. I suppose we can hold the fort without you."

M rs. Ramoškienė!"
A piercing light struck one of Sigita's eyes. She tried to twist away but found she couldn't, someone was holding her, someone held her head in a firm grip.

"Mrs. Ramoškienė, can you hear me?"

She was unable to answer. She couldn't even open her eyes on her own.

"It's no use," said a different voice. "She's out of it."

"Whew. That's a bit ripe."

Yes, thought Sigita dizzily. There really was a foul odor, of raw spirits and vomit. Someone ought to clean this place up.

"Mrs. Ramoškienė. It will be a lot easier if you can do some of it yourself."

Do what? She didn't understand. Where was she? Where was Mikas?

"We have to insert a tube in your throat. If you can swallow as we push, it will be less uncomfortable."

Tube? Why would she want to swallow a tube? Her confused brain took her back to the absurd bets of the schoolyard. Here's a litas if you eat this slug. Here's a litas that says you're too chicken to swallow the earthworm alive. Then a grain of logic asserted itself. She must be in a hospital. She was in a hospital, and they wanted her to swallow a plastic tube. But why?

She couldn't swallow, as it turned out. Couldn't help. Couldn't stop herself from struggling, which brought a new pain, sharp enough to pierce the fog of her confusion. Her arm. Oh God, her arm.

It is very hard to scream with a plastic tube in your throat, she discovered.

"Mikas."

"What is she saying?"

"Where is Mikas?"

She opened her eyes. They felt thickened and strange, but she forced them to open all the same. The light was blinding, and white as milk. She could only just make out two women, darker shapes amidst the whiteness. Nurses, or aides, she couldn't make out the details. They were making the bed next to hers.

"Where is Mikas?" she said, as clearly as she was able.

"You must be quiet, Mrs. Ramoškienė."

An accident, she thought, I've been in an accident. A car, or perhaps the trolley bus. That's why I can't remember anything. Then came the fear. What had happened to Mikas? Was he hurt? *Was he dead?*

"Where is my son?" she screamed. "What have you done with him?"

"Please calm yourself, ma'am. Mrs. Ramoškienė, will you *please* lie down!"

One of them tried to restrain her, but she was too afraid to let herself be restrained. She got up. One arm was heavier than the other, and a bitter green wave of nausea washed over her. Acid burned her much-abused esophagus, and the pain took her legs from her, took away all control, so that she ended up on the floor next to the bed, clutching at the sheets, still struggling to get up.

"Mikas. Let me see Mikas!"

"He's not here, Mrs. Ramoškienė. He is

41

probably with your mother, or with some other relative. Or a neighbor. He is perfectly fine, I tell you. Now will you please lie down and stop screaming so. There are other patients here, some of them seriously ill, and you really mustn't disturb them like this."

The nurse helped her back into the bed. At first she felt simple relief. Mikas was all right! But then she understood that something wasn't quite right, after all. Sigita tried to see the woman's face more clearly. There was something there, in the tone of her voice, in the set of her jaw, that was not compassion, but its opposite. Contempt.

She knows, thought Sigita in confusion. She knows what I did. But how? How could some unfamiliar nurse in a random ward in Vilnius know so much about her? It was so many years ago, after all.

"I have to go home," she said thickly, through the nausea. Mikas couldn't be with her mother, of course. Possibly with Mrs. Mažekienė next door, but she was getting on now and could become peevish and abrupt if the babysitting went on too long. "Mikas needs me."

The other nurse gave her a look from across the neighboring bed, smoothing the pillowcase with sharp, precise movements.

"You might have thought of that before," she said.

"Before . . . before what?" stammered Sigita. Was the accident her fault?

"Before you tried to drink your brains out. Since you ask."

Drink?

"But I don't drink," said Sigita. "Or . . . hardly ever."

"Oh, really. I suppose it was just a mistake, then, that we sent you to have your stomach pumped? Your blood-alcohol level was two point eight."

"But I . . . I really don't."

That couldn't be right. Couldn't be *her*.

"Rest a little," said the first nurse, pulling the blanket across her legs. "Perhaps you will be discharged later, when the doctor comes by again."

"What's wrong with me? What happened?"

"I believe you fell down some stairs. Concussion and a fracture of your lower left arm. And you were lucky it wasn't worse!"

Some stairs? She remembered nothing like that. Nothing since the coffee and the playground and Mikas in the sandbox with his truck.

Getting away from the center was actually a relief, thought Nina, as she drove up the ramp to Magasin's parking garage and eased her small Fiat into the none-too-generous space between a concrete pillar and somebody's wide-arsed Mercedes. Sometimes she got so sick and tired of feeling powerless. What kind of country was this, when young girls like Natasha were compelled to sell themselves to men like the Bastard for the sake of a resident's permit?

She took the elevator to the top floor of the building. As soon as she stepped out of the narrow steel box, the odor of food overwhelmed her—roasted pork, hot grease from the deep-fryer, and the pervasive aroma of coffee. She scanned the cafeteria and finally caught sight of Karin's blond head. She was seated at a table by the window, in a sleeveless white dress that struck Nina as an off-duty version of her nurse's uniform. Instead of one of the chic little handbags she normally sported, one hand rested possessively on the black briefcase on the chair next to her, while the other nervously rotated her coffee cup, back and forth, back and forth.

"Hi," said Nina. "What is it, then?"

Karin looked up. Her eyes were bright and tense with an emotion Nina couldn't quite identify.

"You have to fetch something for me," she said, slapping a small round plastic circle onto the table. A token with a number on it, Nina observed, like the ones used for public lockers.

Nina was starting to feel annoyed.

"Don't be so damned cryptic. What exactly is it I'm supposed to fetch?"

44

Karin hesitated.

"A suitcase," she finally said. "From a locker at the Central Station. Don't open it until you are out of the place. Don't let anyone see you when you do open it. And hurry!"

"Bloody hell, Karin, you make it sound as if it's stuffed full of cocaine, or something!"

Karin shook her head.

"No. It's not like that. It's. . . ." She stopped short, and Nina could see the barely suppressed panic in her. "This wasn't the deal," she said feverishly. "I can't do this. I don't know how. But you do."

Karin got to her feet as if she meant to leave. Nina felt like grabbing her and forcing her to stay, much like she had with Natasha. But she didn't. She looked down at the token on the table between them. 37-43, read the white numbers against the black plastic.

"You're always so keen on saving people, aren't you?" said Karin with a bitter twist to her mouth. "Well, here's your chance. But you have to hurry."

"Where are you going?"

"I'm going home to quit my job," said Karin tightly. "And then I'm going away for a while."

She zigzagged her way to the exit, skirting the other tables. She clutched the briefcase under her arm rather than carry it by the handle. It looked wrong, somehow.

Nina watched her go. Then she looked at the small shiny token. A suitcase. A locker. *You're always so keen on saving people, aren't you?*

"What the hell have you gotten yourself into, Karin?" she muttered to herself. She had a strong feeling that the wisest thing to do would be to leave number 37-43 there on the sticky cafeteria table and just walk away.

"Oh hell," she hissed, and picked up the token.

M rs. Mažekienė? It's Sigita."
There was a moment's silence before Mrs. Mažekienė answered.

"Sigita. Thank the Lord. How are you?"

"Much better now. But they won't let me out of here until tomorrow. Is Mikas with you?"

"Oh no, dear. He is with his father."

"With *Darius?*"

"Yes, of course. He picked him up even before your accident. Don't you remember, dearie?"

"No. They say I'm concussed. There is so much I don't remember."

But . . . Darius was in Germany, working. Or was he? He didn't always tell her when he came home. Officially, they were still only separated, but the only thing they had in common now

46

was Mikas. Might Darius take Mikas back to Germany with him? Or to his mother's house in Tauragė? He didn't have a place of his own in Vilnius, and she very much doubted that the party-crowd friends he occasionally stayed with would welcome a three-year-old boy.

Her head hurt furiously. She couldn't think things through with any clarity, and she didn't feel very reassured by the knowledge that Darius had Mikas, but at least she knew where her son was. Or with whom, at any rate.

"It looked so awful, dearie. I thought you were dead! And to think you had been lying on those stairs all night! Now, you just have a good rest at that fine hospital, and let them look after you until you're better."

"Yes. Thank you, Mrs. Mažekienė."

Sigita snapped her mobile shut. Getting hold of it at all had been a challenge, and smuggling it into the loo with her even more difficult. The use of mobile phones was prohibited inside the hospital, except for a certain area in the lobby, which might as well have been the moon as far as she was concerned—she still couldn't walk without hanging onto the walls.

Awkwardly, she opened the phone again and pressed Darius's number with the thumb of her right hand. She was unable to hold the phone in her plaster-cased left, or at least not in such a way that she was able to operate it.

47

His voice was happy and warm and full of his presence even on a stupid voicemail message.

"You have called Darius Ramoška, but, but, but . . . I'm not here right now. Try again later!"

That was actually completely appropriate, she thought. The story of his life, or at any rate, the story of their relationship. I'm not here right now, try again later.

They had started going out together the summer she was due to finish elementary school, and he was about to begin his second year of secondary school in Tauragė's Education Center. The summer had been unusually hot that year. In the schoolyard, only the most energetic of the little kids felt like playing on the heat-softened tarmac. The older students sat with their backs against the gray cement wall, with rolled up sleeves and jeans, chatting lazily in what they felt was a very grown-up manner.

"Are you going away for the holiday, Sigita?"

It was Milda asking. And she knew very well that the answer was no.

"Maybe," said Sigita. "We haven't really made plans yet."

"We're going to Palanga," said Daiva. "To a hotel!"

"Really?" drawled Milda. "How cool. We're just going to Miami."

All around her, there was a sudden awestruck silence. Envy and respect were almost as visible in the air as the heat shimmer over the asphalt. Miami. Outer space seemed more accessible to most of them. A holiday meant Daiva's fortnight at a Palanga resort hotel, or perhaps a trip to the Black Sea, if they got really lucky. No one in their grade had ever been further away than that.

"Are you sure?" said Daiva.

"Of course I'm sure. The tickets are already booked."

No one asked where the money came from. They all knew—Milda's father and uncle brought used cars home from Germany, fixed them up, and sold them to the Russians. That this was good business had been obvious first from the children's clothes, and Milda's new bike, then from the BMWs they drove, and finally from the big new house they built just outside town. But all the same—Miami.

"I'd rather go to New York," Sigita heard herself say. And immediately wished she could have swallowed every last syllable.

Milda threw back her head and laughed.

"Right, then, you just tell your father that you want to go to New York," she said. "He'll buy the ticket right away . . . just as soon as he sells those shirts."

Sigita felt the heat rise in her cheeks. Those damned shirts. She would never hear the last of it. They would haunt her to the end of her days, she felt sure.

They were everywhere in the flat. Thousands of them. They came from a closed-down factory in Poland, and her father had bought them for "practically nothing," as he put it. Practically nothing had still been enough that they had to sell the car. And even though her father kept talking about "top-shelf merchandise" and "classic design," he had managed to sell fewer than a dozen. For nearly two years they had been hanging there from broomsticks and wires screwed into the ceiling, crackling, plastic-shrouded, and "fresh from the factory," above the couch, above the beds, even in the loo. She never brought friends home anymore; it was simply too embarrassing. But not nearly as embarrassing as being forced to take "samples" with her to class in the hopes that some of her friends' parents would feel a sudden urge to buy one.

Her father had been severely out of his depth since the Russians went home. Back then, in the Soviet era, he had been a controller at the canning factory. It did not pay much better than working on the line, but back then it hadn't been the money that mattered, it had been the connections. No one could just buy what they wanted, it had to be arranged. As often as not, her father had been the man who could arrange it.

Now the factory had closed down. It sat behind

50

its barbed-wire fence, a gray and black hulk with empty window frames, weeds breaking through the concrete paving. The old connections were worthless, or worse than worthless. The people who did well these days were the ones who knew how to trade, fix, and organize—in the black economy as well as in the white.

Sigita got up. The sun hit her like a hammer, and once she was on her feet, she really had no idea where to go.

"Leaving so soon?" said Milda. "Oh, I suppose you are in a hurry to go home and book that New York hotel?"

It was at that moment that he came to her rescue.

"Sigita? Don't forget we're going to Kaliningrad on Saturday, right?"

Darius. Tanned and fair-haired, with that relaxed and well-trained confidence none of the other boys had. His shirt was left casually open to reveal a crisp white T-shirt underneath, and neither garment had come from Poland.

"No," she said. "It'll be fun. Have you heard that Milda is going to Miami for the holidays?"

"Oh," he said. "You must say hello to my uncle, then. He lives there."

It had taken her years to see that Darius's shining armor was eggshell thin. He couldn't rescue her, had never really been able to. God only knew what he was doing with Mikas right now. Had

51

he brought her little boy with him to some bar where Darius's party buddies would let him finish their beers? She shuddered. She *had* to get out of this damned hospital in a hurry.

The railway station was crammed with irritable Monday crowds, and there was a nearly visible mist of exhaled breaths and collective sweat in the great central hall. People were tetchy in the heat, with their clothes and their tempers sticking to them, and over the PA came the announcement that the 13:11 to Elsinore was delayed by approximately twenty minutes. Nina felt a tension that made her unwilling to be so physically close to a lot of strangers. She tried to move so that they wouldn't touch her, but it just wasn't possible. Finally she reached the stairwell leading down to the left luggage cellar. The sharp smell of cleaning chemicals was weaker here and couldn't quite mask the stench of well-aged urine. The scratched metal lockers hugged the walls, long white rows with black numbers on them. 56, 55. . . . She checked the token again. 37-43. Where on earth was section 37?

She found it at last, in a quiet blind alley leading off the more heavily trafficked main corridor.

Right now, there were only two travelers in here —a young couple struggling to fit a large backpack into one of the lockers.

"It won't fit," said the girl. "I told you. It's too big."

By the girl's accent, Nina took them to be American, or perhaps Canadian. Should she wait until they had left? But other tourists would come, and at least these two were intent on their Battle of the Bulging Rucksack. She pushed the token into the automated system controlling section 37, and there was a crisp metallic *click* as locker 43 came open.

Inside was a shiny dark-brown leather suitcase, a little old-fashioned, with a long tear down one side so that the green lining peeked through. Otherwise there was nothing very noticeable about it. No address labels or tags, of course. She knew it would be foolish to open it now. People who pick up their own bags don't open them to check what is inside. And Karin had said the same thing—*don't open it until you're out of there. Don't let anyone see.* Oh, Karin. What are you up to? Nina thought. It was difficult to imagine that it might be anything very sinister or serious. Karin was so . . . "unadventurous" wasn't quite the word, but still. It was just hard to picture easygoing, hedonistic Karin involved in anything dirty, illegal, or dangerous. But there had been that unwonted panic in her voice: *This wasn't the deal.* What had she meant by that?

Nina dragged the suitcase out of the locker. It was heavier than it looked, at least forty pounds, she guessed. Not easily carried for any length of distance, and the underground parking lot in Nyropsgade, where she had left the Fiat, was a couple of blocks away. But Copenhagen's Central Station did not provide complimentary trolleys like those in airports, so there was nothing else for it.

The young couple had begun taking things out of the backpack to slim it sufficiently for the narrow locker. The young man dropped a toilet bag, which hit the floor with a clang and came open. Mascara, eyeliner, hair mousse, and deodorants spilled across the tiles. One of the deodorants curved towards Nina and came to a spinning stop at her feet.

"Oh, hell," he said. "Sorry."

Nina smiled mechanically. Then she took the suitcase in the firmest grip she could manage and began to walk, trying to look halfway natural. Sweet Jesus, it was heavy. What on earth was in it?

It was only when she reached the car-park that she opened it. And found the boy.

He was unconscious. His skin was cool, but not alarmingly cold. Some automated professional part of her noted that his pulse was slow, but again not dangerously so, his respiration deep and also slow, his pupils slightly contracted. There was little doubt that he had been drugged, she thought. He wasn't about to die on her, but he needed treatment—fluids, and perhaps an antidote, if they could work out what had been used on him. She seized her mobile and pressed the first two emergency digits, then paused before the final one.

Her eyes fell on the suitcase. So ordinary. Normal. The tear in the leather had made it easier for the boy to breathe, but there was no way to tell whether it had been made intentionally to ensure him a certain supply of oxygen. People who put little children in suitcases do not, Nina thought, care terribly about their welfare.

Steps somewhere, and the slamming of car doors, then the growl of an engine starting up. The sounds echoed back from the concrete walls, and she ducked instinctively behind the dumpster so as not to be seen. Why? Why didn't she get up instead and call for help? But she didn't. She caught a glimpse of silver metal and shiny hubcaps, then the car was gone.

She had to get the child to her own car, but how? She could not bear to close the suitcase and carry him like that, as if he were baggage. She ran to the Fiat instead, and got a checkered picnic blanket from the trunk, tucked it around him, and carried him against her shoulder. Mother and child, she thought. If anyone sees me, I'm just a mommy who has just picked up her exhausted toddler from kindergarten.

He seemed feather light, much less of a weight than he had been in the suitcase. She could feel his breath against the side of her neck, a small warm puffing. Dear sweet Jesus. Who would do this to a child?

She lowered him onto the back seat and checked his pulse once more. A little faster already, as if he were reacting to his surroundings. She grabbed the plastic water bottle from between the front seats and moistened his lips with a wet finger. His tongue moved. He was not deeply unconscious.

Hospital, police. Police, hospital. But if it was just a question of calling 911, why hadn't Karin done it herself? Bloody hell, Karin, Nina cursed silently. Are you mixed up in this? "I can't do anything, but you can," Karin had said. But just what the *hell* was it she was supposed to be doing?

Monday morning, Sigita was finally released. She had called Darius at least a dozen times, but all she got was the stupid answering machine.

She still didn't understand what had happened. She really didn't drink, certainly not to the point of falling down stairs in a state of blind oblivion. And why had she let Darius take Mikas away? That had happened before the stairs, so Mrs. Mažekienė had said. Sigita felt a tiny persistent sting of fear. What if Darius would not give Mikas back to her? And how was it that she had ended up at the foot of the stairs with a broken arm and a concussion? Darius had never hit her, not once, not even during the bitterest of their fights. She couldn't believe he had done so now. But perhaps some accident . . . ? If there was one person on God's green earth who could inspire her to get drunk, it was surely Darius.

She considered taking a taxi back home to Pašilaičiai, but the habits acquired through years of enforced parsimony were not easily shaken. After all, the trolley bus stopped practically at her doorstep. For the first few stops, inside Vilnius proper, the bus was crowded to sardine-tin capacity; her plaster cast got her the offer of a seat, which she gratefully accepted, but even so, the pressure of other human bodies made nausea rise in her gullet until she was afraid she would not be able to contain it. One more stop, she told herself. If it doesn't get better after that, I'll get off and call for a cab. But the pressure did ease as they left the center of the city and the rush-hour current ran the other way. When she finally got off by Žemynos gatvė, she had to sit on the bus-stop bench and just breathe for a little while before she was able to walk on.

She rang the bell by Mrs. Mažekienė's front door before going into her own flat.

"Oh, it's you, dearie. Good to see you on your feet again. What a to-do!"

"Yes. But, Mrs. Mažekienė, exactly when did Darius pick up Mikas?"

"Saturday. How peculiar that you don't remember."

"When on Saturday?"

"A little past noon, I think. Yes. I had just had my lunch when I saw them."

"Them? Was someone with him?"

Mrs. Mažekienė bit her lip, looking as if she thought she might have said too much.

"Well, yes. There was this lady. . . ."

It stung, even though Sigita had been the one to kick Darius out, and not the other way around. But of course there was a "lady." Had she really imagined there wouldn't be?

"What did she look like?" she asked, in the unlikely case that it had been Darius's mother or sister.

"Very nice. Quite young. Tall and fair-haired, with nice clothes. Not tarted up like some," said Mrs. Mažekienė.

Which meant it wasn't Darius's sister, for sure.

Then another thought came to her. A nice-looking, tall, fair-haired young woman. Quite a few of those around, of course, but still. . . .

"Can you remember what she was wearing?"

"A light summer coat. One of those cotton coats, I think. And a scarf."

The woman from the playground. The one who wanted a child so badly. Sigita felt a chill go through her. What if Darius had a girlfriend now who longed for children. . . . Sigita remembered the silver gleam of the chocolate wrapping, Mikas's chocolate-smeared cheeks. The sly, ingratiating bitch. Watching them, watching Mikas, worming her way into his trust with the forbidden chocolate gift. Suppose it hadn't been a Russian accent after all, but a German one. Some Irmgard he had picked up where he worked now.

"Dearie, are you all right?"

"Yes," said Sigita through her teeth, though nausea sloshed in her throat like water in a bucket. "But I think I had better go lie down all the same."

The flat looked the way it always did. Clean and white and modern, light-years away from the shirt-ridden hell of Tauragė. Even Mikas's toys were lined up in tidy rows on the shelves. Only one alien object disturbed the symmetry: an empty vodka bottle glared at her from the kitchen worktop, next to the sink.

She tossed it into the bin with unnecessary force. Did they get her drunk first? She didn't believe, *couldn't* believe, that she had just let

Darius and his German slut waltz off with Mikas in tow.

Her mobile rang.

"Sigita, where the hell are you? Dobrovolskij will be here in half an hour, and we need those figures!"

It was Algirdas. Algirdas Janusevičius, one half of Janus Constructions, and her immediate boss.

"Sorry," she said. "I just got out of hospital."

"Hospital?" Irritation was clear in his voice at first, but he managed a more suitably worried tone when he spoke again. "Nothing serious, I hope?"

"No," she said. "I fell down some stairs. But I won't be in for a few days."

His silence was palpable at the other end of the line.

"Sorry," she said again.

"Yes. Well. It can't be helped. But . . . the figures?"

"There's a green folder in the cabinet behind my desk, under Dobrovolskij. The accounts are almost the first thing you'll come across."

"Sigita, for God's sake. Not *those* figures."

She knew what he meant, of course. When one worked for Dobrovolskij, there were unwritten accounts as well, numbers and sums that never made it into the official records. The reason Sigita had become indispensable to Algirdas so quickly was that she was able to hold it all in her head.

Even old man Dobrovolskij himself, who was not easy to please, had come to trust in Sigita's accuracy. She knew what had been agreed, down to the last litas.

Except that right now she would have some trouble remembering her own phone number. The only thing her head held at the moment was a gray fog of nausea and confusion.

"I'm really sorry," she said. "I'm a little concussed."

This time, the silence was even heavier. She could almost hear the panic in Algirdas's breathing.

"How long . . . ?" he asked cautiously.

"They say most people get their full memory back inside a few weeks."

"A few *weeks!*"

"Algirdas, I didn't do it on purpose."

"No . . . no. Of course not. We will just have to manage somehow. But. . . ."

"Yes. As soon as I can."

"Take care." He hung up. She let the hand holding the phone sink into her lap.

Her head hurt. It was as though some great fist were squeezing it in rhythmic throbs, to match the beating of her pulse. She tapped out Darius's number again.

"You have called Darius Ramoška. . . ."

She sat for a long time in one of the white wooden chairs by the kitchen table, trying to think.

Then she called the police.

The boy lay unconscious on the back seat, with the checkered picnic blanket covering his thin, unmoving body. And Karin wasn't answering her phone.

Nina closed her eyes, trying to concentrate. 1:35. It should be 1:35. . . . Her hands shook slightly as she turned her wrist to check her watch. 1:36, stated the stark, digital numbers. Close enough. Relief flooded through her, making it a bit easier to think.

Sorry, Karin, she silently told her friend. You ask too much, this time.

She pulled the blanket a little higher so that it was not immediately obvious a child was asleep beneath it. Rolled down the window just a notch, so air would get into the car. Locked the Fiat and left, walking with long, quick strides she knew were nearly as fast as running.

She cut through the central hall of the railway station, heading for the green and white sign that proclaimed the local police presence. She entered the small office, wondering what one actually said in such a situation. Good afternoon, I've just found a child?

62

The officer at the reception desk looked tired. Not the easiest job in Copenhagen, probably.

"What can I do for you?" she asked.

"Err . . . I have a child in my car—"

Nina's hesitant explanation was interrupted by a crackle from the woman's radio. Nina couldn't hear what was being said at the other end, but the officer snapped a hasty "Copy that. I'm on my way," and headed for the door at a run.

"Please wait here," she called over her shoulder, but Nina had already followed her back into the central hall. She watched the officer and one of her uniformed colleagues fairly sprint for the stairwell leading down to the left luggage lockers. Following still further, into the basement, was not actually a conscious decision.

She heard the racket as soon as she started down the stairs. Everyone in the facility had stopped their various baggage maneuvers, and some had already gathered at the entrance to the passage where locker number 37-43 was situated. Nina felt a warning flutter along her spine, like an insect moving over her skin, but she still had to look.

A man was kicking at the metal doors with frightening ferocity. She caught a brief glimpse of the back of his head, hair clipped so short it looked almost shaved, and of a set of enormous shoulders encased in a shiny brown leather jacket that was surely too hot for this weather. When the officers reached him, he shook off

63

the first one as if she were a child he no longer wanted to play with. Then he seemed to collect himself.

"Sorry, sorry," he said, rolling his r's in a way that almost made them into d's. He stood quite still, letting the police officers calm down from violence alert to dialogue mode. "I pay. Is broken, I pay."

Then he suddenly turned his head, looking directly at her. She didn't know what made him pick her out of the crowd, but she saw his muscles bunch tensely as fury tightened his face and narrowed his eyes. He remained still, and didn't speak, but even so she sensed the violence he was holding in check.

What had she done to deserve such rage? She had never seen the man before.

But of course the locker he had been kicking to pieces was not just any locker. It was number 37-43. And she suddenly knew where the rage had come from.

She had taken something that was his.

She had to employ every shred of self-control she possessed to stop herself from running all the way back to the car. He won't be able to follow, she told herself, the police are there. She walked as quickly as she could without turning heads.

But she remembered how he had shaken them

off like a dog shakes a flea from its fur, and the only plan she was able to form was that they had to get away, she and the boy, as far away from that man as they could possibly get.

When the stolen Nokia beeped in his briefcase more than three hours later, Jan's plane was still sitting on the pavement, and he was still in his business class seat, sweating like a pig. This time no flight attendant swooped down on him when he pulled out his phone. Cabin personnel had long since given up on that particular score, and at least twenty other people around him were engaged in multilingual phone calls, explaining why they would be delayed.

"Mr. Marquart." In spite of the hiss and crackle of a bad connection, the man's fury came through loud and clear, not so much in his words as in his tone of voice.

"Yes. . . ."

"I delivered. As agreed. The woman came and took the goods. But she left no money. You did not pay."

What?

Jan protested. He himself was stuck in a plane, he explained, but he had directed his assistant to go in his stead, and he was sure she had followed his instructions.

"Mr. Marquart. There was no money."

Jan tried to imagine what could have happened.

"There must be some misunderstanding," he said. "As soon as I get back, I'll clear it up."

"That would be a very good idea," said the man, and cut the connection. The very restraint of his phrase sent a chill through Jan even in the midst of the overheated cabin. It signaled that this was a man who did not have to resort to threats. A man best not angered.

Jan jabbed out Karin's number with some ferocity. She didn't answer, and he left no message apart from a curt "Call me!"

He stared sightlessly at the back of the seat in front of him. Sweated. Sipped the water, and the lukewarm gin and tonic he had accepted a few hours ago when he thought he had accomplished a feasible Plan B. It took him nearly half an hour to accept that he would have to call Anne.

"Have you seen Karin?" he asked. And listened, while Anne's soft voice told him that yes, Karin had returned, but had left again rather quickly. She had been in her flat above the garage for only a few minutes.

"Was she carrying anything?" he asked. "When she arrived? And when she left?"

"I really don't know," said Anne vaguely. "Were you thinking of anything in particular?"

"No," he said. "It's nothing. It'll have to wait till I get back."

As the plane finally started to taxi out onto the runway, he leaned back against the blue leather upholstery, wondering feverishly how he could have been so wrong about her.

I should have done it myself, he thought bitterly. But that is just so typical. You make immaculate plans. You are in control. And then a fucking *seagull* wrecks it all.

The villa in Vedbæk was perfectly situated, thought Nina.

It had neither ocean view nor idyllic woods in the background, but for privacy it couldn't be matched. Neatly clipped hedges screened the sprawling redbrick and the graveled parking lot from prying eyes, and the surrounding well-to-do family homes oozed respectability. Whether that had been at the front of Allan's mind when he chose to buy his way into this particular general practice in the northern suburbs was dubious, as it had never really been part of his plan to moonlight as a medical resource for illegal immigrants; but it suited Nina's purpose beautifully.

She checked the rearview mirror. The boy

hadn't moved in all the time she had had him in the car, nor made a sound. The blanket was undisturbed, and only a few wisps of blond hair poked from its folds.

Tock, tock.

A measured rapping against the window glass made Nina jerk. It was Allan. His tall, gangly form cut off the sun as he bent to peer into the car. Then he rapped on the glass once more, but before she had time to react, he moved on, and was now trying to open the rear door, in vain. She must have locked it without thinking. She realized she was still gripping the steering wheel, fingers locked whitely around the rim, and it took her a second to make her hands unclench. She reached back and unlocked the rear door with stiff fingers, then got out of the car her-self.

Allan had already lifted the boy gently out of the car, the blanket still wrapped around him. He held the child against his shoulder.

"What do you know?"

He was headed for the house, and Nina had to lengthen her stride to keep up.

"Nothing. Or almost nothing. Someone left him in a suitcase!"

Nina closed the door behind them and followed Allan as he strode towards his office. Jolly children's drawings decorated the walls, and behind his computer sat a small gnome-like clown doll, obviously intended for the cheering up of young patients.

The clown would not serve them now. The suitcase boy hung limply in Allan's arms, like one of Ida's cast-off Raggedy Anns, thought Nina, with a familiar taste of metal in her mouth. It was her personal taste of fear. It always came to her when adrenalin rushed through her body, into every last cell of it, reminding her of the camps at Dadaab and Zwangheli and other hellholes in which she had lived and looked after the children of others. (And it reminded her of the day he died.)

Nina pushed away the thought as soon as it entered her mind and instead locked her focus on Allan and the boy. Allan had rolled the small, soft body gently onto the couch, his middle and index finger resting against the side of his neck. His face was alight with concentration, and she saw a single bead of sweat trickle down his throat and into the open neck of his white shirt. This was not the time to talk to him.

The sphygmomanometer sat on Allan's desk, within handy reach, but the cuff was much too big for the boy's thin arm. She found a smaller one and attached it. The child did not react to the high-pitched whine, or to the pressure from the inflating cuff. 90/52. She turned the display so that the digital numbers were visible to Allan.

Allan frowned and slid his hand across the

boy's chest, setting the stethoscope against the smooth, white skin of the chest, and then, in a quick precise move, to the abdominal cavity. He then rolled the boy onto his side with a gentleness that, for a moment, caused a strange tender warmth in Nina's own chest. He listened again, and finally let the boy slip down to his original position, resting on his back with his arms spread wide.

Still this disturbing lack of life, thought Nina. As if he were caught in some limbo, neither dead nor alive, simply a thing. Allan cautiously lifted one eyelid and shone his pen-sized flashlight at the boy's pupil.

"He has been drugged," he said. "I don't know with what, but it doesn't seem to be exactly life-threatening."

"Should we give him naloxone?" asked Nina.

Allan shook his head.

"His respiration is okay. Blood pressure is a little on the low side, and he is somewhat dehydrated, but I think he will simply sleep off whatever it is and wake naturally. And in any case, we can't give an antidote when we have no idea what the original substance was."

Nina nodded slowly, dodging Allan's gaze. She knew what he had to say next.

"You will of course take him to a hospital."

"But you said he would wake on his own. . . ."

Allan gestured, indicating his collection of medical reference books.

"There's a million drugs out there that someone could have given him, and I have no idea what is really wrong with him, nor do I have the facilities to do the proper tests. You simply have to take him to Hvidovre."

Nina made no reply at first.

She had had so little time to look at the child. At first she had thought him to be barely three years old, but now, examining his face, she thought he was merely small for his age. Closer to four, perhaps. She touched his cheek gently, tracing the soft lines of the mouth. His hair was short and so fair it was nearly white, the skin parchment thin and almost bluish in the light streaming through the blinds.

"I don't know where he's from," she said. "I don't think he is Danish, and I know someone is looking for him. Someone who wants to . . . use him for something."

Again, Allan frowned.

"Pedophilia?"

Nina shrugged, trying to recall as much as she could about the man who had been kicking at the locker. Huge. That was the main impression. Perhaps thirty years old, with hair so short it hardly left an impression of color. Brown, perhaps? Like the weather-inappropriate leather jacket. She tried to imagine the police issuing an APB and knew immediately that this description would match any number of large men. And she pictured the boy, alone in a hospital room, while some social worker or child care specialist sat in the staff room filling out endless forms. Would they be able to protect the boy against the rage she had seen in the man's eyes? Once he woke up, what would the Danish authorities do with him? Send him to some institution or refugee center like the Coal-House Camp? Nina suppressed a shudder. Natasha's bastard of a fiancé had sauntered straight into the camp to pick up Rina without anyone even notic-ing she had gone. Far too many of the so-called unaccompanied minors simply disappeared from the camps after a few days. They were collected by their owners.

"I'm not letting them take him to the camps," she snapped, glancing around the office. "Children vanish from them almost every day. He's not going to any of those places."

Finally she saw what she was looking for. Behind the matte glass doors of the cabinets by the door she made out the contours of Allan's special emergency kit, which she knew to contain a couple of bags of IV fluid.

Last year, Allan had gone with her to attend an elderly man who had fled the Sandholm asylum center and was hiding with some relatives in the city. He had been due to be sent back to some refugee camp in Lebanon, but instead he was slumped on a mattress in a loft above an old tenement flat in Nørrebro. It was at least 115 degrees Fahrenheit up there under the rafters, and in other circumstances it might have been a rather trivial case of heat stroke. But because they didn't have the range of equipment an ordinary ambu-lance would have had, they nearly lost him. Since then, the infusion sets had been a fixture in Allan's emergency bag. As yet, he had not had to use them, as far as she knew. He wanted out. In fact, he had wanted out for a long time, but there was not exactly a waiting list for the unofficial post of MD to the illegal immigrants that the network struggled to aid, and Nina had hung on to his phone number. Just in case, she thought with a sardonic inner smile that didn't quite reach her lips. Just in case she came across a three-year-old boy in a suitcase.

She grabbed the infusion set and the IV bag off the shelf and felt a sense of calm descend as the familiar equipment came into her hands. She had done this a thousand times. Torn the clear wrapping in a single jerk, freed the needle, uncoiled the plastic tubing. She cast around for something to place the bag on, so that it would be higher than the boy, and finally cleared a space for it on the shelf above the couch, where various toys resided. Then she took hold of the boy's inanimate arm, exposed the veins under the white skin, and let the needle slide in.

Allan, standing next to her, shook his head and sighed.

"I'll lose my license if they find out about this. If anything happens to him. . . ."

"They won't. Why should they? And I'll take good care of him," said Nina. "He'll be all right."

Allan looked at her with a strange uncertainty Nina wasn't sure she cared for. Then he turned to the boy again, this time completely removing the blanket, which until now had shrouded the boy's lower body.

"Did you find him like this?" he asked.

Nina nodded.

"Would you be able to tell whether anything has been done to him?" she asked. "Whether he has been . . . abused?"

Allan gave a partial shrug and rolled the boy onto his side again, so that his back was turned to them. Nina again felt the sour metallic taste in her mouth, and turned to look out the window. There was a slight breeze now, and she could hear the leaves of the large chestnut tree outside rustle in the hot wind. Except for that, there was barely a sound. No voices, no cars, no children. People in Vedbæk obviously weren't as noisy as those in the inner city, she thought, suddenly aware of the sweaty stickiness that made her T-shirt cling to her back.

Behind her, Allan spoke in carefully measured tones.

"I see no evidence of abuse, but one can never tell with complete certainty. People can be horribly inventive about such things."

Allan pulled off the thin white plastic gloves with a snap, covered the boy to the waist once more, and gently stroked his forehead.

"This is my professional advice to you, Nina," he said, looking at her directly for the first time. His eyes were the color of corroded steel. For God's sake, thought Nina, the man might have stepped right off the pages of a Harlequin romance, fit and tanned in an affluent kind of way that spoke of tennis courts and long sailing trips in the boat she knew he kept in Vedbæk harbor. A note of casual ease was introduced by the dark blue denim jeans, trendily scuffed at the knees to just the right degree. A handsome, humane suburban GP who did everything right and proper, even running great personal risks by doing his bit for the network. His place in the practice was on the line, she thought. This was so obviously a good man.

And yet she felt a guttering animosity. In a minute, this nice, humane man would tell her that he couldn't help her anymore. That there was nothing further he could do for the boy.

Allan sighed again, a mere exhalation of breath.

"My professional advice is that you take this boy to Hvidovre Hospital. And if anything goes wrong. . . ."

Nina knew what he was about to say, but now it didn't matter, because she also knew she had won the essential victory: he wouldn't call the police.

"If anything goes wrong, and questions are asked of me and this practice, then that is the advice I have given you. And I want to hear you accept it."

She nodded quickly.

"I'll take him to Hvidovre Hospital," she obediently replied, with a quick glance at her watch.

3:09.

She had been there for more than thirty minutes.

Allan looked at her again with the skeptical expression that reminded her so much of her long, exhausted fights with Morten. Morten, who seemed to think that she could no longer be trusted to handle anything alone. Least of all the children. He didn't say it outright, but she could hear it in the way he spoke when he gave her detailed instructions on how to make Ida's lunch box, or how to dress Anton for school. He spoke slowly and clearly, enunciating each syllable, all the while trying to fix her eyes on him as though she were hard of hearing, or mentally defective, or both. More than anything, she could see it in his eyes when he packed his bags for his monthly shifts on the company's North Sea oil rigs. Leaving her alone with the children had begun to scare him.

He no longer believed her. He no longer believed in anything she said.

Nor did Allan, it would seem. But at least he

was not about to stop her. The suitcase boy was not his responsibility, and never would be. Only for that reason was he letting her go.

"Keep the IV going until the unit is empty," said Allan. "After that, I want you gone. Don't let anyone see you leave. And Nina. . . ."

He caught her eyes again, and she could see that his impatient irritation had returned.

"I'm through with this," he said. "Don't come back."

A nd it is your claim that your husband has abducted Mikas?"

Evaldas Gužas from the Department of Missing Persons looked at Sigita with visible skepticism.

"We are separated," she said.

"But he is the father of the child?"

She could feel herself blushing. "Of course."

The office was stifling in the summer heat, and a house fly buzzed desperately in the window overlooking the street, caught between the net curtain and the glass. Gužas's desk looked to be a scarred veteran of the Soviet era, several years older than Gužas himself was. Sigita would have preferred an older policeman, not this young, black-haired, sharp-featured man of thirty at the

77

most. He had doffed his blue-gray jacket and loosened his burgundy tie, so that he looked for all the world like a café patron on holiday. It didn't give a serious impression, she thought. She wanted experience, steadfastness, and efficiency, and she wasn't sure she was getting it.

"And this alleged abduction . . . you say it happened Saturday?"

"Saturday afternoon. Yes."

"And you waited two days to come to us because . . . ?"

He left his unfinished sentence hanging in the humid air.

She nearly lowered her eyes, but resisted the impulse. He would only see it as uncertainty and become even more skeptical than he already was.

"I was in hospital until this morning."

"I see. Can you relate to me the circumstances of the alleged abduction?" he asked.

"My neighbor saw my husband and a strange young woman take Mikas to a car and drive off with him."

"Did the child resist?"

"Not . . . not as far as Mrs. Mažekienė was able to see. But you see, the woman has been spying on us for some time, at least two or three days, and she gave Mikas chocolate. That's not normal!"

He clicked his ballpoint pen a couple of times, watching her all the while.

"And where were you when this happened?"

Now she could not keep the uncertainty from coming out in her voice.

"I . . . I don't remember clearly," she said. "I've suffered a concussion. Perhaps . . . perhaps they attacked me."

The words felt odd in her mouth because she didn't herself believe that Darius was capable of something like that. But the woman. She didn't know the woman, did she?

"And at which hospital were you treated?"

Her heart dropped like a stone. "Vilkpėdės," she said, hoping that would be the end of it. But of course it wasn't. He reached for the phone.

"Which ward?"

"M1."

She sat there on the uncomfortable plastic chair, frustrated and powerless, as he was put through to the ward and had a brief conversation with some-one at the other end. The fly kept buzzing and bumping into the glass. Gužas listened more than he talked, but she could guess what he was being told. Alcohol content in the blood, fall on the stairs.

"Mrs. Ramoškienė," he said, replacing the receiver. "Don't you think you should simply go home and wait for your husband to call?"

"I don't drink!" She blurted out the words even though she knew they would only confirm his suspicion.

"Please go home now, Mrs. Ramoškienė."

•••

Mechanically, she got on the number 17 trolley bus at T. Ševčenkos gatvė. Several stops too late, she realized that she had failed to get off at Aguonų gatvė to change lines. It was as if the city in which she had lived for more than eight years had suddenly become strange to her. The sunlight pierced her eyes like needles. Only once before in her life had she felt this helpless.

Please go home now, Mrs. Ramoškienė. But to what? Without Mikas, the whole thing made no sense—the flat, the furniture, all the clean and new things she had fought so hard for.

God's punishment, a voice whispered inside her.

"Shut up," she said under her breath, but it did no good.

She hadn't attended mass since leaving Tauragė. Not once in eight years. She didn't *want* to believe in God, but it was as if it wouldn't let her go—the hot, waxy scent of the candles, the old women who could barely kneel but insisted on doing so all the same, the flowers on the altar, the sense of solemnity that had made her sit quietly even when she had been so young her legs dangled from the pews in white stockings and shiny black shoes—that one day of the week one should make the effort, her mother said, and dress in one's best. Her first communion . . . she had felt so grown-up, so important. She was old enough to *sin*. The word unfolded inside her, releasing a scent of darkness and sulphur, of guilt and lost souls. But above all, sin was *interesting*. Interesting like Mama's sister, Aunt Jolita, who lived in Vilnius and had done things that no one would explain to Sigita. Sinners were far more interesting than ordinary people—it even said so in the Bible. Now this world of sin and confession had opened to her, too. It was peculiarly intoxicating to be a part of the chorus of response when the congregation murmured its *"Esu kaltas, esu kaltas, esu labai kaltas."* I am guilty, I am very guilty. She went at it with a will.

"Shhhh," said her mother, twitching her scarf into place. "Not so loud!"

By and by she learned the correct volume—not self-promotingly loud and shrill, nor so low that it sounded reluctant; a sincere murmur reaching the nearest without echoing through the dome. Esu kaltas. There was a beauty, a sweetness to it.

Until the day when she actually had something relevant to confess and couldn't bring herself to say it. At first she had tried for teenage rebellion by stating flatly that she wasn't going. Had it been only her mother, she might have carried it off. But when Granny Julija looked at her and asked her if anything was wrong, her weak attempt at mutiny collapsed. No, there was nothing wrong. Nothing at all. Granny Julija had patted her arm and told her that she was a good girl. It was all right to doubt a little sometimes, she said. God could take it. Then Sigita had had to hurry up and change into her Sunday best, so that they wouldn't be late. On the outside, everything was the way it had always been. On the inside, the world had come to an end.

The church of St. Kazimiero was silent and nearly empty now. Two older women were busy cleaning. Volunteers, probably, like they would have been at home in Tauragė, thought Sigita. One of them asked if Sigita needed anything.

"Thank you, no," said Sigita. "I just want to sit here for a while."

They nodded kindly. The need to "sit for a while" was understood by any true believer. Sigita felt like a fraud. She was no longer a believer of any kind.

If that is so, what are you doing here? whispered the voice inside her.

She couldn't explain it. She felt as if she was standing at the edge of an abyss, but she was in no way counting on God to rescue her. On the contrary. *I don't believe in any of it. Not anymore.* But when she looked up at the image of the Holy Virgin, she could no longer hold it back. The Madonna cradled the Baby Jesus tenderly, her face aglow with love. And Sigita fell to her knees on the cold flag stones and wept helplessly, hard involuntary sobs that echoed harshly under the vaulted ceilings. Esu kaltas. Esu labai kaltas.

• • •

She had only just left the church when her mobile phone started vibrating in her bag. She fumbled through the contents one-handedly, with the bag hanging from her plaster-encased lower arm, until wallet and makeup purse and throat lozenges tipped out onto the pavement and rolled in all directions. She had eyes for nothing except the phone. The call was from Darius, she noticed, as she snatched it from the ground.

"What's up with you?" he said in his usual happy warm voice. "You've called about a million times."

"You have to bring him back here. Now!" she snapped.

"What are you talking about?"

"Mikas! If you don't bring him back, I'll call the police." She neglected to tell him that she had in fact already done so. They just didn't want to know.

"Sigita. Sweetie. I have no idea what you're talking about. What is wrong with Mikas?"

Years of training had made her an expert. She was able to tell, by now, if he was lying or telling the truth. And the confusion in his voice sounded one hundred percent genuine.

Strength drained from her legs like water from a bath tub, and she dropped to her knees for the second time, in the middle of the sidewalk, surrounded by the debris from her bag. A distantly tinny Darius-voice was shouting at her from somewhere: "Sigita. Sigita, what is it? Where is Mikas?"

She was no longer at the edge of the abyss. It had already swallowed her. Because if Darius did not have Mikas, who did?

5 :10 p.m.

Whose turn was it to pick up Anton today? Suddenly Nina couldn't remember, and felt a long, cold tug in the pit of her stomach, as though she was about to be pulled under by some deep, chill current. The after-school child care program provided by the city would have closed at 5:00. Her son might be standing by the gate right now, accompanied by a seriously cross member of the staff.

She had seated herself on the couch with the unknown boy half in her lap, his bare white body curled against her. A few damp streaks had appeared in his hair. His skin felt warmer now, and after the fluid had begun to run into him, he seemed more alive. Not awake, but alive, at least. Once, he whimpered in his sleep, turned a wrist, moved his leg a bit. It had to be a good sign, thought Nina. She had done the right thing in staying away from the hospital, and even though she had felt her resolution firm every time she thought of the furious man at the railway station, it was still an enormous relief. The boy hadn't died. He lived, and she could tell by the tiny twitches beneath his eyelids that he was on his way back up from the deep darkness he had rested in.

Yet mixed with the relief was a new sense of panic, as thoughts beyond mere survival started to surface. What on earth had she been thinking since she fled from the railway station?

Not a damn thing, she thought sardonically, running a finger under the strap of her wristwatch to ease it away from the overheated skin underneath. There hadn't been a single thought in her head apart from the panicked urge to get away. Bring him to safety. And now she would soon have a wide-awake naked boy in her arms, and absolutely no idea what she was going to do with him.

She needed to buy time. She leaned over and tugged her bag toward her, fumbling inside for her mobile. Thank God Morten was home this week. He would have to deal with things until. . . .

Her finger hovered over the Place Call button for a few seconds while she prepared herself as best she could. She had never been particularly good at lying to Morten, and time hadn't improved her skills, despite frequent practice. It wasn't that she wanted to be able to lie to him about important things. Just little everyday fibs that would make life run so much more smoothly. Like being able to say that her new top had cost 200 kroner rather than 450, or that it hadn't been she who had forgotten the picnic invitation from Anton's school. Other people got away with such things, why couldn't she? She was an adequate liar with everyone but Morten, she thought. But Morten saw through her feeble attempts in seconds. Somehow, she lacked her usual protective coloration when she was with him. It seemed to her that he could look directly into the bubbling mass of unfinished thoughts churning inside her. It was why she had fallen in love with him, and why he was so hard to live with now. Sometimes a lie would go by without comment, but it didn't feel like success; it was more as if he couldn't really be bothered to discuss it with her. He let her off the hook.

Nina touched the call button tentatively; the phone was already damp from the heat of her hands. Then she pressed it, and raised the phone to her ear, careful not to disturb the boy with her shift of position.

There was a tiny click as he answered, followed by a faint, surf-like noise. She could hear Morten's fumbling with the phone, and distant children's voices in the background. Thank God. He was picking up Anton, then. It might even be his turn today. Her mind felt curiously blank when she tried to remember.

"Yes." Morten's voice succeeded in being angry and resigned at the same time. "Where are you?"

It was the voice of a man who felt that she no longer deserved to be talked to as an equal. Or even as an adult.

Nina moistened her lips, looking down at the child in her arms. She had to come up with something not too far from the truth, she thought, or he would slice her explanations into ribbons before they were half finished.

"Karin called me, earlier today," she finally said. "She wasn't feeling very well. She really needed help. I've had to stay with her so that I can take her to a doctor if it becomes necessary."

Silence at the other end. Then she could hear shouting again, and Anton's thin voice asking for something.

"No," said Morten without putting down the phone, "No ice cream. It's Monday, and you know the rules." In the background Nina could hear Anton's voice rising, getting ready for the full campaign. Which might be her good luck.

"Okay," said Morten. "But I didn't think the two of you were that close anymore?"

He didn't sound angry anymore, just a little tired.

"I've known her for fifteen years. With history like that, you don't just turn your back on people."

"It's okay," he said. "But perhaps you might have called me, instead of leaving that to the staff here."

Damn. Nina shrunk a little. It *had* been her turn, had to have been, and somehow she would have felt better about it, more secure, if Morten had thrown a fit. Now there was just the unrythmic rattle of the receiver and the indistinct snatches of a new heated argument between Morten and Anton. Morten had already forgotten she was there.

"I'm sorry," she murmured, trying to press her ear more closely to the phone. "I just forgot."

"Yes, I suppose you did," he said, his voice cold and weary. "I thought things were better. I thought you were going to stop forgetting your own family. Any idea when you will be home?"

Nina swallowed. The boy had turned slightly, and one small hand opened and then closed around her arm. His eyes were still closed.

"Oh, I suppose I can leave here around eight," she said, trying to sound carefree and unworried. "It won't be very late, I promise."

Again the static hiss of wind and a connection on the point of breaking up.

"I'll see you when I see you," said Morten, the last few words nearly lost in the roar of the wind and the sound of Anton's eager pestering. "Or not. It's up to you."

Morten's voice had gone dark and distant. Then

there was just silence, real silence, as the connection was finally severed.

Nina exhaled soundlessly and let the phone slip back into her bag on the floor. Then she eased herself away from the boy and stood up. Her heart beat a hard, cantering rhythm, and she needed to move, as if the disquiet she felt could be dispelled by mere motion. She stooped to snatch up the phone once more and pressed a new number while pacing up and down, imposing her own restless-ness on the whole room.

He was listed merely as "Peter" in her phone book, and actually that was almost as much as she knew about him, except that he lived some-where in Vanløse. He was the only contact in the network whose number she had. Normally it was the other way around—they called her. The people the network looked after could not saunter into the office of their local GP, or take their children to the emergency room if they were ill. Could not, in fact, approach authority in any form. So when there was need, Nina was sent for, or Allan. Or so it had been. Might she perhaps ask Magnus to step in, if Allan was serious about quitting? Unfortunately, though, Magnus did not have access to a handily secluded private practice in Vedbæk.

"Hi, this is Peter," announced a happy-sounding voice, and Nina nearly said "Hi" herself when the voice went on without pausing: "I am on holiday from the fifteenth of August to the twenty-ninth, so you'll just have to do without me!"

Bloody hell. Nina rested her forehead against the wall, closing her eyes for a minute. She had never done this bit before. Not with an unaccompanied child. The network would sometimes find some basement room or empty summerhouse for a family to stay in, or help them across to Sweden —that wasn't too complicated. Such people could, after all, look after themselves in most respects. But was there anyone out there who would take on an abandoned three-year-old? And if there was, how would she find them?

Nina opened her eyes, examining the boy in a slightly different way. He could come from anywhere, she thought. Anywhere in Northern or Eastern Europe. Denmark, Sweden, Poland, Germany. She drew a hand through her own short, dark hair, which felt sticky and damp in the humid air. She would be wiser once the boy woke up, she supposed; meanwhile, she just had to get hold of Karin. She was the one who had started all this, and Nina had no doubts that Karin knew more than she had been willing to say when she'd sat there in Magasin's cafeteria, nervously twisting her coffee cup.

This time, she let the phone ring until it stopped, but Karin still didn't answer, and Nina brushed at the faintly lit display with a restless finger, as if to clear away invisible dust.

The boy stirred, and the blanket slipped to reveal a naked shoulder.

Clothes, thought Nina, and felt relief at having a practical solution to focus on. She had to get some clothes for the boy so they wouldn't draw any more attention than they had to. She peered at the IV bag. Nearly empty, which meant she would be able to get out of here soon.

She tried Karin once more. Same depressing lack of results.

"Why the hell couldn't the woman just answer her phone?

Jučas knew his rage was both a weakness and a strength. When he was training he could sometimes use it to wring the last reserves from his body, and achieve those explosions of force that made his blood throb in a way that was almost better than sex. Following a set like that, he could *see* it: the veins lay on top of his muscles like plastic tubing, and the pump was visible, bang bang bang, just as he felt it in every fiber. God, he loved that feeling. In such moments he felt strong, and he had to suppress a desire to leap onto the bench and yell out his invulnerability to the world, like some action hero from the American films he liked to watch: *You don't fuck with me, man.*

At other times, the rage helped him do things he didn't really like doing. It was always there, just under the surface, a hidden power he could call on at need. Then the men became swine, and the women bitches, and he could do what had to be done. But it was dangerous to unleash it, because it also meant a loss of control. He couldn't always stop once he had started, and he didn't think as clearly as he normally did. Once he had hit the man who was the swine at that moment so hard that the guy never really recovered, and Klimka had told him that if that happened again, Jučas would be fired. In the most permanent way. It was just about then that he realized the rage could kill him one day if he wasn't careful, and he had actually stopped taking both the andros and the durabolines immediately, because they made the rage that much harder to control. It was around that time he had met Barbara, too.

When he was with Barbara, the rage was sometimes so distant he could pretend it had gone away. It might even *be* gone one day, he thought, when he never had to work for Klimka again, when he and Barbara had their house just outside Krakow, and he could spend his days doing ordinary things like mowing the lawn, putting up shelves, eating dinners Barbara made him, and making love to the woman he wanted to spend the rest of his life with.

But there hadn't been any money. Every time he thought of the empty locker, fury sent accurate little stabs through him like a nail gun. God, he could have smashed the bitch's skull in.

He had deliberately chosen a locker in the was out of sight of the staff in the security booth. At first he had taken up position in the actual basement, so that he would be able to see when the suitcase was picked up, and by whom. But he had been there only about ten minutes when the security staff began to get nervous. He could tell they were watching him, taking turns at it, first one, then the other. They put their heads together and talked. Then one of them reached for the phone. Damn. He got out his own mobile and held it so that it shielded part of his face as he went past their window and up the stairs to the central hall.

In the end, he'd had to station Barbara there, while he himself tried to watch both the other two exits from the car. It was far from perfect. If only it had been the Dane himself, whom he knew by sight. But now it was to be some female Jučas had never laid eyes on. Oh, well. He would be able to recognize the suitcase, at least.

Twelve o'clock came and went with no suitcase-dragging woman in sight. He kept phoning Barbara, just to be sure, but he could hear that he was only making her nervous. He decided to give it an hour; after all, the Dane had had to make contingency plans, so some delay was under-standable. But in the end, he had to send Barbara down to check on the locker.

A few minutes later, she came up the stairs by the street exit, and he could see it a mile off: something was wrong. She was walking with tense little reluctant steps, her shoulders hunched. ."It wasn't there," she said.

So he had to go see for himself, of course. And she was right. Somehow, the woman must have gotten past either him or Barbara. The suitcase was gone, and no money had been left in its place. When he saw that, he lost it for a moment so that the uniformed piglets got all scared, and he had to smile and pay to calm their frightened little hearts.

And in the middle of all that, he had felt it. Her eyes on him. She might have been any old tourist except for the intensity of her gaze, but he picked her out of the crowd immediately. The woman. She had been scared, too. And more than that. He had seen her note what locker it was he had been smashing. When she turned and ran, he was sure. She was the one. She had taken the suitcase. But why had she come back? Did she think she could come here to gloat, and he wouldn't know? He would show her differently. Even through the rage, he saw her clearly. Thin as a boy, with very short dark hair; for a moment he imagined sticking his cock into something like that, but who would want to, unless they were queer?

Bloody boy-bitch. He would stick her, all right, but with something else.

He called the Dane right away. Was fed a truckload of excuses about delays and honest intentions. Could he believe the man? He didn't know. Anger was still guttering in his stomach as he walked up the steps to the street, past three Russians engaged in a blatant dope deal. Morons. Couldn't they be just a little discrete? The biggest one, obviously meant to be the muscle, cast a nervous eye over Jučas. It improved his mood a fraction. Look your fill, he thought. I'm bigger than you are, pal.

Outside in the street, heat surged from the pavement and the sun-warmed bricks. The leather jacket had been a bad choice, but he'd thought Denmark would be colder, and now he didn't really feel he could take it off. He sweated a lot, people did when they were in good shape, and he didn't like Barbara to see him with huge underarm stains on his shirt.

"Andrius?" Barbara called to him through the open car window. "Is it okay?"

He forced himself to take long deep breaths. Couldn't quite produce a smile, but he did manage to ease his grip on the car keys.

"Yes." Deep breaths. Easy now. "He says it's a mistake. He is on his way home, and when he gets here, we will get our money."

"That's good." Barbara was watching him with her head cocked slightly to one side. For some reason, it made her neck look even longer. More elegant. She was the only one who ever called him by his given name. Everyone else just called him Jučas. He didn't even think of himself as Andrius, and hadn't since his Granny died and he was sent to Vilnius to live with his father because no one had any idea what else might be done with him. His father rarely called him by name at all, it had been either "boy" or "brat," according to his mood. Later, in the orphanage, everyone had gone by their last name.

He let himself drop into the front seat next to her, wincing at the contact with the sun-scorched fabric. The Mitsubishi had a certain lived-in appearance after two days on the road. Paper mugs and sandwich bags from German Raststellen littered the floor, and the food-smeared car seat the boy had been strapped into gave off a sour odor of pee. He really ought to dismantle it and sling it in the back of the van, but right now the fug was too much for him and he didn't want to spend another minute in the car.

"Are you hungry?" he said. "We might as well do something while we wait for him to call."

Suddenly, Barbara's face came alive.

"Tivoli!" she said. "Could we go there? I was looking through the fence earlier, and it all looks so beautiful."

He had not the slightest wish to endure the wait surrounded by screaming toddlers, cotton candy, and balloon vendors, but the surge of expectation in her eyes melted his resolve. They paid a day's wage to get in, and ate a pizza that only set him back about seven or eight times as much as it would have cost him in Vilnius. But Barbara was loving every minute. She smiled more than she had done at any time during the long tense drive here, and his nerves began to settle. Perhaps everything would still be all right in the end. It might be just a misunderstanding. After all, if the Dane was stuck in a plane and couldn't do much, it wasn't surprising somebody screwed up. He would pay. He had said so. And if he didn't, Jučas knew where he lived.

"There's a bit of oregano on your chin," said Barbara. "No, let me. . . ." She blotted the corner of his mouth gently with the red-and-white-checkered napkin, smiling into his eyes so that the rage curled up inside him and went to sleep.

Later they walked around a ridiculous little lake in which someone had placed a disproportionate schooner, so large it would hardly be able to turn if anyone had the misguided idea to try to actually sail it. Barbara put two fat Danish coins into an automat and was rewarded with a small bag of fish fodder. As soon as they heard the click from the automat, the fish in the lake surged forward so that the water literally boiled with their huge writing bodies. The sight turned his gut, he wasn't quite sure why. At that moment, the phone finally rang.

"I just got home," said the man at the other end. "There is no sign of the goods or the money. Nor of the person I sent to do the trade."

Bitch. Swine.

"I delivered," he said, with as much calm as he could muster. "Now you must pay."

The man was silent for a while. Then he said:

"When you give me what I paid for, you will get the rest of the money."

Jučas was struggling both with his temper and his English vocabulary. Only Barbara's hand on his arm made it possible to win at least one of those battles.

"You sent the woman. If she don't do what you say, is not my problem."

Again, the silence. Even longer, this time.

"She took a company car," the Dane finally said. "We have GPS tracking on all of them. If I tell you where she is, will you go and get her? She must have either the money or the goods, or both. Or she must know where they are. Bring her back to me."

"Is not what we agreed," said Jučas through clenched teeth. He wanted his money, and he wanted to get out of this stinking, stupidly expensive country where even the fish were fat.

"Ten thousand dollars extra," said the man

promptly. "To get the money and the goods, and bring her back."

The screaming from the roller coaster was getting on his nerves. But ten thousand dollars was ten thousand dollars.

"Okay," he said. "You tell me where she is."

Nina wrapped the blanket more tightly about the boy, picked him up, and left Allan's office with the skinny body in her arms. He felt feather light compared to Anton, but of course Anton was no longer a toddler. He went to school. He was a big boy now.

She was careful to make sure that the lock on the main door of the practice clicked behind her. The parking lot, thank God, was still empty. She levered the body carefully into the back seat and closed the door with a soft push. It was 6:44.

"What do I do now?" she muttered, then caught herself with some irritation. Talking to herself now. Not cool. She hadn't done that much since she started secondary school and had had to leave that and other childish habits behind if she wanted to survive socially. But sometimes, under pressure, it came back. It seemed to help her concentrate.

She started the car and let it roll down the graveled drive. Her hands were shaking again. She noted it with the same detached interest she would have awarded a rare bird at her bird feeder. She had to lock her fingers around the rim of the steering wheel to stop the annoying quiver that spread through her arms, then her palms to the tips of her fingers.

Karin had not returned any of her calls. Nor had Morten. Nor had there been any sign of police or other authorities. The last would of course have been unlikely, but the sense of being hunted would not leave her. It just didn't seem right that she could be driving around for hours with a three-year-old boy who wasn't hers. Somebody had to be missing him—someone other than the furious man at the railway station.

Nina turned up the volume of the car radio to be ready to catch the news. It was 6:46 according to the display on her mobile. She slowed slightly and regained enough control of her fingers to tap out Karin's number once more.

After seven long rings, there was, finally, an answer.

"Hello?"

Karin's voice sounded both hopeful and reserved.

Nina took a deep breath. It would be so easy for Karin to cut the connection if Nina came on too strongly. She had to be careful. Had to coax Karin into giving the answers she needed.

"Karin."

Nina softened her tone persuasively. Like she did when Anton was in the grip of one of his nightmares—gently, gently.

"Karin, it's Nina. I have the boy with me here in the car. He is okay."

Silence. Then a long hiccoughing breath and a heavy sigh. Karin was battling to control her voice.

"Oh, thank God. Nina, thank you so much for getting him out of there."

Another long silence. That seemed to be it. Nina cursed inwardly. Thank you for getting him out of there? How about an explanation? How about a bit of help? Something, anything, that would tell her what to do with her three-year-old burden.

"I have to know something about him," she said. "I have no idea what to do with him. Do you want me to take him to the police? Do you know where he comes from?"

Nina heard the rising shrillness in her own voice, and for a moment she was afraid Karin had gotten spooked and hung up. Then she heard a faint, wet snuffling, as if from a cornered and wounded animal.

"I really don't know, Nina. I thought you had contacts . . . that your network would be able to help him."

Nina sighed.

"I have no one," she said, and felt the truth of it for the first time, at the very pit of her stomach. "Look, we need to talk properly. Where can I find you?"

Karin hesitated, and Nina could practically hear the doubts and fears ripping away at her.

"I'm in a summer cottage."

"Where?"

Nina waited tensely, while Karin fumbled with her phone.

"I don't want to be involved in this. I can't. It wasn't supposed to be a *child*."

The last word was nearly a wail, a high-pitched hysterical whimper, and Karin could no longer control the violent sobbing that Nina guessed had been coming even before she answered the phone.

"Where is the cottage?" she repeated, striving for a note of calm authority. "Tell me where you are, Karin, and I will come to you. It will be all right."

Karin's breath came in harsh bursts, and her silence this time was so long that Nina might have ended the call, had she not been so desperate herself.

"Tisvildeleje."

Karin's voice was so faint that Nina could barely make it out.

"I've borrowed the cottage from my cousin, and it's. . . ." There was a crackling sound as

102

Karin fumbled for something, possibly a piece of paper. "Twelve Skovbakken. It's at the very end, the last house before the woods."

There was a click, and this time, she really was gone.

Nina turned to the sleeping child with the first real smile she had been able to manage during the six hours that had passed since she opened a suitcase and found a boy.

"I've got it covered," she said, feeling her hands unclench on their own. "Now we will go find out what has happened, and then I will see to it that you get back home where you belong."

S igita was desperate enough to ask him to come. Darius's mobile phone voice became ill at ease.

"Sigita. . . . You know I can't."

"Why not?"

"My job."

He worked for a construction company in Germany. Not as an engineer, as he sometimes told people, but as a plumber.

"This is *Mikas*, Darius."

"Yes. But. . . ."

She ought to have known. When had she ever

been able to count on him? But Mikas . . . she hadn't imagined that Mikas meant so little. Darius liked the boy and often played with him for anything up to an hour at a time. And Mikas worshiped his father, who would always appear at the oddest times, carrying armfuls of cellophane-wrapped toys.

"Are other people's toilets really more important to you than your son?" she choked.

"Sigita. . . ."

She hung up. She knew it wasn't his job that was stopping him. If it had been something he really wanted to do, like a football match or something, then he called in sick without worrying about it. He was not a career chaser. His job didn't mean all *that* much to him.

It wasn't because he couldn't, it was because he wouldn't. He wanted to stay in his new life, probably with a new girlfriend, too, and had no wish to be drawn back to Vilnius and Tauragė, to Sigita and her tiresome demands.

Pling-pliiing. The mobile gave off its tinny "Message received" signal. The text message was from Darius.

Call me when Mikas comes home, it said.

As though Mikas were a runaway dog who would appear on her doorstep when it became sufficiently hungry.

"Are you all right, madam?"

She looked up. An elderly gentleman in a gray

suit stood watching her from a few yards away, supported by a black cane.

"Yes," she said. "It's . . . it was just . . . it's over now."

He helped her to her feet and began to collect her scattered belongings.

"It's important to drink enough when it is this hot," he said kindly. "Or so my doctor is always telling me. I often forget."

"Yes. Yes, you are quite right."

He tipped his pale gray Fedora to her as he left. "Good afternoon, madam."

She went back to the police station in Birželio 23-iosios gatvė. Sergeant Gužas's face took on a look of resignation when he saw her in his doorway.

"Mrs. Ramoškienė. I thought you were going home."

"It's not him. Darius didn't take him," she said. "Don't you understand that my son has been kid-napped?"

Resignation gave way to tiredness.

"Mrs. Ramoškienė, a few hours ago you claimed that your husband had taken the boy. Am I to understand that this isn't so?"

"Yes! That's what I'm telling you."

"But your neighbor saw—"

"She must have made a mistake. She's old, her eyesight is not very good. And I think she has only met Darius once."

105

Click, click, click. The point of his ballpen appeared and disappeared, appeared and disappeared. A habit of his, it seemed, when he was trying to think. Sigita could barely stand it. She wanted to tear the pen away from him, and only the need to appear rational and sober held her back. He simply *has* to believe me, she thought. He has to.

Finally, he reached for a notepad.

"Sit down, Mrs. Ramoškienė. Give me your description of the chain of events once more."

She complied, doing the best she could to reconstruct what had happened. Described to him the tall, fair-haired woman in the cotton coat. Told him about the chocolate. But then she reached the gap. The black hole in her mind into which nearly twenty-four hours had disappeared.

"What's the name of the kindergarten?"

"Voveraitė. He is in the Chipmunk Group."

"Is there a phone number?"

She gave it to him. Soon he was talking to the director herself, Mrs. Šaraškienė. The compact ladylike form of the director popped into Sigita's mind's eye. Always immaculately dressed in jacket and matching skirt, nylons and low-heeled black pumps, as if she were on her way to a board meeting in a company of some size. She was about fifty, with short chestnut hair and a natural air of authority that instantly silenced even the wildest games whenever she entered one of the homerooms. Sigita was just a little bit afraid of her.

Gužas explained his errand; a child, Mikas Ramoška, had been reported missing. A woman involved in the matter might have made contact with the boy in the kindergarten playgrounds. Was it possible that one or more of the staff had observed this woman, or any other stranger, talking to the children or watching them, perhaps?

"The chocolate," said Sigita. "Don't forget the chocolate."

He nodded absently while listening to Mrs. Šaraskienė's reply.

Then he asked directly, apparently completely unaffected by Sigita's presence: "What is your impression of Mikas Ramoška's mother?"

Sigita felt heat rush into her face. The nerve! What would Mrs. Šaraškienė think!

"Thank you. I would like to talk to the group leader in question. Would you ask her to call this number as soon as possible? Thank you very much for your time."

He hung up.

"It seems one of the staff has in fact noticed your fair-haired woman and has told her not to give the children sweets. But Mikas wasn't the only child she contacted."

"Maybe not. But Mikas is the only one who is gone!"

"Yes."

She wasn't going to ask. She didn't *want* to ask. But she blurted it out anyway:

"What did she say about me?"

The tiniest of smiles curled his upper lip, the first sign of humanity she had observed in him.

"That you were a good mother and a responsible person. One of those who pay. She appreciates your commitment."

There was no fee as such to be paid for Mikas's basic care, but the kindergarten had an optional program funded by parents who paid a certain sum into the program's account every month. The money was used for maintenance and improvements, and for cultural activities with the children —things for which the city did not provide a budget. It had been a sacrifice, especially the first year after she had bought the flat, but to Sigita it was important to be "one of those who pay."

"Do you believe me now?"

He considered her for a while. Click, click went the damned pen.

"Your statement has been corroborated on certain points," he said, seeming almost reluctant.

"Then will you please *do* something!" She could no longer contain her despair. "You have to find him!"

Click, click, click.

"I've taken your statement now, and we will of course send out a missing persons bulletin on Mikas," he said. "We'll look for him."

At first Sigita felt a vast relief at being *believed.* She opened her purse and pushed the picture of Mikas out of its plastic pocket. The picture had been taken at the kindergarten's midsummer celebration, and Mikas was in his Sunday best, with a garland of oak leaves clutched in his hands and an uncertain smile on his face. He had objected to wearing the garland in his hair because he didn't want to look like a girl, she recalled.

"Thank you," she said. "Will this do? It's a good likeness."

She put it on the desk in front of Gužas. He took it, but there was something in the way he did it, a certain hesitation, as if he wasn't sure how much use it was going to be. It was then she realized that it was much too soon to feel any kind of relief.

"Mrs. Ramoškienė . . . is there any chance that the couple who took the boy are someone you know, or perhaps someone you are related to?"

"No, I . . . don't think so. I certainly didn't know the woman. But I didn't really ask Mrs. Mažekienė about the man because I thought it was Darius."

"We will try to get a description from your neighbor. Have the kidnappers tried to contact you in any way? Any demands, or threats? And can you think of anyone who might want to pressure you for any reason?"

She shook her head silently. The only thing she could think of was that it might be something to do with Janus Construction, with Dobrovolskij and other clients like him, and the figures she kept only in her head. But how? It didn't make sense. And in any case, no one had said a thing. No threats. No demands.

She realized that he was watching her intently, and that the clicking of the pen had finally ceased.

"What do they want with him?" she said softly, hardly daring to say it out loud, because it made it that much more real. "Why do people steal someone else's child?"

"When a child is taken, it is often personal—aimed at a specific child, for specific reasons that might be to do with custody rights, or with something the kidnappers want from the parents. But there is a second category. One where the motives are less personal, and in those cases. . . ." He hesitated, and she had to prod him on.

"What then?"

"In those cases, the perpetrators just take a child. Any child."

He didn't come right out and say it, but she knew immediately what he meant. She knew that children were sold in the same way some people sold women. A crushed and wordless whimper forced itself out of her. Esu kaltas, esu kaltas, esu labai kaltas. It's all my fault. Desperately, she tried to stop the images that flickered through her head. She wouldn't, she couldn't think of Mikas in the hands of people like that. It would destroy her.

"Please. Please, will you find him for me?" she begged, through a hot flood of tears that blurred the room and made intelligible speech almost impossible.

"We will try," he said. "But let us hope that Mikas belongs to the first category. They are often found, sooner or later."

Again he didn't say it, but she could hear the unspoken words all the same: we never find the others.

She didn't really have the time.
Nina's sense of urgency made it feel all wrong to contemplate a mundane shopping expedition, but the devil did, after all, reside in the details, and at a minimum she needed one set of T-shirt, shorts, and sandals sized for a three-year-old if she and the boy were to remain relatively secure and invisible for a while.

She scanned the storefronts on Stationsvej and cursed softly to herself at the lack of choice. There weren't all that many shops to begin with, and most of them now had closed doors and dead, unlit windows. But as she approached the end of the street, more appeared, and two of them, amazingly enough, sold children's clothes. Both clearly saw themselves as up-market; one even had a French name—La Maison Des Petites. Outside, the racks sported brightly colored rompers in a trendy retro '70s style, and when she peered through the window, she spotted a mannequin that looked to be about the right size. *And* the shop was still open. A big retail chain like Kvickly would have been better, not to mention cheaper, but so far all she had seen along the way had been a co-op with nothing much but food products. She was running out of time. The boy was lying on the back seat like a small, ticking bomb; traveling discretely with a screaming three-year-old in tow was difficult enough in itself—if the child was naked, it would be plain impossible. First rule of survival: don't draw attention to your-self.

She turned into Olgasvej and squeezed the antiquated little Fiat into a space between two larger cars parked along the curb. She twisted in her seat to draw the blanket more thoroughly over the boy, who already seemed too close to the surface. One small arm came up to tug reflexively at the woolly material, pulling it off his face again.

Nina got out of the car, quickly scanning her surroundings. On a day as hot as this, presumably most of the inhabitants of Vedbæk would have retired to the beach, or to shady gardens and barbecued patio meals. But there were still people in the streets. On the opposite sidewalk, a suburban family sauntered past, the father thin-legged in shorts that were *too* short, the mother in a white summery top exposing her sunburnt, peeling shoulders. Their two young daughters both held giant ice cream cones, and the parents were engaged in heated conversation. A little further up the street on Nina's side, a senior citizen was walking a heavy-set basset hound, and a tight little group of long-haired teenagers had just turned the corner from Stationsvej and were headed Nina's way.

"All right," said Nina, deliberately leaning across the back seat through the open door. "I'll get you an ice cream, but that's it, okay? No more pestering." She paused artistically, covertly eying the dog walker, who was now within easy hearing, but moving at a draggingly slow pace. "Mama will be back in a jiffy."

She locked the doors quickly, then trotted resolutely back towards Stationsvej. The teenagers seemed not to have noticed her, or the little show she had provided. They moved only enough for her to edge past them and forge on. Behind her she heard their odd mix of conversation and intense texting. Good, she thought. Much too self-absorbed to be a problem.

La Maison Des Petites seemed to think that what every parent really wanted was to dress their offspring like small replicas of the children they themselves had been in the '70s. The colors were bright and loud, the fabrics mostly linen and organically produced cotton, so that the little ones were not exposed to unwanted chemicals. All very well-intentioned, but Nina winced at the thought of what it would do to her bank balance.

A discretely perfumed young mother, hair tucked back by the big dark fashionable sunglasses riding on top of her head, glided past with a fat baby on her hip. Again, Nina became conscious of her sticky T-shirt and the far from fragrant odor of sweat she projected. And of fear, probably. Right now she fitted into this affluent suburban idyll about as well as a Saint Bernard in a two-room flat.

She dug out five pairs of underpants from a jumble box of Summer Sale offers in the middle of the shop. Then she rifled through the piles of jeans and T-shirts. How many days should she plan for? How long would he have to stay with her?

She had no idea, but decided to err on the side of optimism. One pair of jeans, one pair of shorts, and two light long-sleeved cotton shirts. . . . That would have to do for now. Biting her lip, Nina eyed the footwear shelves. A pair of sandals were really a necessity. She piled the goods onto the counter and tried to look as little as possible at the salesperson as she ran the scanner over the brightly colored price tags.

"That'll be two thousand four hundred fifty-eight kroner," said the young woman behind the counter, smiling with superficial courtesy. Nina forced herself to return the smile. Overcoming her reluctance, she tapped her credit card pin-code into the register and received the big white carrier bag with a measured nod.

Outside, the heat was unremitting. Nina checked her watch. 7:02. She had been gone from the car for twelve minutes. She crossed to the corner of Stationsvej and Olgasvej and looked toward the Fiat. No signs of unusual activity. No collection of worried onlookers, no curious faces. An elderly man in an oversized T-shirt shuffled past the car without giving it a second glance. The boy must still be asleep, thought Nina in relief. There was a supermarket just across the street. If she hurried, she might have time to pick up a few groceries. She wasn't exactly hungry, but she had had nothing since breakfast, and she knew she would have to eat something soon.

It didn't take her long to grab a loaf of white bread, a bag of apples, and two bottles of water. That was all she could think of, until she was approaching the exit and her eyes fell on the ice cream freezer next to the toiletry section. Cold, she thought. Sweet. Plenty of calories. Just the thing. She transferred a foil-wrapped ice cream cone from the freezer to her basket and began to load her purchases onto the conveyor belt. The pimply teenage girl at the register was the only living, breathing human in sight. For some reason Nina couldn't take her eyes off the girl's unusually long, square nails as they clicked against the display.

Nina piled her purchases into a yellow plastic bag and hurried back into the brightness of the sunlight. She had been gone for sixteen minutes now, and she suddenly knew sixteen minutes was too long. She had the horrible sensation that time, vitally important time, had once again slipped through her fingers, and she headed for the Fiat at a near-run.

The car was where she had left it, of course, but something was wrong all the same. A woman with a thumb-sucking toddler in a stroller had taken up position a few feet from the car and was anxiously scouting up and down Olgasvej. Nina's stomach dropped, but she still managed to slow to a speed she thought more appropriate for her role as a slightly frazzled but responsible mother.

"Is that your car? Is that your boy in there?"

The woman's voice rose into an indignant descant the moment she caught sight of Nina.

Nina only nodded. The distance to the car seemed to stretch into infinity, and now that the woman had found someone to focus her outrage on, her temper was visibly rising like the tide. Close up, she was older than she had appeared at a distance, one of those thirty-something women who took such infinite care with their appearance that only faint lines at the corner of their eyes betrayed their age when they smiled or frowned. Now indignant anger narrowed her eyes and added years to her face. It didn't become her, thought Nina, and felt her own muscles tense in response.

The stroller was parked so that it blocked the entire sidewalk, and the woman had her hands set on her hips in a confident stance.

"I've stood here waiting for you for nearly twenty minutes," she announced, pointing demonstratively at her watch. "You don't just leave a child in a car like this. And in this heat! He might die of heat stroke. It's completely irresponsible, and frankly dangerous."

Nina considered her strategy. The woman had not been there for twenty minutes, and Nina had made sure the Fiat was shaded by one of the big chestnut trees along the road, and had left all the windows ajar. The boy was in no danger of dying from the heat in such a short time, and nobody knew it better than Nina. She had seen children lie for days without proper shelter in 120° weather and still live long enough to die from malnutrition. The outraged mother was clearly one of those overzealous idiots who enjoyed showing others what a wonderful parent she herself happened to be. But knowing this was of little use. The main objective was to get away without drawing any more attention to herself or the boy. Nina lowered her eyes and forced a contrite smile.

"I had promised him an ice cream cone, and there was a line at the check-out," she said, trying to edge past the aggressively parked stroller.

"Oh? And I suppose the Maison Des Petites was terribly busy too?" countered the woman, and Nina cursed under her breath. The big white carrier bag from the fashion boutique was hard to explain away, and she decided not to try. Instead, she turned her back firmly on the indignant woman, unlocked the car—and came close to knocking down both woman and stroller as she took a startled pace backwards.

The boy was sitting up.

The blanket was still wrapped about his legs, and he was staring at her through the half-open window with huge dark blue eyes.

Nina forced herself to stand still while possibilities and half-formed plans flitted feverishly through her head. Should she simply get into the car and drive away? Should she speak to him? And if she did, what would happen if he answered?

Then she recalled the ice cream cone.

She tore her attention away from the confused, fearful gaze of the boy for as long as it took to rummage through the yellow plastic bag and fish it out. She peeled off the shiny blue wrapper and held out the cone to him through the open window, hardly daring to meet his eyes again. Apparently, she didn't have to. She saw instead how a small pale hand slowly moved toward the rim of the rolled-down window and took hold of the ice cream.

"Atju."

The boy's voice was faint, but he spoke the word slowly and clearly, as if to make sure she didn't misunderstand.

"No," she said quickly. "They were all out of those. You'll have to make do with this one instead."

Then she marched around the front end of the car as quickly as she could and got into the driver's seat. The indignant voice followed her as she backed and turned, sounding loud and clear through the open windows.

"You don't even have a proper car seat for him," shrilled the woman. "I simply don't understand how someone like you can call herself a mother. I simply don't. . . ."

Sigita would have liked to stay at the police station, but Gužas evicted her politely but firmly. He had her phone number, he would call. He repeated his exhortation to go home.

"But perhaps you shouldn't be alone. The boy's father?"

"He works in Germany. He's not coming."

"Well, a relative, then. Or a friend."

She just nodded, as if she were still someone who possessed such things. She did not want to admit to him just how alone she was. It felt shameful, like some embarrassing disease.

Her headache was so strong now that it hovered like a black ring at the edge of her field of vision; her nausea swelled once more. She ought to eat something, or at least drink a little, like the old man had told her to: *It's important to drink enough when it is this hot.* She bought a small square carton of orange juice at tourist price from a man selling candy and postcards and amber jewelry at a bright green cart. The juice was lukewarm and didn't taste particularly nice, and the citric acid burned her sore throat.

They'll find him, she whispered to herself. They will find him, and he will be all right.

There was no conviction in the words. Normally, she didn't see herself as a person with a very lively imagination. She was much better at recalling facts and figures than at picturing places she had never been, or people she had never seen. She didn't read a lot of novels, and saw only the films that were shown on TV.

But right now she could imagine Mikas. Mikas in a car, hidden under a rug. Mikas wriggling and crying while strangers held him down. Mikas calling for his mother, and getting no answer.

What had they done to him? And why had they taken him?

Her legs shook. She sat down on the wide stone steps leading to the river. A couple of years ago, the city had put up benches here, but they quickly became a magnet for addicts and homeless people, and now the seats had been removed, so that only the galvanized steel supports bristled from the concrete like stubble. Below, the Neris moved sluggishly in its concrete bed, brown and shrunken and tame compared to its winter wildness.

Her first summer with Darius, the river had been their secret place. If you followed the bank far enough away from the bridge, the paved pathway gave way to a muddy trail through the jungle of reeds. Insects buzzed and whirred, gnats and tiny black flies, but there were no people, no prying eyes or wagging tongues, and that was a rarity in Tauragė. They could even bathe. Together.

She didn't know anyone else like him. The other boys were idiots—giggling and drawing crude pictures of penises on school books. Milda's older brother had once pinched Sigita's left nipple and tried to kiss her; he was basically just as mean as Milda, only in a slightly different way.

121

Darius was completely different. He seemed utterly relaxed and at ease with himself, and so much more mature than any of the others. He told her he had been named after the hero pilot Steponas Darius, just like Tauragė's mainstreet, Dariaus ir Girėno gatvė. That was rather fitting, she thought. She could easily imagine Darius doing great things one day.

When he wanted to take off her blouse, she stiffened, at first. He stopped what he was doing, and slid both hands down to her waist.

"You are so tiny," he said. "My hands go almost all the way around you."

A deep shudder went through her that had nothing to do with cold. His hands moved up inside her blouse and brushed her breasts very lightly, very gently. She raised her face to the sun. Don't do that, said Granny Julija's voice in her head, you will go blind. But she let the sunlight blind her for a few more moments before she closed her eyes. Her hands spasmed into fists, clutching two handfuls of shirt from his back, and his tongue touched hers, then her lips, then the inside of her mouth. He had given up on the blouse and concentrated his efforts on her skirt and knickers. She stumbled and was thrown off balance, and he did nothing to hold her, but let himself fall with her instead, so that they hit mud and sun-warmed river water with a wet thud. His weight came down on top of her so hard that she was too winded to move or speak, which he took for acceptance.

"God, you're fine," he whispered, spreading her thighs with eager hands.

She could have stopped him. But she wanted it too. Her body wanted it. Even her head wanted it, in a way. She wanted to know what it was like—this sinning business. And it was good that she didn't really have to *do* anything except lie there and let him at her. She was prepared for pain; there had been whispers and sniggers in the girls' lavatories at school, that the first time was difficult, and that it hurt.

But it didn't. It was almost too easy, too right, to lie with him like this, pushed down into the soft warm mud by the weight of him, to feel him move between her legs and then inside her, like a welcome guest that might have stayed for so much longer than the brief moment it actually took.

He hunched over her, and then slid out. Lay there completely spent for a while, as the buzzing of the insects slowly returned, and the sound of the train on the railway bridge in the distance, and the rustle of the reeds in the wind. For an instant, a dazzling blue dragonfly hovered over his shoulder before zooming away.

Was that it? thought Sigita. Was that really all?

He rolled off her. He hadn't taken off any of his clothes; only his fly was open. She, on the other hand, was suddenly conscious of how inelegant she looked, with her knickers round one ankle and her skirt rucked up so that her entire pelvis was exposed. Somehow, he had also managed to push up both her blouse and her bra to get at her breasts, something she had barely noticed because so much else was going on. She hastily tugged her skirt into place and wanted to pull down her blouse also.

But this was when he did something that none of the other boys would have done. The thing that was just Darius. He pushed her gently back into the mud. He kissed her, a deep wet kiss that went on till she could hardly breathe. And then he touched her, outside and in, so that she gasped in surprise.

"Darius. . . ."

"Shhh," he said. "Wait."

He used only his hands and his mouth. And he kept at it till the light and the sounds went away. Till she shuddered from head to foot. Till something wild and unfamiliar throbbed inside her, over and over, and she knew for certain that she was no longer any kind of virgin, and never would be again.

She felt no guilt at that moment, nor did she think of shame, or sin, or consequences. That came later.

August twilight had begun to gather over the bay when Nina turned off the former fishing village's main street and continued up the sparsely paved road that led through the near-deserted holiday cottage park. Tisvildeleje these days was populated mainly by commuters and tourists, and now that the school holidays had ended, most of the visitors had left. There were still a few cars with German license plates outside the biggest and most luxurious of the houses, and a couple of children whacked away at a tetherball, the pole wobbling ominously with each swing. Except for that, the lawns lay deserted and scorched from the unremitting sun of this late, hot summer. Last year had been rainy and dull, but this year the sky had seemed permanently blue since May, and by now leaves, shrubbery, and grass had long since lost any vestige of lushness and formed a dry landscape of burnt yellows and dusty greens. Nina checked her watch. Exactly 8:20.

She parked in the lane by the mailbox, behind a blue VW Golf with a streamer in the rear window. *M-Tech*, it said. *Solutions That Work*. Was it Karin's? It didn't seem like the kind of car she would choose, but Nina could see no other, more likely vehicle. She peered up the long winding drive. The cottage looked to be quite old; it was painted a deep dark red, with white frames and tiny romantic window panes from before the age of double glazing. It was set some distance from its neighbors—the last one before the woods, just as Karin had said.

Nina jammed her keys and her mobile phone into the pockets of her jeans and got out. The boy was watching her covertly, beneath half-closed eyelids. She opened the rear door and touched his wrist gently. He felt warm now, but not fevered, she noted with professional routine. There was no doubt that he was fully conscious, even though he was lying very still, the now somewhat greasy blanket wound around his legs.

He is trying to disappear, thought Nina. Like the baby hare she had once come across as a child, in the back garden, where it had been desperately trying to hide. When she had picked it up, it hadn't struggled or resisted. It just crouched in her hands, feather-light and downy. In her six-year-old ignorance, she had thought it liked her. But when she put it on her bed, it had already had the same distant look as the boy in the back seat, and later that night, she found it limp and dead in the shoe box she had provided for it.

Was the boy giving up in the same way?

Nina shivered, and not entirely because the day had finally begun to cool. She couldn't leave the boy in the car, she decided. He was awake, and even though he didn't know her from Adam, coming with her had to be better than the alternative—being left locked in a car in the gathering darkness, not knowing where or why.

He hadn't moved a muscle, but as she reached for him now, he suddenly scooted back with such abruptness that the blanket slipped off him and dropped onto the floor of the car.

Nina hesitated.

She didn't want the child to be afraid of her. She didn't like that he looked at her as if she might be a monster little different from the man in the railway station, but she had no idea how to win his trust.

"What on earth have they done to you?" she whispered, sinking down onto her haunches and trying to catch his eyes. "Where do you come from, sweetie?"

The boy made no answer, only curled himself into a tighter ball at the opposite end of the seat, as far away from her as he could get. She could see a dark stain on the seat where the blanket had slipped, and the boy smelled unpleasantly of body sweat and old urine. Nina felt a surge of tenderness, just as she did when Anton or Ida had a temperature or threw up, back home in the Østerbro flat. She would bring them crushed ice, berry juice, and damp cloths; the urge to be good to them and make them well again was so overpowering it filled her entire being. So simple to be a good mother then, she thought. It was everything else that got to be so complicated.

She pointed to the house, then put her hands together like a statue of a praying saint and rested her cheek against them in a parody of sleep.

"First, we'll get you something to eat," she said, trying to smile. "And then we'll find a bed for you to sleep in. And after that, we'll see."

The boy made no sound, but she had to have done something right after all, because he uncurled and slid an inch or two in her direction.

"Good boy," she said. She remembered an article she had read a few years back about children's ability to survive in even the most brutal of environments. They were like little heat-seeking missiles, it had said, aiming themselves at the nearest source of warmth. If a child lost its mother, it would reach for its father. If the father disappeared, the child would head for the next grown-up in the line, and then the next, seeking any adult who would provide survival, and perhaps even love.

She showed him the clothes she had bought, and when she began to dress him, he helped. He obediently held out his arms so that she could put them into the sleeves of the new T-shirt, and ducked his head so that it was easier for her to pull it on. A clean pair of underpants followed. That would have to do for now, but even that much suddenly made him seem much more like a normal three-year-old. He came into her arms easily, as she lifted him from the car. Again she was struck by the difference between his weight and Anton's.

Now that he was awake, he didn't allow her to hold him against her shoulder. He sat warily straight on her left hip as she walked up the gravel path to the veranda.

"Hey, little one," murmured Nina, softening her voice into a maternal cooing. "No need to be afraid anymore."

His warm breath came quickly and carried a sour smell of fear and vomit.

On the veranda, someone had arranged a row of large pots containing herbs and pansies; their well-watered plumpness looked odd against the aridness of the rest of the garden. By the half-open door, a pair of bright yellow galoshes sat next to a small pet carrier. Nina remembered that Karin had spoken of a cat, at that drunken Christmas party. Mr. Kitty, she had called him. She had acquired this male presence when she'd decided once and for all that she was tired of looking for Mr. Right and the two point one children she was statistically entitled to.

At the moment, Nina could detect no sign of either kitty or Karin.

She raised her free hand to knock on the door, but it moved as she touched it, swinging open at her first knock. Unhindered, Nina stepped right into the little darkened hallway. There was a clean detergent-borne scent of citrus and vinegar, and Karin's shoes and boots were lined up neatly by the half-open kitchen door.

It was very quiet.

"Karin?"

Nina's foot came down on something soft, which gave way under her heel with a slight crunch. Startled, she backed up and steadied herself against the wall.

"Karin?" she called again, but this time with little expectation of an answer. She inched forward, running her hand over the door frame until she felt the sharp plastic contours of a switch. The light came on with a faint click, revealing a half-eaten sandwich on the floor. It was still partially wrapped, and had been acquired from the deli of the local Kvickly, she could see.

Nina felt a sharp cold jab in her stomach. It was possible that Mr. Kitty had made illegal forays into the groceries and dragged his booty into the hallway, but the house was entirely too silent considering the distraught and loudly sobbing Karin that Nina had been talking to just ninety minutes ago.

She lowered the boy to the floor of the hallway and stood undecided on the threshold.

"Stay here," she whispered, pointing at the floor. "Don't go anywhere."

The boy made no reply, only looked at her with solemn eyes. New cracks of black fear had begun to open in his gaze; he had been frightened to begin with, and her indecision was not improving matters. She had to do something quickly.

"Karin!"

Nina walked quickly through the kitchen and into the compact living room. Karin had turned on a small, green lamp above the settee. The television was on, but with the sound turned down. TV2 News. Nina recognized the scarlet banner headlines and the usual respectable suit of the anchor.

She strode across to the window, which overlooked the garden on the other side of the house. She could see very little, only the tall pines of the plantation behind the cottage, and an unkempt lawn littered with leaves and pine cones. Nina dug into her pocket for her mobile phone, pressed the recall button and waited for the call tone. Immediately, there was an answering trill from a real phone somewhere in the house. The sound seemed to be coming from behind a closed door that probably led to the bedroom, and although the distance couldn't be great, it sounded oddly muffled, as if someone had dropped it into a bucket. A quick glance assured her that the boy's small straight form was still standing motionless by the kitchen door. She looked at the phone again. 8:28.

The numbers on the pale blue display had a calming effect on her. She slid the phone back into her pocket and pushed open the bedroom door.

Karin lay curled on the bed, with her forehead resting against her knees, as though she had been practicing some advanced form of yoga. But Nina saw it the second the image was processed against her retina.

Death.

There was a peculiar quality about dead people. Little things that seemed insignificant on their own, but added up to an unmistakable impact, so that Nina was never in any doubt when she encountered it. The slight out-turned wrist. The leg that had slipped limply from its original position, and the head resting much too heavily against the mattress.

Nina felt the first rush from her flight instinct. She forced herself to approach the bed, while new details flooded her senses. Karin's fair hair spread around her head like a flaxen halo mixed with red and dark brown nuances. The sheet beneath her had soaked up far too much blood, and when Nina carefully turned Karin's upper body, Karin's mouth opened, and vomit mixed with blood sloshed over her lower lip and ran down her chin and into the soft folds of her throat. Two of her teeth were missing, and there was red and purple bruising on her face and neck. A lot of the blood seemed to come from a wound above the hairline, at her left temple, and when Nina probed it cautiously, the skull gave beneath her fingers, too soft and flat. Death had not been instantaneous, thought Nina. She had had time to curl up here, like a wounded animal that left the herd to die alone.

And now. So much blood.

She didn't mind blood, she reminded herself soothingly. She was okay with it, had, as a matter of fact, been one of the most steadfast at nursing school when it came to dealing with bodily fluids. (Since that day twenty-three years ago she had become very good at it. She had decided to become good at it, and it had worked.)

Nina stepped back from the bed and managed to twist to one side before she threw up, in short, painful heaves. She had eaten nothing since this morning, and all that sploshed onto the clean wooden floor was dark yellow gall and grayish water.

It was then she heard the scream. A shrill, heart-rending note of terror, like the scream you hear in the night when a hare is caught by the fox.

Sigita was sitting on the stone steps by the river, waiting for the nausea and headache to subside enough so she could walk on. Her good hand was clenched around her mobile. It had to ring. It had to ring so that she would know Mikas was all right. Or so she knew at least he wasn't what Gužas called the second category; those who were never found.

No. Don't even think it. Don't think about what strangers might do to the perfect, tiny body, don't let the thought in even for a second. It would only make it real. It would break her, it would tear her open and rip out her heart so that she wouldn't be able to breathe, let alone act. She clung to the phone like an exhausted swimmer to a buoy.

It didn't ring. In the end she pressed a number herself. Mrs. Mažekienė's.

"Mrs. Mažekienė. The man who took Mikas— what did he look like?"

The old woman's confusion was obvious, even over the phone.

"Look like? But it was his father."

"No, Mrs. Mažekienė. It wasn't. Darius is still in Germany."

There was a long silence.

"Mrs. Mažekienė?"

"Well, I did think that he must have gained some weight. He looked bigger than I remembered."

"How big?"

"I don't know . . . big and tall, now that I think about it. And hardly any hair, the way it had been cropped. But that's all the rage these days, isn't it?"

"Why did you think it was Mikas's father, then?"

"The car looked like his. And who else would be going off with the boy?"

Sigita bit down hard on her lip to avoid saying something unforgivable. She is just an old woman, she told herself. She didn't do it on purpose. But Mrs. Mažekienė's mistake had cost them nearly 48 hours, and that was very hard to forget.

"What kind of car was it?" she asked, once she had regained some self-control.

"It was gray," Mrs. Mažekienė answered vaguely.

"What make of car?" But she knew even as she asked that it was hopeless.

"I don't know much about cars," said Mrs. Mažekienė helplessly. "It was . . . ordinary, like. Like Mikas's father's car."

The last time Sigita had seen Darius, he had been driving a dark-gray Suzuki Grand Vitara. So presumably it was a gray SUV of some kind, or perhaps a station wagon. Or a van. If Mrs.

135

Mažekienė couldn't tell Darius's rather slender form from what sounded like that of a crew-cut doorman's, then there was no reason to think that she could distinguish between an off-roader and a Peugeot Partner. It wasn't much to go on.

"It had a baggage box on the roof," said Mrs. Mažekienė suddenly. "I remember that!"

Dobrovolskij's eldest son, Pavel, sometimes drove a silver Porsche Cayenne. It resembled the Vitara about as much as a Shetland pony resembles a Shire horse, and she had never seen it with a baggage box on its expensive roof. But it was enough to make her call Algirdas.

"Hi," he said. "Are you feeling better?"

She didn't reply to that.

"How did the meeting with Dobrovolskij go?" she asked instead.

"So-so. He wasn't happy that you weren't there."

"But there wasn't any . . . trouble?"

"Sigita, what is it you want?"

She didn't know how much to say. She had never told Algirdas much about her personal life, and it seemed awkward to start now. But what if? What if Mikas's disappearance had something to do with her job?

"Mikas is gone."

He knew, she thought, that she had a son. She had brought Mikas along to the Christmas pantomime last year, when Janus Corporation had suddenly decided it needed to do something for the children of its employees.

"Mikas? Your little boy?"

"Yes. Someone has taken him."

There was an awkward pause. She could almost hear the gears click inside Algirdas's mind as he tried to work out whether this would rock *his* boat in any way. Algirdas was a pleasant enough employer most of the time, friendly, informal, not a bully or a tyrant. But she sometimes thought that he felt the same way about his staff as she did about computers: they were just supposed to work—he didn't care what was inside.

And now I don't work anymore, she thought. And he doesn't know whom to call in order to get me repaired.

"Does this have anything to do with your concussion?" he finally asked.

"Possibly. I don't remember what happened. I thought Mikas was with Darius, but he isn't."

"But why are you asking about Dobrovolskij?"

"Pavel Dobrovolskij has a silver Cayenne. And Mikas was taken away in a gray or silver SUV." She was aware that she was twisting facts to provide more substance for her suspicions than they really warranted. But if it was Dobrovolskij, then Mikas didn't belong to the second category. If it was Dobrovolskij, one could find out what he wanted, and then do whatever it took to get Mikas back.

"Sorry, Sigita, but you're off your head. Why the hell would Dobrovolskij take your boy? Besides, I think Pavel sold the Cayenne. He said it was easier to fit an elephant into a matchbox than to park that monstrosity in downtown Vilnius. Did you tell the police?"

"Yes."

"Let them deal with it, then."

"But they're not doing anything! There's just this one pathetic man clicking his bloody ballpoint pen!"

"What does his pen have to with anything?"

"And he says they will look for Mikas now, but I don't think anything is really happening. They're never found. Not the ones where it's not personal." She realized she was being incoherent. Knew, too, that this was entirely the wrong way to be with Algirdas, that it would only make him retreat. She forced herself to breathe more calmly, waiting until the words presented themselves in the proper order. "Algirdas, I have to know if you are involved in something that Dobrovolskij wouldn't like. Or if any of the payments have been incorrect."

"Bloody hell, Sigita. It's your autistic head that's keeping track of everything. I just pony up when you tell me to."

Normally, she would be able to remember. Normally she would know if even a single litas was missing.

"Besides, you're making him sound like a gangster. He isn't."

"But he knows people who are," she said stubbornly. In the river below the steps, a black plastic garbage bag was floating past, buoyed up by the air trapped inside. For one horrible moment all Sigita could think about was that it was large enough to contain a dead child.

"Look, Sigita. I'm really sorry your boy has disappeared, but Dobrovolskij can't possibly be involved. For God's sake, don't get him mixed up in this."

She didn't say goodbye. She barely managed to turn off the mobile before her abdomen contracted, and she threw up orange juice and warm stomach acids all over her skirt and bare legs.

Nina turned just quickly enough to see the boy's shadow disappear from the doorway. She heard the rapid patter of his bare feet through the living room, then the creak of a door. Her own legs were momentarily paralyzed by a hot, melting sensation, and when she finally managed to move, her ankles and knees wobbled dangerously.

A couple of long strides took her through the door, and then into the kitchen. Out of the

139

window above the sink she saw his flaxen head bobbing past in the darkness; he was running away. She continued her wobbly flight through the hallway and out onto the veranda. In the humid air outside, her face and throat felt flushed and pulsing with heat.

The black pines in the plantation behind the house were blurred by mist; she couldn't see the boy anywhere, but she heard the snapping of branches as he fled among the trees. Following the sound, she took off at the fastest run she could manage.

Pine boughs whipped against her face, and the tall, dry grass at the forest's edge was a rustling, prickly barrier, impeding her steps. Fortunately, she could now see the boy's white hair like a will-o'-the-wisp among the black tree trunks in the gathering darkness. She was closing in on him.

She ducked the low branches as best she could, then had to veer sharply to one side to avoid the bristling remnants of a fallen tree. Her right ankle protested, but she did manage a second burst of speed. She snatched at the boy's shoulder, but lost her grip again, and he stumbled on. Her next attempt was more successful. She caught his arm and clung to it, forcing him to stop.

Wordlessly, she pulled him down onto the mossy grass and closed her arms around him. Under the twisted T-shirt, his heart was beating fast and hard against his bared ribs, and his breath was a hot flush against her neck.

Then she heard it.

It might have been a completely insignificant sound. A faint click, as of a door being cautiously closed, somewhere in the summer night. The sound could come from any of the other cottages skirting the forest's edge, thought Nina, as she inched backwards into deeper cover, pulling the boy with her. She could no longer see Karin's cousin's cottage, but at the end of the winding drive her own red Fiat was perfectly visible.

More sounds. Footsteps, this time, and a rustling as if someone was moving through tall, dry grass. Nina saw the man from the railway station in her mind's eye. The pale, narrowed eyes, the tense jaw, the ferocity of the kicks he aimed at the busted locker.

Had he found Karin and unleashed that fury in her?

Nina looked at her watch.

8:36.

Her watch was usually 29 seconds slower than the more accurate time given by her mobile. For some reason she hadn't corrected that imprecision. She rather liked having to figure out what time it really was.

She hugged the boy tight against her chest. His little warm body was twitching, small jerks of protest, but he made no sound. Did he understand the need for silence, or was it merely traumatized resignation?

She listened again, but the rustle of the footsteps, if that was what they were, had stopped. Should she call the police? She fumbled at the pockets of her jeans, first on the right, then on the left.

No phone.

She checked again, but knew it was futile. She had dropped it. Where and when, she had no idea.

New little bursts of adrenalin exploded in her head. The phone had been her only line of contact to the real world—to Morten, to the network and her job, and now to the police. She was alone now. Completely alone with the boy.

The crash of a door being slammed rang through the silence.

Her heart gave a wild leap and raced even faster under her sweat-soaked T-shirt. She stumbled to her feet, still with the boy locked in her arms.

And then she ran.

The boy's body was tense with resistance and difficult to manage, and she felt the extra weight now in her knees and ankles. She was getting older, she thought, too old to be fleeing with a child in her arms.

Seconds later, she reached the Fiat and yanked open the door to the driver's seat. She glanced up at the cottage through the foliage of the birches flanking the drive. She could see no signs of any human presence up there, and for a moment she began to doubt her senses. Had the footsteps really been footsteps? Or had it really just been the wind rustling the grass, or perhaps Mr. Kitty? Her phone. Should she go back and look for it? Did she dare? She felt an irrational urge to protect the still, unliving body in there, to guard it against. . . .

Against what? It was too late. For Karin, everything was too late. Now Nina had to think of the boy, and of herself. Yet still she hesitated, child on her hip, as she peered through the dusty, dry leaves. Then she froze. A light had come on in the kitchen, and she saw someone move about in there. Then the dark form seemed to grow bigger as it approached the window, and for a moment, she saw the pale outline of a face.

Nina practically threw the boy into the passenger seat. She thrust the key into the ignition with frantic haste, and the second the engine caught, she backed wildly down the lane, careening from one side of the road to the other. The long grass hissed against the sides of the car, and once, a stone or a root knocked against the undercarriage. The other cottages all had black, dark windows and empty drives. No help to be had there. Gravel from the road whipped up against the windscreen when she finally managed to turn the car around and continued, still at much too furious a speed, down the partially paved road towards the sea. It was only then she realized that she had forgotten to turn on the headlights. The boy next to her had begun to scream so loudly that anyone would think she was trying to kill him.

Nina forced a deep breath into her abdomen, slowed the car a fraction, and turned on the lights with a dry little click. The boy's screaming softened into sobs, but he was now crouched on the floor of the car, his arms clutched around his head. And suddenly, amidst the soft, gurgling sobs, intelligible words began to form.

"Mama. Noriu pas Mama!"

Sweet Jesus, she thought. He has a mother somewhere.

Jan had decided to spend the night in the company's downtown flat in Laksegade. This was mainly in order to avoid Anne. With her peculiar Anne-radar she had naturally spotted something wasn't going quite according to plan, and right now he had to keep his distance from her, or she might realize just how much of a shambles the whole thing was. Besides, it would be much easier to deal with Karin without Anne somewhere in the vicinity.

He bought a TV dinner in Magasin's delicatessen and heated it in the microwave of the small kitchen. Karin's betrayal still left a bitterness in his mouth. How he could be so wrong? But it would seem she was both less loyal and more mercenary than he would have guessed. At home, in her flat above the garage, he had found only two things worth noticing: the empty briefcase and a note announcing in bold letters, "I QUIT."

So that was gratitude for you. Normally, he was a better judge of whom to guard against, and whom to trust. And Karin had known what was at stake. Even now, he couldn't quite rid himself of the feeling that it was all a misunderstanding. That once he got to talk to her, everything would work itself out.

But the Lithuanian hadn't called, which had to mean he hadn't found her. Jan felt his stomach cramp at the thought of what this would do to him and his life. The chances that it would ever be normal again lessened with each hour that went by. He didn't exactly have all the time in the world—didn't she understand that?

He made himself a cup of coffee and tried to watch the news, but he couldn't concentrate. Perhaps he should go for a run in Kongens Have? But he hadn't brought his running clothes or shoes, and although Magasin's Men's Department was just around the corner, he didn't feel like another shopping expedition. He had already purchased a shirt and some underwear for tomorrow, the way he often did when he had been working so late that making the drive back to the house wasn't practical.

The flat was cramped as a coffin compared to the house, but there was something about it that he liked. His assistant, Marianne, had seen to the redecoration, and she had hit a note that made him feel comfortable here. Sort of a luxury version of a student's digs. Old armchairs draped with pale rugs. Retro lamps she had found in flea markets. Seven different plates, rather than a single pattern, and equally unmatching coffee mugs. Marianne liked doing that kind of thing. "It needs personality," she had said. "Or you might as well put people up in a hotel." Perhaps the place reminded him of the small flat he had shared with his student friend Kristian, back when the world was new, when they both had dreams of becoming IT millionaires. Briefly, he wondered what Kristian was doing now. As far as he knew, Jan had been the only one to make the millionaire dream come true.

What an absolutely bloody day. He stretched, and felt a twinge from the operation scar just above his hip. He scratched it reflexively. What the hell was the Lithuanian doing? And what the hell was Karin thinking?

Suddenly, the door phone buzzed aggressively. Jan set the mug on the worktop and went to press the button.

"Yes."

"It's Inger."

A fraction of a second ticked by before he realized which Inger. His mother-in-law.

"Inger," he said, trying to put a smile into his voice. "Come in!"

She was slim and fair like Anne, exactly the same figure. Right now she was wearing one of her bright African dresses, her bare, tanned arms sporting four or five carved ebony bracelets. This was the sort of thing Inger could carry off—making something like that look exactly right.

"Anne said you were here," she said. "So I thought I would seize the moment."

"What a lovely surprise," said Jan. "Would you like a cup of coffee?"

"No thank you," she said. "I just want to talk to you."

"Oh dear," he said, trying for a humorous note. "What have I done now?"

She didn't buy his attempt at levity.

"Anne is upset," she said.

"Did she say that?"

"Of course not. Anne is Anne. She would never say a thing like that. But something isn't right with her, and I am asking you now. Is it Aleksander?"

His heart pounded madly.

"No, no," he said. "That's all been taken care of."

She looked at him directly. Her eyes weren't

147

quite as blue as Anne's were; there was more gray in them.

"What, then?" she asked. "Is there something wrong between the two of you?"

His smile felt as if it were glued to his face, and he was sure the lack of naturalness was showing. Why could he never do things right? He admired Inger. She was a wonderful woman, feminine and strong at the same time, just the sort of soulmate a man like Keld deserved. He so wanted her to *like* him.

"I would never hurt Anne," he said.

Her eyebrows shot up.

"No," she said. "I didn't think you would. But that wasn't the question I asked."

Wrong again. Sometimes he felt as if there were a little man inside his head with one of those ear-splitting buzzers they used on quiz shows whenever a contestant got it wrong.

"Then I'm not sure I know what you mean," he said. "We're fine."

She sighed. Shook her head.

"Do you know," she said. "I don't think so." She got up, hitching the strap from her stylishly fringed handbag onto one bare shoulder.

"Are you leaving already?" he said.

"There doesn't seem to be much point in staying," she said, and again, he had the feeling that he had failed some test he didn't really understand.

"Have you talked to Keld about this?" he burst out.

Again, she gave him one of those very direct, gray-blue looks. She shook her head once more, but he wasn't certain it meant no. What if she had been sitting out there in the Taarbæk villa, discussing it with Keld, in the conservatory, perhaps, over a glass of late evening wine and some really good cheese, talking about him, about him and Anne and their marriage, wondering if everything were the way it should be . . . his stomach became a small, rock-solid lump at the thought.

"Goodnight," she said. "I hope you work it out." She put a hand on his arm for a moment before she left, and he was pretty sure that there was pity in her glance.

He stood by the window, watching her walk down the street. From the rear, she could still pass for a young woman, her stride full of energy and grace, her feet turned slightly out. Once, she had laughingly told him she had been a ballet child for three whole years before they kicked her out. "And you never stop walking like a duck after that." She still took some kind of dancing class in the evenings.

He discovered he was shaking all over. Stop it, he told himself. In a little while, the Lithuanian will call. He will have found Karin. And there is still time. It will all be fine.

Just before midnight, the phone rang, but it wasn't the Nokia. It was Anne, on his personal mobile.

"The police have been here," she said, and he could hear the fragile cracks in her voice. "They say that Karin is dead."

The Dobrovolskijs were Russian, but not from the Soviet era. The family had lived in Vilnius for more than a hundred years, and old man Dobrovolskij himself, the present patriarch, still inhabited one of the old wooden mansions behind Znamenskaya, the Orthodox Church of the Apparition of the Holy Mother of God. Sigita had been there once before, with Algirdas, and they had been served black Russian tea on the porch, in tall glasses so gilded that they were only barely transparent.

Sigita paused by the garden gate, suddenly indecisive. Now that she was actually here, it was hard to imagine that the Dobrovolskijs could be holding Mikas somewhere in that beautiful, freshly painted house. And there was no silver Cayenne parked by the curb.

If Dobrovolskij had anything to do with this, he wouldn't do it here. Not in his childhood home, so close to the Church its huge silvery dome could be seen through the treetops. Where others tore down the old wooden houses and built modern brick monstrosities as soon as they came into money, Dobrovolskij had instead carefully renovated. The delicately carved trimmings shone with fresh yellow paint, the intricate window frames and shutters likewise; and though there might still be a well in the garden outside, it was for decorative purposes only. Sigita knew for a fact that there were three shiny new bathrooms in the house—that had been part of the agreement between Janus Construction and the old man.

She had stood there long enough to be noticed. The white lace curtain in one window twitched, and a little later a young dark-haired girl came out onto the porch.

"Mrs. Dobrovolskaja is asking whether there is anything we can do for you?" she said, her Lithuanian heavily accented. Her slim, girlish figure was dressed in a white T-shirt and a pair of black Calvin Kleins, and Sigita guessed her to be some kind of Russian relative, or perhaps an au pair. Or both.

Sigita cleared her throat.

"I'm sorry. This may sound odd. But do you know if Pavel Dobrovolskij still owns a silver Porsche Cayenne?"

"Has something happened?" The girl focused on Sigita's plaster cast. "An accident? Is he all right?"

"No, nothing has happened . . . or, not in that way. I had a fall on the stairs."

"Is it broken?"

"Yes."

"What a pity. I hope it will soon be new again." She smiled awkwardly. "Forgive me. My Lithuanian is not yet very good. I am Anna, Pavel's fiancée. How do you know Pavel?"

"It's really more my boss who knows him. Algirdas Janusevičius. They do projects together from time to time. My name is Sigita."

They shook hands.

"The Porsche?" said Sigita. "He still has it?"

Anna smiled.

"He's trying to sell it. He calls it an elephant. But no one has bought it yet. If you're interested, you can see it in Super Auto's showroom in Pusu gatvė. It's only two blocks from here."

The Porche Cayenne stood proudly in the best window at Super Auto, behind bars and armored glass, and without license plates. A price sticker announced that Sigita could become the happy owner of this vehicle if only she were willing to pay six years' wages for it. Algirdas had been right, thought Sigita miserably. There was absolutely no evidence that Dobrovolskij had taken Mikas, or had anything to do with his disappearance.

Not until she felt that straw break did she realize

how hard she had been clinging to it. It had to be Dobrovolskij because Dobrovolskij was someone she knew, he had a face, she knew where he lived. If it was Dobrovolskij, Mikas would come back to her.

But it wasn't Dobrovolskij.

Sigita walked to the nearest trolley stop on legs that felt disconnected. The trolley stop did not represent a conscious decision, more a conditioned reflex. She had lived in this neighbor-hood herself, once, in two attic rooms in one of the wooden houses where the well was anything but decorative. For three years she had climbed the narrow stairs every day with a couple of ten-liter plastic water containers in her hands, one for Mrs. Jovaišienė, who owned the house, and one for herself. If she needed to bathe, she had to use the public facilities some blocks away, so usually she took sponge baths and relied heavily on a wonder-product called Nuvola, which came in an aerosol can; one sprayed it into one's hair, waited for a few minutes, and then brushed vigorously, after which everything would be as clean as if one had just showered. Or that was the theory. Once a week she borrowed Mrs. Jovaišienė's little hand-cranked washing machine, but most of the time she just washed her clothes in the sink, like they had done back home in Tauragė.

Mrs. Jovaišienė was probably dead by now. She had been over ninety. Sigita deliberately avoided Vykinto gatvė, where the house was, although that would have been the shorter route. She didn't want to see it. Didn't want to be reminded of that time. Mikas was all that mattered now, she told herself.

Back home in Pašilaičiai, the flat was unchanged. White. New. Empty. She closed the blinds to the afternoon sun and lay down on the bed with all her clothes on. A few seconds later, she was asleep.

The year Sigita became pregnant, winter had come early to Tauragė. The first snows fell at the end of October. Her father had just taken over the position of caretaker in their building, after Bronislavas Tomkus had moved out. In practice, this meant that Sigita had to help her mother shovel the walks before she could go off to school and her mother could leave for her job at the post office. Her father had "the thing with his back," of course. He did insist on directing his troops, though, entertaining them with a series of humorous remarks to keep up morale.

"It's the secret weapon of the Russians, that is," he said, pointing to the packed snow. "Direct from Siberia. But they won't get us down while we have good, strong women like you!"

He jokingly praised Sigita and her mother as

brave defenders of the Independence to every-one passing on the half-cleared sidewalk. It was all rather unbearable.

At least the cold weather meant that Sigita could wear heavy sweaters without arousing comment. She had begun to cut all phys-ed classes, but she knew it was only a matter of time before Miss Bendikaitė would contact the head-master, who in his turn would contact her parents.

Sexual education was not in any way part of the curriculum at Tauragė Primary and Secondary School, but Sigita did realize what it meant when she had missed her period in August, and again in September. She just wasn't exactly sure what to do about it. Theoretically, she could have bought a pregnancy test at the pharmacy in City Square, but Mrs. Raguckienė, who sat at the register, had gone to school with her mother. And in any case, what good would a test do? She already knew what was wrong.

She hadn't told Darius. By the end of August, he had been sent to the States to stay with his uncle and attend an American high school for a year. Sigita rather thought that this unprecedented generosity owed much to the fact that his mother didn't consider Sigita a suitable girlfriend for her golden boy. Sigita had written him a letter, but without mentioning her condition. Her own mother sorted all mail outbound from Tauragė, and the airmail paper was so terribly, trans-parently thin.

She missed him. She missed him so much it made her breasts and her abdomen ache. She counted this longing as one more item on the list of sins she had omitted to tell Father Paulius about, but she had no plans to confess. Eventually she realized that the tenderness in her breasts meant something other than merely thwarted passion. But to write the words: *I am pregnant,* or, *You're going to be a father. . . .* No. She just couldn't do it.

One Thursday night in the beginning of December she packed as many clothes as she could fit into her gym bag. It had to be the gym bag, because the suitcases were kept in a locked storage room in the building's long, windowless attic, and besides, walking down Dariaus ir Giréno gatvé with a suit-case would definitely cause eyebrows to lift. Someone might even try to stop her. It also had to be Thursday, because that was the day when her mother went to visit Granny Julija, and her father always took that opportunity to go play cards with some of his old mates from the canning factory.

She left no letter. She would have had no idea what to say in it. Only her little brother Tomas saw her leave.

"Where are you going?" he asked.

"Out," she said, unable to even look at him.

"Mama said you had to mind me."

"You are twelve years old, Tomas. You can mind yourself by now."

She caught the last bus to Vilnius. It took nearly five hours to get there, by which time it was past midnight, and the big city of her dreams had closed for the night. There were no trolley busses, and she couldn't afford a taxi. She asked the busdriver for directions and began to walk through the silent streets, with the freezing snow crunching under the soles of her boots.

Her aunt was astonished to see her. She had to say her name twice before Jolita even recognized her.

"But Sigita. What are you doing here? Why didn't your mother call me?"

"I wanted to visit you. Mama doesn't know."

Jolita was older than her mother, but looked younger. The hair brushing her shoulders was a uniform black, and a pair of huge golden loops dangled from her earlobes. She was wearing a royal blue kimono dressing gown, but despite this, it didn't seem that she had been in bed when Sigita rang the bell. From the flat behind her came a series of soft jazz notes and the smell of cigarette smoke.

Jolita's penciled eyebrows shot up.

"You wanted to *visit* me?" she said.

"Yes," said Sigita. And then she started crying.

"Little darling. . . ."

"You have to help me," sobbed Sigita. "I'm going to have a baby."

"Oh dear Lord, sweetheart," said Tante Jolita, drawing her into a silky, tobacco-scented, and very comforting embrace.

K arin is dead. Karin is dead. Karin is dead.
The thought was pounding away inside
Nina's skull as she turned onto Kildevej and
headed back toward Copenhagen. She was nearly
certain now that no one had followed her from
the cottage. The first harried miles on the narrow
road through Tibirke, she had checked her mirror
every other second.

Karin is dead, she thought, gripping the steering
wheel still harder. She had tried to wipe her
hands on a crumbled, jellybean-sticky tissue she
had found in the glove compartment, but the
blood had had time to dry and lay like a thin rust-
colored film over her palm and fingertips.

Unbidden, the feel of Karin's skull came back to
her. Like one of those big, luxurious, foil-wrapped
Easter eggs Morten's parents always bought for
Ida and Anton, and which always got dropped on
the floor somehow. The shell under the foil would
feel flattened and frail, just like Karin's head. She
had been able to feel individual fragments of
bone moving under the scalp as she probed.

She had been killed. Beaten to death. Someone
had hit her until she was dead.

Nina hunched over the steering wheel, trying to

158

control her nausea. Why would anyone want to kill Karin? Karin was one of the least dangerous people Nina had ever met, big-bosomed in a rather maternal way that had always made Nina think of warm milk and homemade bread. Secure. She had always been secure.

Nina wiped her eyes with one hand; she felt her gaze drawn to the unwinding ribbon of the road's central white line and had to yank it back up with an act of will.

They had always stuck together, back at nursing school. Studied together, gone to parties and Friday drinks together, even though on the face of it they didn't have much in common. Nina was small and skinny and went in for the pale, doomed, and emaciated look. Karin, on the other hand, would have looked completely at home in a propaganda film from the Third Reich. Tall, blond, and buxom, with generous hips and smooth, golden skin. And she had been so wonderfully uncomplicated. Not stupid, not at all, just—uncomplicated, and with an overwhelming potential for happiness. Or that, at least, was how Nina had seen her, and it might have been why she stuck around, hoping for some of that happiness potential to rub off, needing to be with someone whose world was just as round and perfect as Karin herself was.

That Karin, in the end, had been the one who found it most difficult to realize her dream of a family, of husband and children, had always been a mystery to Nina. But for some reason or other, the men around Karin never stayed. Nina was the one who had acquired the whole package without ever really wanting it, and that may have been what came between them in the end.

While Nina had had her first child and gone off to save the world in foreign climes, Karin had worked as a private nurse to a Danish family stationed in Brussels, and later at some posh and probably hair-raisingly expensive clinic in Switzerland. They tried to meet during those interludes when they were both in Denmark at the same time, but it became more and more obvious that the distance between them was growing.

Like the time when she had been pregnant with Anton. Very pregnant, actually, and very nearly due. She could still recall the hurt, offended look in Karin's eyes when Nina opened the door to her in the new flat in Østerbro she and Morten had just moved into. It had been that rarest of times when everything seemed right with the world, and she had felt, perhaps for the first and only time in her life, at peace with herself. She had gained fifty-five pounds and enjoyed every ounce of it, feeling pleasantly round, firm and soft at the same time.

Karin hadn't said anything. Not even congratulations.

Since that visit, the phone calls had come at greater and greater intervals, and when she had seen Karin at that ill-fated Christmas party, already a little soused and wearing a pair of glittery reindeer antlers on a headband, it had been four years since they had last met.

Nina, too, had become rather drunk rather quickly, but she did remember Karin telling her that she was home to stay. That she had found a great job near . . . Kalundborg, wasn't it? And what else?

Nina frowned, trying to recall the scene more precisely. There had been little handcrafted schnapps glasses and chubby Santa-shaped candles on the table, vats of beer, and for some reason the kind of confetti people usually used for New Year's.

Karin was a private nurse again, she had said, and she was raking it in. Nina suddenly remembered seeing a peculiar weariness in Karin's eyes. She had had entirely too much schnapps, and she sat there twisting a plastic beer glass between her hands and telling Nina exactly how much she brought home every month, after taxes. And that she didn't even have to pay rent because there was this great flat that went with the job, with a brilliant view of the bay. The dim light deepened the furrows on her brow and made little vertical lines appear around her mouth, and for the first time ever, Nina had felt a dislike for her friend. It was as if she didn't know her anymore, and as the evening wore on, she had been full of contempt for the choices Karin had made. They were both dead drunk by then, even more so than when they used to party together when they were students. And Nina was feeling tired, and mean, and sick at heart.

Perhaps that was why she had said it. That she was still saving the world. That she was happy. That she had the perfect family, and the perfect husband, and that she spent her spare time helping all the children, women, and crippled little men no one else in all of fucking Denmark seemed to care about.

She had told Karin about the network.

The first part of it was a pack of lies, but it felt fantastic to say it. The rest was true. She did spend a lot of time on the network. Too much, thought Morten. Sometimes he complained that she was only in it for the adrenalin fix, but it was more than that; she still needed to save the world, still needed to feel that she wasn't powerless.

Nina wiped her eyes again, and eased her foot off the accelerator. This was not a motorway, although she was not the only driver who seemed to be driving like it was. The boy was quiet now. He crouched on the seat next to her, his knees drawn up to his chest, staring wide-eyed at the fields slipping past, and the dark forms of dozing horses under the trees.

She thought of the words that had tumbled out of him in that desperate wail, and tried to recall the unfamiliar sounds. The word "Mama" had been easily distinguishable, but other than that Nina could not identify a single syllable. Not one. Nor could she recognize the general tone of it. It was probably some Eastern European language, she thought, especially considering the boy's fair hair and skin. On the other hand, she didn't think it was either Russian or Polish. Not enough z-sounds. She cursed at her lack of linguistic skill and rubbed the bridge of her nose with one hand. God, she was tired. It felt as if she had been awake for days, and she had to force her eyes to focus on the digits of the car's clock.

8:58.

She wondered what Morten and the children were doing now. Ida would probably be in her room, hypnotized by one of her endless computer games. And Anton would be in bed, bedtime story over and done with. If Morten had been in a mood to read to him, of course. He might have been too angry. He had asked Nina to stay away, hadn't he? Or what was it he had said? Nina could no longer recall the exact words.

Had he asked her to come home?

Probably not. Nina felt a clean, cold calm spread from her chest to her stomach.

Morten didn't get angry very often.

In many ways, he reminded her of those big, soft dogs who let their ears get nipped and their tails get tugged day in and day out. The kind of animal you are completely certain is the nicest dog in the world, until one day it explodes in a fit of rage and sinks its teeth into the leg of the pesky seven-year-old boy next door.

Morten was actually capable of scaring Nina a little on such occasions, especially because his anger was directed at the whole world even though the spark that triggered it was usually something she had done. When they had had a bad fight, he became curt and dismissive with Ida and Anton. As if they were an extension of her and all the things about her that he couldn't stand.

On such rare days Morten found it hard to cope with Anton, and Ida was asked to turn off the television in her room for no better reason than that it annoyed him that it was on.

Nina pictured him now, sitting alone on the sofa with the laptop open on the low coffee table in front of him, restlessly surfing job ads, trekking equipment and cheap trips to Borneo or Novo Sibirsk. Anything that would give him a fleeting sense of what life could be like without her.

Her skin suddenly felt chill despite the muggy heat still trapped in the car. What was she going to do? She would learn nothing more from Karin now than she already had, and that was practically nothing.

She left route 16 by Farum and stopped at a Q8. Stiffly, she turned in her seat to look at the boy.

His eyes were closed now, and he lay huddled against the opposite door like small, limp animal. He must be completely exhausted, she thought.

She was no more than a few minutes away from the Coal-House Camp. And what then? Tuck him into one of the baby blue cots in Ellen's House? Sit by his bedside, praying and hoping that the man from the railway station wouldn't find them?

He had already found Karin. She was almost certain about that. Found her and killed her, despite the fact that Karin had left her job and the flat with the great view of the bay and had tried to hide in a small summer cottage on the Northern coast.

The boy didn't stir as she got out of the car. She closed the door as gently as possible so as not to wake him, edged past the trailers for rent, and headed for the store. To one side of the door was a wooden pallet loaded with firewood bagged in purple sacking, on the other a huge metal basket full of sprinkler fluid promising to be especially effective against dead insects on the windshield. Right now it seemed completely absurd that there were people in the world who cared deeply about such things.

Inside, the boy behind the counter, much too young for his job, eyed her with the special wariness convenience store staff acquire after dark: Is this it? Is this where it gets unpleasant and dangerous, is this where armed strangers stick a gun in my face and tell me to open the till? The fact that she was female immediately lowered his anxiety levels, and she tried to smile disarmingly to soothe him even further, but the smile felt more like a rictus.

Oh hell, she thought. I still have blood on my hands. Maybe on the T-shirt too. She hadn't even thought to check. What the hell was she using for brains? She tucked her hands into her pockets and asked to borrow a telephone. And perhaps a bathroom?

Helpfully, he showed her into a small lounge-like area at the back of the store. She opted for the bathroom first, and used the cloyingly perfumed soap from the dispenser to rub the last rusty remnant from her nails and the wrinkles on her knuckles. Miraculously, the T-shirt had escaped smears and stains. She didn't have the patience to use the blower, but wiped her hands on her jeans instead.

Then the telephone.

She dialed the number for North-Zealand Police, helpfully provided on the message board by the phone together with details on how to reach the local cab company, Auto-Aid, hospital emergency room and other useful services. But as the line established the connection with a click, she caught sight of herself on a surveillance monitor mounted above the counter.

"Nordsjælland Police."

Nina stood motionless while clumsy thoughts waddled through her tired brain. These days, there was no such thing as a truly anonymous call.

"Hello? This is Nordsjælland Police, how can I help you?"

You can't, thought Nina, and hung up. The certain knowledge that there was nothing more she could do for Karin came back to her. She had to concentrate on the boy.

He hadn't moved. He was still curled against the door of the car, and she wondered if she should put him in the back seat instead, where he would be more comfortable. But the feeling of being hunted and observed had come back. She started the Fiat and turned onto Frederiksborgvej. At least she felt more awake now, and coherent thought no longer appeared an unsurmountable task. She hit the motorway at the Værløse exit and joined the flow of cars gliding towards the city in the dense, warm summer night. One thing, at least, was clear now. Her only key to the mystery of where the boy came from was the boy himself.

The phone woke her. It was Darius.

"Sigita, damnit. You set the cops on me!"

"No. Or . . . I went back and told them it wasn't you. That you didn't have him."

"Then kindly explain why two not very civil gentlemen from the Polizei were here a moment ago, turning over the whole place!"

He was really mad at her, she could tell. But she was pleased. Gužas was actually doing something, she thought. Ballpoint-clicking Gužas. He had contacted the police in Düsseldorf, which was where Darius lived at the moment.

"Darius, they have to check. When the parents are divorced, that's the first thing they think of."

"We're not divorced."

"Separated, then."

"Did you really think I would take him away from you?"

She tried to tell him about the woman in the cotton coat and the mistaken conclusions drawn by Mrs. Mažekienė, but he was too angry to listen.

"Honestly, Sigita. This is too fucking much!"

Click. He was gone.

Dizzy and disoriented, she sat on the bed for a little while. She had been asleep for less than an hour. It was still afternoon. And she still had a headache. She opened the door to the balcony, hoping it would clear the air, and more importantly, her mind.

That seemed to be a signal Mrs. Mažekienė had been waiting for for a while. She was sitting outside on her own balcony, surrounded by a jungle of tomato plants and hydrangeas.

"Oh, you're home," she said. "Any news?"

"No."

"The police were here," she said. "I had to make a statement!" She sounded proud of the fact.

"What did you tell them?"

"I told them about the young couple, and about the car. And . . . erh . . . they asked about you, too."

"I imagine they would."

"If there were other boyfriends, and so on. Now that you're on your own again."

"And what did you tell them about that?"

"God bless us, but I'm not one to gossip. In this building, we mind our own business, is what I told them."

"I think you know that I don't have a boyfriend. Why didn't you just say so?"

"And how would I know such a thing, dear? It's not as if I watch your door, or anything. I'm no Peeping Tom!"

"No," sighed Sigita. "Of course not."

Mrs. Mažekienė leaned over the railing. "I've

169

made cepelinai," she said. "Would you like some, dearie?"

The mere thought of doughy yellow-white potato balls made nausea rise in her throat again.

"That's very kind of you, but no thanks."

"Don't forget your stomach just because your heart is heavy," said Mrs. Mažekienė. "That's what *my* dear mother always used to say, God rest her soul."

My heart isn't heavy, thought Sigita. It is black. The blackness was back inside her, and she suddenly couldn't stand another second of Mrs. Mažekienė's well-intentioned intrusions.

"I'm sorry," she said abruptly. "I have to. . . ."

She fled into the flat without even pausing to close the balcony door. It wasn't nausea that seized her, but weeping. It ripped at her gut and tore long, howling sobs from her, and she had to lean over the sink, supporting herself with her good hand, as though she were in fact about to throw up.

Several minutes passed before she could breathe again. She knew that Mrs. Mažekienė was absorbed in the spectacle from the vantage of her own balcony, because she could still hear a soft litany of "There, there. There, there, now," as if the old lady were trying to comfort her by remote control.

"There is no harder thing," said Mrs. Mažekienė, when she heard the sobbing ease a

170

little. "Than losing a child, I mean."

Sigita's head came up as if someone had taken a cattle prod to her.

"I have not lost a child!" she said angrily, and marched over to close the balcony door with a bang that made the glass quiver.

But the double lie cut at her like a knife.

Aunt Jolita worked at the University of Vilnius. She was a secretary with the Department of Mathematics, but in reality her job consisted mostly of assisting a certain Professor Žiemys. The reason she and Sigita's mother were no longer on speaking terms became obvious fairly quickly. Every Monday and every Thursday, the Professor came to see Jolita. On the Thursday Sigita arrived, Jolita had just kissed him goodbye by her front door. It had been his cigarettes Sigita had smelled.

At first, Sigita couldn't understand why this should shock her so. Jolita wasn't married and could do what she wanted. This was not Tauragė. The Professor did have a wife, but surely that was his business.

In the end she came to the conclusion that the shocking thing was that it was all so *petty*. She had always known Jolita had done something awful, something Sigita's mother could not condone in the depth of her Catholic heart. Jolita had sinned, but no one had been willing to explain to Sigita precisely how and why. As a child, she had vaguely imagined something to do with dancing on a table while drunken men looked on. She had no idea where that peculiar vision had come from. Probably some film or other.

And now, the reality had proved to be so mundane and regulated. Every Monday, every Thursday. A bearded, stooping man more than fifteen years her senior, who always forgot at least one pair of glasses if Jolita did not remind him. She might as well have been married, or nearly so. It might all have been youthful and passionate once, but if so, that was a very long time ago.

Sigita had fled to Vilnius to escape Tauragė's judgment. To be free of prying and gossip, of moralizing parochial prejudice. Of everything *provincial*. Since she was nine or ten, she had been a highly secret admirer of Jolita's courage; she imagined that her aunt had done everything she herself dreamed of: that she had broken free and made a life for herself on her own terms, up there in the impossibly distant big city. This was why Sigita had sought her out. Jolita would understand. She would be able to see they had kindred souls, rebellious and free. And when Jolita had embraced her and let her move in with no questions asked, it had seemed an affirmation of everything she had dreamed.

But on Mondays and Thursdays, Jolita became anxious. She cleaned the flat. She bought wine. She awkwardly told Sigita she couldn't stay in the flat, but must keep away from five in the afternoon until midnight at the earliest. Highly embarrassing, it would seem, if the Professor were to meet Jolita's uncouth country niece, who had been so stupid as to get herself knocked up at age fifteen. If Sigita didn't leave quickly enough, Jolita's gestures became increasingly jerky and hectic. She would press money on Sigita, so she could buy herself a meal somewhere, go out on the town, see a film, that would be nice, darling, wouldn't it? Damp, crumpled notes would be pushed into Sigita's hands as Jolita damn near forced her out the door. Sigita saw a lot of films that winter.

It occurred to her that Jolita was not free or independent at all. She hadn't acquired her job by sleeping with the Professor—the job came first, and the Professor later—but that was seventeen years ago, and no one remembered that now. If the Professor were to lose his position, Jolita would be sacked as a matter of course. For the university, as for many others, the Independence hadn't been all sweetness and light and patriotic hymns. Funds were at a minimum, and everyone fought like hyenas for the pitiful scraps and jobs that there were. Jolita's whole life dangled by the thinnest of cobweb threads. Her position, her salary, her flat, her entire way of life . . . everything depended on him. Mondays and Thursdays.

Jolita didn't think Sigita should go to school.

"You can do that next year, darling, when this is all over and done with," she said, jiggling the coffee pot to try to gauge its contents. "Another cup?"

"No, thank you," said Sigita distractedly. She was seated on one of the ramshackle wooden chairs in the kitchen; she had to sit with her legs apart to accommodate her belly. "But Jolita. There will be a baby, then."

Jolita froze for a minute, with the coffee pot raised in front of her as though it was an offensive weapon. She looked at Sigita seriously.

"Little darling," she said. "You're an intelligent girl. Surely you don't imagine that you'll be able to keep it?"

The clinic had recently been established in a big old villa in the Žvėrynas Quarter. There was a smell of fresh paint and new linoleum, and the chairs in the waiting room were so new that some of them still sported their plastic covers. Sigita sat heavily on one of them, squatting like a constipated cow. Sweat trickled down her back, soaking into the awful, bright yellow maternity dress Jolita had acquired through a friend at the University. For the past four weeks, this had been the only garment that would fit Sigita's bloated body, and she hated it with a will.

At least it will soon be over, thought Sigita. And clung to that thought as the next spasm gripped

174

her. A deep grunting sound escaped her, and she felt like an animal. A cow, a whale, an elephant. How the *hell* had it come to this? She gripped the edge of the table and tried to inhale and exhale, all the way, all the way, as she had been taught, but it made not the slightest bit of difference.

"Aaaaah. Aaaaaah. Aaaaaah."

I don't want to be an animal, she thought. I want to be Sigita again!

Jolita came back, accompanied by a slight, red-haired woman in a pale green uniform. Why not white? Perhaps it was meant to match the new mint green paint on the walls.

"I'm Julija," she said, holding out her hand. Sigita couldn't release her grip on the table, so the woman's gesture transformed itself into a small pat on the shoulder, presumably meant to be soothing. "We have a room ready for you. If you can walk, that will probably be the most comfortable for you."

"I. Can. Walk." Sigita hauled herself upright without letting go of the table. She began to waddle after the woman whose name was the same as Granny Julija's. Then she discovered that Jolita wasn't following. Sigita stopped.

Jolita was wringing her hands. Literally. One slim-fingered hand kept stroking the other, as though it were a glass she was polishing.

"You'll be fine, darling," she said. "And I'm coming back later."

Sigita stood utterly paralyzed. She couldn't mean . . . surely, she couldn't expect Sigita to go through this alone? Unthinkingly, she reached for her aunt with a begging gesture she regretted seconds later. Jolita backed away, staying out of reach.

"I'll bring you some chocolate," she said, smiling with unnatural brightness. "And some cola. It's good for when you're feeling poorly." And then she left, walking so quickly she was nearly sprinting. And Sigita suddenly realized why.

It was Thursday.

Nina parked the Fiat in the narrow, cobble-stoned part of Reventlowsgade, squeezed in between a row of classic Vesterbro tenements on one side and the Tietgensgade embankment on the other. On top of the embankment, the traffic moved past in uneven, noisy jerks.

The boy wriggled as she pulled the shorts up around his skinny waist, but he was apparently pleased with the slightly over-sized sandals. He picked at the velcro straps with his short, soft fingers, and Nina cautiously stroked his hair. She found the water bottles, unscrewed the cap of one of them, and held it out to him.

"Atju."

The boy accepted the bottle earnestly, and drank with clumsy greed. Some of the water sloshed onto his chin and the new T-shirt, and he silently wiped his mouth with the back of his hand.

The motion was so familiar that for a split second, Nina felt as if she might be sitting in a car with an ordinary child on their way home from a long day at the kindergarten. Slowly, she repeated the word to herself. Atju. Wasn't that the same thing he had said when she gave him the ice cream earlier?

It had to mean thank you.

Nina recognized the slight nod and lowered eyes that most children learn to produce as an automatic reaction. "Thank you" was the first phrase taught by any parents with the slightest ambition to raise a polite child. It couldn't be a coincidence, thought Nina. Both times, she had been giving him something. The word was clearly designed for such situations. So, thank you. It made her task a little easier, as "Mama" was probably too universal to be much use.

Nina opened the door and got out of the car. Heat still clung to the pavement and brick walls, and the heavy diesel fumes rising from the central railway station stung her nostrils with every breath. A faint puff of wind whirled a scrunched-up cigarette pack along the curb, until it came to rest against a tuft of yellow grass poking up between the paving stones.

The boy permitted her to lift him from the car only with reluctance, and once out, insisted on walking himself. He became tense and unmanageable in her arms, arching his spine and throwing back his head in silent protest, and when she gave in and let him slide to the sidewalk, she thought she had caught a glint of triumph in his tired eyes. He landed neatly, his new sandals meeting the pavement with a crisp and satisfied smack. Then he reached for her hand as though that was the most natural thing in the world. He was used to walking this way, thought Nina. He was used to holding someone's hand.

They walked up Stampesgade and turned right along Colbjørnsensgade, and then on to Istedgade. The boy's hand rested in hers, lightly as a butterfly, as they slowly moved past Kakadu Bar and Saga Hotel. There were still quite a few people about in the warm, dark night; outside the cafés, the guests were sipping beers and lattes and colas, barefooted in sandals, and still dressed only in light summer dresses or shorts.

The first prostitutes Nina saw were African. Two of them, both of them rather solidly built, and dressed in high boots and brightly colored skirts stretched tightly over muscular, firm thighs. The women stood less than five yards from each other, yet they didn't talk. One had propped herself against a wall with a cigarette between pursed lips, and rummaged hectically through her bag at regular intervals. The other did nothing at all except stand there, watching every car that turned the corner.

No one took any notice of Nina and the boy, and it struck her that they must look relatively normal, walking together like this. A little late to be out and about, certainly, considering the usual bed-time of children his age, but nothing that would raise eyebrows. Vesterbro might contain Copen-hagen's red light district, but it was also a neighborhood full of ordinary families, some of them with young children. Vesterbro was becoming hip, and fashionable cafés had sprung up among the topless bars and porn shops.

The boy dragged his feet a little, but she still felt no resistance in the hand resting confidently in hers. In a doorway a little further down the street, two women argued heatedly. They were both blond, with skinny legs and remarkably similar emaciated faces. The argument stopped abruptly, as suddenly as it has begun, and one of them reached into her handbag and handed a can of beer to the other.

Nina paused, and the boy stood obediently quiet at her side while she tried to obtain eye contact with one of the women, the one now holding the beer can. She, in her turn, ignored Nina and looked at the boy instead.

"Hi there, sweetheart."

Her voice was blurred and bubbly, as though she were talking to them from the bottom of a well. When the boy didn't react and Nina kept standing there, she finally raised her eyes to Nina's, with a grimace of confusion on her face.

"Yes?"

Nina took a deep breath. "I'm looking for. . . ." Nina hesitated, fumbling for the right words. The woman's gaze was already wandering again. "The Eastern European girls, where are they? Do you know?"

The woman's pale blue eyes widened in astonishment and distrust. Her pupils moved in tiny rapid jerks, and her mouth tightened. Nina realized she must look like the enemy, that the woman might consider her world to be under attack from the semi-detached, permanent-income, husband-toting kind of person who would condescend to and disapprove of people like her. She might suspect Nina of being a journalist, or an outraged wife, or even a tourist vicariously fascinated by the prospect of sleaze and degradation. In any case, the woman clearly did not relish the role of practical guide to Vesterbro's night life. Her eyes glinted aggressively.

"Why the hell are you asking?"

She moved half a step closer, and Nina felt the heaviness of her breath waver in the air between them.

Truth, she thought. I'll give her the truth, or a small part of it, at any rate.

"The boy needs his mother," she said, pulling the child onto her arm. "I have to find her."

For a few wobbly seconds, the woman maintained her stance, chest pushed forward and eyes glinting. Then the appeal to the maternal instinct had its effect. She slumped, taking another sip of her lager, and studied the boy with renewed interest.

"Poor little dear," she said, reaching out to touch his cheek with a bony finger.

He jerked his head out of reach and hid his face against Nina's shoulder, which made the beer-can woman scowl. She teetered off, pulling her friend with her. But she did answer the question as she went.

"They're everywhere at the moment," she said. "Some in Skelbæksgade, some at Halmtorvet. There are probably some in Helgolandsgade, too. They're bloody everywhere, and you have a long night ahead of you if you don't know her usual spot."

"Where do they come from, do you know?"

Nina wasn't sure the woman heard her, but just before they turned the corner, her friend twisted to look at Nina.

"Most of the white girls are from Russia," she said. "But there are others, too. Prices are way down because of them. The stupid little tarts ruin it for everyone else."

The door buzzer let off a snarl, startling Sigita out of a strange sort of absence. Not sleep. Nothing as peaceful as sleep.

"This is Evaldas Gužas, from the Department of Missing Persons. May we come in?"

She buzzed them through. Her heart had begun to pound so hard that the material of her shirt was actually quivering with each beat. They have found him, she thought. Holy Virgin, Mother of Christ. Please let it be so. They have found him, and he is all right.

But as soon as she opened her door to Gužas and his companion, she could tell that he was not the bearer of such good news. She still couldn't help asking.

"Have you found him?"

"No," said Gužas. "I'm afraid not. But we do have a possible lead. This is my colleague, Detective Sergeant Martynas Valionis. When I told him about the case, it rang a few bells."

Valionis shook Sigita's hand.

"May we sit down for a moment?"

"Yes, of course," said Sigita politely, all the while silently screaming *get on with it*.

Valionis perched on the edge of the white

couch, put his briefcase on the coffee table, aligning it with the edge with unconscious perfectionism, and brought out a plastic folder.

"I am about to show you some photographs, Mrs. Ramoškienė. Do you recognize any of these women?"

The photos were not glossy portrait shots, but printed hastily on a none-too-efficient inkjet, it seemed. He held them out to her one at a time.

"No," she said, to the first one. And the next.

The third photograph showed the woman with the chocolate.

Sigita clenched the paper so hard that she scrunched it.

"It's her," she said. "She's the one who took Mikas."

Valionis nodded in satisfaction.

"Barbara Woronska," he said. "From Poland, born in Krakow in 1972. Apparently she has lived in this country for some years, and officially she is working for a company selling alarm and security systems."

"And unofficially?"

"She came to our attention for the first time two years ago when a Belgian businessman made a complaint that she had tried to blackmail him. It would appear that the company uses her as an escort for their clients, particularly the foreign ones, when they visit Vilnius."

"She's a *prostitute?*" Sigita never would have guessed.

"That is perhaps a little too simple. Our impression is that she works as what's known as a honey trap. She certainly seems to have an uncommonly high consumption of prescription eyedrops."

Sigita didn't understand.

"Eyedrops?"

"Yes. Medicinally, they are used to relax the muscles of the eyes, which is useful in certain instances. But if they are ingested, in a drink, for instance, they have the rather peculiar side effect of causing unconsciousness and deep sleep within a short time. It's not uncommon for a hard-partying businessman to wake up in some hotel room, picked clean of his Oyster Rolex, cash, and credit cards. But Miss Woronska and her backers seem to have refined the technique a bit. They arrange so-called compromising photographs while our man is unconscious, and afterwards suggest to him that he agrees to an export deal on, shall we say, very lucrative terms for the Lithuanian companies involved. Only this time, the Belgian got stubborn, told them to publish and be damned, and came to us. Miss Woronska was one of the participants in the arranged photograph. The other was some little girl who could hardly have been more than twelve years old. One quite understands why the police have not heard from their other victims."

Hardly more than twelve . . . Sigita tried to push away the mental images. She couldn't make it square with the neat and elegant woman in the cotton coat. When people did something like that for a living, shouldn't it somehow show? She stared at the printed page. It was not a classic identification photo of the kind made after arrests. Barbara Woronska was not looking directly at the photographer, her head was turned slightly to the left, bringing out the elegance of her long neck. The quality was grainy, as if the picture had been too much enlarged, and the expression on her face was . . . peculiar. Her mouth was half open, her eyes stared blankly. Even though only her face and neck were showing in the photo, Sigita suddenly felt convinced that Woronska was not wearing any clothes, and that this was a detail from one of the "compromising photographs."

"But why . . . what made you think that she was the one who took Mikas?"

"Two things," explained Valionis. "Item one: the Belgian had an alarming alcohol content in his blood in spite of swearing to us that he had had only one drink in the company of the delectable Miss Woronska. When our doctor examined him, he found lesions in the man's throat consistent with intubation—in other words, someone could have inserted a tube and poured alcohol directly into his stomach while he was unconscious. It's a good way of demoralizing and incapacitating someone, if you are willing to take the risk. People have been known to die from it, from acute alcohol poisoning."

Sigita's head came up.

"But . . . but that is. . . ."

Evaldas Gužas nodded. "Yes. I'm sorry no one believed you. At this stage, unfortunately, we cannot prove that this was what was done to you, as it is not now possible to distinguish any original injury from those stemming from the intubation you had to undergo at the hospital. But everyone I have spoken to has characterized you as a sober and responsible person, so. . . ." He left the conclusion hanging in the air, unsaid.

Some of Sigita's general misery eased a little. At least they believed her now. At least they would be serious about looking for Mikas.

"And . . . Mikas?"

"The other thing that rang a bell was the fact that Barbara Woronska had been identified as one of four possible suspects in another case involving the disappearance of a child," said Valionis, consulting his notebook briefly.

Sigita's hands shook.

"A child?"

Valionis nodded.

"A little over a month ago, a desperate mother reported her eight-year-old daughter missing. She had been picked up from the music school where she took piano lessons twice a week by an unknown woman who presented herself as a neighbor. The piano teacher was not suspicious, as the mother works as a nurse and has often sent others to pick up the child when she herself has a late shift. Unfortunately, the piano teacher was not able to give us a very good description and would only say that it might be one of these four women." He tapped the photographs with one forefinger.

"But where is she now?" said Sigita. "Haven't you arrested her?"

"Unfortunately not," said Gužas. "Her place of employment tells us that they haven't seen her since Thursday, and she has apparently not been living at her official address since March."

"But how come she is not in jail? With all this, how come she is still out there, stealing other people's children?"

Valionis shook his head with a disgusted grimace.

"Both cases were dropped. The Belgian went home very suddenly, and all we got from him was a letter from his lawyer to the effect that his client was dropping all charges. And the nurse just as suddenly maintained that it had all been a misunderstanding, and the child was home and quite safe."

"Isn't that a little odd?" asked Sigita.

"Yes. We are convinced that they both gave

in to some form of pressure." Evaldas Gužas's gaze rested on her with an ungentle emphasis. "Which is why I have to ask you yet again, Mrs. Ramoškienė. Does anyone have any reason to subject you to that kind of pressure?"

Sigita shook her head numbly. If it hadn't been Dobrovolskij, she couldn't imagine anyone else feeling any need to pressure or threaten her.

"Surely they would say something?" she said. "I haven't heard a thing."

Helplessness gripped her once more. Again, an unbearable image flitted through her mind: Mikas in a basement somewhere, on a dirty mattress, crying, afraid. How can anyone stand this? she thought. I can't. It will kill me.

"I implore you to contact us if you hear anything at all," said Gužas. "It's impossible for us to stop people like this if no one will talk to us."

She nodded heavily. But she knew that if it became a choice between saving Mikas and telling the police, the police didn't have a prayer.

Valionis closed his briefcase with a crisp snap. The two officers got to their feet, Valionis gave her his card, and Gužas shook her hand.

"There is hope," he said. "Remember that. Julija Baronienė got her daughter back."

Sigita felt a brief spasm in her chest.

"Who, did you say?"

"Julija Baronienė. The nurse. Do you know her?"

Sigita's heart leaped and fluttered.

"No," she said. "Not at all."

She stood on her balcony and watched the two men cross the parking lot below, get into a black car, and leave. Her right hand had come to rest just under her navel, without any directions from her. Certain things are never entirely forgotten by the body.

Contrary to everything Sigita had heard about first-time births, it had been quick, and very, very violent. In the beginning she had yelled at everyone in sight, telling them to do something. In the end she just screamed, for four hours straight. It was Julija's hand she clung to, the nurse who was somehow also Granny; and Julija stayed with her so that she felt at times that this was the only thing that held her to this world: Julija's strong, square hands, Julija's voice, and Julija's face. Her eyes were dark, the color of prunes, and she did not let go, nor did she let Sigita do so.

"You just keep at it," she said. "You just keep at it until you finish this."

But when the baby did come, Sigita could hold on no longer. She slipped, and something flowed out of her, something wet and dark and warm, so that there was only cold emptiness left.

"Sigita. . . ."

But Julija's voice was already distant.

"She's hemorrhaging," said one of the other sisters. "Get the doctor, *now!*"

Sigita kept on slipping, into the chill and empty dark.

It was nearly a day and a night before she came back. She was in a small, windowless room lit by fluorescent ceiling lights. It was the light that had woken her. Her eyelids felt like rubber mats, her throat was sore. One arm had been tied to the side of the bed, and fluids were slowly dripping into her vein from a bag on a thin metal pole. Her body felt heavy and alien to her.

"Are you awake, little darling?"

Her aunt Jolita was by the bedside. The fluorescent lights bleached her skin and dug deep shadowed pits beneath her eyes. She looked like a tired old woman, thought Sigita.

"Would you like some water?"

Sigita nodded. She wasn't certain she could talk, but in the end she tried anyway.

"Where is Julija?"

Jolita frowned, her penciled brows nearly meeting in the middle.

"Your grandmother?"

"No. The other Julija."

"I don't know who you mean, darling. Here, have a sip. Now all you have to do is rest up and get better, so that we can get you home."

That was when it happened. When Jolita said

190

the word *home*. Something huge and black exploded in her head, her breasts, her belly. Its edges were so sharp and *evil* that it felt as if something was there, even though she knew that it happened because something was lacking. Because some-thing had been taken out of her.

"Is it a boy or a girl?" she asked.

"Don't think about it," said Jolita. "The quicker you forget about the whole thing, the better. It will have a good life. With rich people."

Sigita felt tears slide down her nose. They felt scalding hot because the rest of her was so cold.

"Rich people," she repeated, testing to see if that might make the Blackness go away.

Jolita nodded. "From Denmark," she said brightly, as if this was something special.

The Blackness was still there.

Two days later, Sigita was standing next to the bed in a gray sweatshirt and a pair of jeans she hadn't been able to fit into for months. Standing was tiring, but she still couldn't sit, and getting out of bed was so painful that she didn't want to lie down again. Finally Jolita returned, accompanied by a fair-haired woman in a white lab coat. Sigita had never seen the woman before.

"Goodbye then, Sigita, and good luck," she said, holding out her hand.

It felt odd, being called by her first name by

someone she didn't know at all. Sigita nodded awkwardly, but returned the handshake. The woman handed Jolita a brown envelope.

"There is a small deduction for the extra days," she said. "Normally, our girls leave us inside a day."

Jolita nodded absently. She opened the brown envelope, peeked inside, then closed it again.

"I'll need your signature here."

Jolita took the pen.

"Shouldn't I be the one to sign it?" asked Sigita.

Jolita hesitated. "If you wish," she said. "But I can do it too."

Sigita looked at the paper. It wasn't an adoption form. It was a receipt. For payment received on delivery of "Ass. herbs for the production of natural remedies." The amount signed for was 14.426 litai.

This is no adoption, thought Sigita suddenly, with glacial clarity. This is a purchase. Strangers have bought my child and paid for it, and this is my share of the loot.

"Can't I at least see it?" she asked. "And meet the people who are taking it?" Her breasts were swollen and throbbed painfully. Julija had provided her with a tight elastic bandage that she was to keep wrapped around her torso for at least a week, she had been told, to stop the milk from coming.

The woman in the white coat shook her head. "They left the clinic yesterday. But in our

192

experience, that's best for both parties anyway."

The Blackness stirred inside her, carving new passages in her body, flowing into her veins. She could feel the chill beneath her skin. It was already done, she thought. Now all that was left was the money. She held out a hand toward Jolita.

"Give it to me."

"Little darling. . . ." Jolita looked at her in confusion. "You make it sound as if I was about to steal it!"

Sigita merely waited. In the end, Jolita passed her the envelope. It was thick and heavy with the notes inside it. Sigita clutched it in one hand and waddled for the exit. The stitches stung with every stride.

"Sigita, wait," said Jolita. "The receipt!"

"You sign it," she said, over her shoulder. "It was all your idea anyway."

Jolita scribbled a hasty signature and said good-bye to the woman. Sigita just walked on. Into the corridor, through the waiting room, and out the door.

Jolita caught up with her on the rain-drenched pavement.

"Let's get a taxi," she said. "Let me take you home."

Sigita stopped. She turned and looked at Jolita with all the new coldness she now possessed. "You go home," she said. "I'm going to a hotel. I don't want to see you again. Ever."

∙ ∙ ∙

There were four Baronienė in the Vilnius phone book. Sigita called them all, asking for Julija. No result. Then she tried Baronas, in case the telephone was registered to the husband only. Eight of those. Two didn't answer, one had an answering machine that made no mention of any Julija, two said they didn't know anyone of that name. The sixth call was answered by a woman's voice with a cautious "Yes?"

Sigita listened intently, but she wasn't sure whether she recognized the voice.

"Is this Julija?" she asked.

"Yes. To whom am I speaking?"

"Sigita Ramoškienė. I would just like to—"

She got no further. The connection was severed with an abrupt click.

Jučas drove the car all the way down onto the beach. It was dark now, and there were no people. Behind him, the thicket of pines formed a black wall. He took off all his clothes except his underpants. The sand was still warm beneath the soles of his feet, and the water tepid and so shallow that he had to wade several hundred feet before it became deep enough for him to swim.

There was no significant surf, no suction. Just this flat, lukewarm water that could not give him the stinging shock he craved. It had to be there, he thought, further out—the cold, the undertow, the powers. He considered quite soberly the possibility of simply continuing until he met something stronger than he was.

Barbara was waiting at the hotel. He hadn't told her much, just that he had to help the Dane with something before they could get their money.

There would be no Krakow now, he thought, digging into the water with furious strokes that did, after all, make his muscles burn a little. In his mind he could still see the smiling family, the mother, the father, the two children, but large brown rats had begun to gnaw at the house so that it was disappearing bite by bite, and now one of the rats had started on the leg of the smallest child, without causing the child or the parents to smile any less.

He stopped his progress abruptly, treading water. He knew where those rats came from. Could still remember them scuttling away as he had come into the stable with the lantern and had found Gran on the floor next to the feed bin. No one had ever thought it necessary to tell him what she had died from. But dead she was, even a seven-year-old boy could tell as much. And the rats had known it, too.

He had succeeded in finding waters too deep for him to touch bottom. But he began to swim for the coast, this time with smooth, methodical strokes. He would not let the rats win. And there was still a trail of sorts that he might follow.

He thought about his clothes. What to do with them. In the end he dipped the sleeve of his shirt into the petrol tank of the car and made a small bonfire on the beach. He had only vague notions of DNA and microscopic fibers, but surely fire would deal with most of that.

The first thing to go wrong had been the woman herself. It hadn't been the one he had seen in the railway station—the bony, crew-cut boy-bitch. This one was fair-haired like Barbara and had even bigger breasts. It would have been so much easier if it had only been the other one.

But she tried to run the minute she saw him, and surely she wouldn't have done that if she had been innocent? His reflexes took over, and he hit her a few times on the arms and legs when he caught her, just to stop her from trying to run again. She was terrified. She gabbled at him in a language that was probably Danish, then seemed to realize that he didn't understand. She began speaking English instead. Asked him who he was, and what he was doing there? But he could tell from her eyes that she knew precisely why he had come. And she was so scared that a trickle of yellow pee ran down one leg and made a damp spot in the middle of her white dress.

Why wouldn't the stupid woman just *tell* him,

he thought? What was she thinking? That if she said "no" enough times, he would apologize for the inconvenience and go away?

There always came a point when they knew. Some tried to escape, or scream and beg. Others simply gave up. But the time always came when they knew. Once he had torn away all the things they used for protection—nice clothes, perhaps, or an immaculate home, courtesy and starched curtains, a name, a position, an illusion of power and security: *this can't be happening to us . . .* once he had made them understand that yes, it was happening, it could happen to anybody, and right now it's happening to you. Once the disbelief had vanished. Then there was only one raw reality left: that he would not stop until they gave him what he had come for.

Despite her terror, it took a long while for the fair-haired Danish woman to get to that point. Much longer than he was used to in Lithuania. Perhaps the layer of security was thicker here, like the layer of fat on the fish in the Tivoli lake. Peeling it off took time. But in the end she was just trying to figure out what he wanted her to say.

He asked about the money. I put it back, she said. Jan has it. She kept saying that, so it might be true.

Then he asked about the boy. Who was the bitch who had collected him? Where was he now? Who had him?

That was when he came upon a core of resistance in the middle of all that soft blondness. She wouldn't tell him. Lied to him, saying she didn't know. And that was when he became angry.

He had had to leave her for a while, afraid of losing it, afraid that he had already lost it. He'd stood outside on the porch for some minutes, just breathing, listening to the irritating whine of the mosquitoes, as if they all had little miniature engines that were tuned too high. A small gray tabby suddenly appeared from under the bushes on the opposite side of the lawn. It stopped some distance away, meowing with a curious questioning intonation. But it seemed to realize something was wrong, because it came no closer, and immediately afterwards darted back into the shrubbery and was gone.

When he went back in, she had succeeded in crawling onto the bed. Her breathing sounded wrong, too wet and bubbly, and she didn't react when he came into the room.

"Ni-na," she gurgled. "Ni-na."

He wasn't even sure whether it was in answer to the questions he had asked, or whether she was just calling for someone she imagined might help her. But he took her mobile from the bedside table to check if there was a Nina. There was. He took down both the number and her last name and tossed the phone on the bed.

"Ni-na," she said once more.

She doesn't even know I'm here, he thought. Then he saw the pool of blood spreading beneath her head.

The flames were dying. He kicked some sand over the embers, then decided to bury the remains of the bonfire properly. With a bit of luck they would never be found. Then he got himself a clean dry shirt from his bag in the car.

He tried to view the situation with a clear mind. One had to. At the moment, he didn't know where the money was. The blonde had said she had given it back to the Dane. The Dane said the blonde had it. Jučas believed the blonde more than he believed the Dane.

And the boy? Perhaps that gurgling "Ni-na" had actually been the answer. Maybe she was called Nina, the dark-haired boy-bitch who had ogled him back at the railway station. What if she had the brat, and this was why the Dane was suddenly so uncooperative about paying? At the price they had set, it wasn't too surprising if he wanted delivery of the goods before he handed over the cash.

Once Jučas was fully dressed again, he called Barbara. He had checked her into a hotel before leaving the city. More unnecessary expense, but he couldn't take her with him.

"Is there a phone book in the room?" he asked.

She said there was.

"I need you to find an address for me," he said.

"But don't call Directory Enquiries, and don't ask the operator. Is that clear?"

"When will you be back?" she asked, and he could hear the anxiety in her voice.

"Soon. But you have to do as I say, it's important."

"Yes. Yes, okay. What is it you want me to do?"

"Look up someone in the phone book. See if there's a listing for a Nina Borg."

Helgolandsgade.

The street was narrow and a bit claustrophobic. On one side was the newly refurbished Hotel Axel with its brilliant white facade and a big golden dragonfly hovering above the entrance. It had become trendy, thought Nina, to spend the night in Vesterbro, with a view of hookers and pick-pockets.

A group of teenage girls had taken up position directly opposite the hotel's entrance. They looked like ordinary school girls, thought Nina in surprise. No leather, no fishnet stockings or bleached hair. They looked like regular young people ready for a night on the town. And yet, there was somehow no doubt what they were here for.

The four girls all checked the street regularly,

eyeing the passersby. Every little while, one would separate herself from the herd, walk a few steps, perhaps get out her mobile, but without ever calling someone. Then she'd return to lean on the small black motor scooter they were all gathered around. While everyone else moved on, they stayed.

Nina gripped the boy's hand a little more tightly, then approached them. A couple of phrases in accented English rose above the noisy conversation of a couple of drunks going the other way.

"Nineteen. You owe me."

One of the girls laughed loudly, and took a couple of tottering steps backwards, on heels that were far too high for her.

They had been betting on her age, thought Nina, but she couldn't tell whether the others had guessed too high or too low. She shivered. Ida would be fourteen at her next birthday.

"Excuse me?"

Nina deliberately made her voice soft and neutral. These girls wouldn't want to talk to anyone except for necessary business, her instincts told her.

All the girls turned to regard her, and once more, Nina was struck by their youth. The heavy makeup and pale glittery lip gloss just made them look like little girls disguised as grown-ups. Nina half expected some tinny voice to announce that these were the contestants in some bizarre

American Little Miss beauty pageant, so that any minute now, one of them might break into song.

One of the four took up a stance directly in front of her, legs apart and arms crossed over her chest, presumably in an effort to look menacing. She was small and very slim, her dark eyes darting nervously.

"I need some help with this boy," said Nina. "I need to know if you can understand him."

The girl cast a glance up the street, then looked at Nina again, her skepticism obvious.

"Atju," said Nina, pointing at the boy. "Do you know what it means? Do you know which language?"

Something moved in the girl's sullen face. Nina could practically see her deliberating the pros and cons, and separating them into two untidy piles. Nina quickly stuck her hand into the pockets of her jeans and came up with a crumbled hundred-kroner note. That obviously helped. The girl discreetly transferred the note to her own pocket.

"I'm not sure. I think maybe Lithuanian."

Nina nodded, smiling as softly as she knew how. She was definitively out of cash now.

"And you are not from Lithuania?"

The answer was self-evident, but Nina wanted to keep the conversation going, to hang on to the slight thread of a chance she had been offered.

"Latvia." The girl shrugged. "Marija is Lithuanian."

She stepped aside a little, indicating the tall, gangly girl who had laughed before, and who might or might not be nineteen years old. She had long dark hair, gathered in a ponytail at the back of her head. There was something coltish about her, thought Nina. Her legs seemed too long for her body, the knees wide and bony in comparison, and her movements had all the gawky awkwardness of a growing teenager.

Her face, too, was sullen, and she looked uncertainly at Nina.

"Do you know the word *atju*?" asked Nina.

An involuntary smile flashed across the girl's face, probably at Nina's attempt at pronunciation.

"It's *ačiu. Ačiū.*"

Her A was a little longer than Nina's, and it sounded exactly right in a way Nina's attempt had not. Something soft and girlish came into the young woman's face as she repeated the word, and she exposed a row of perfect white teeth still too big and too new, somehow, for the adult makeup.

"That is Lithuanian," she said, smiling again, and raising a flat hand to her chest. "I am from Lithuania."

Again, Nina pointed to the boy.

"I need to talk to this boy. I think maybe he is Lithuanian too."

If the girl would help her, she would be able to get information from the boy. He might even be able to tell her how he had ended up in a suitcase in a baggage locker at the central railway station. If only the girl would agree to go somewhere a little more quiet.

"Could you help me talk to him?"

The girl cast a quick look over her shoulder, and now there was a wary expression on her face. She was having second thoughts, and when a young man in a black T-shirt suddenly crossed Helgolandsgade and headed their way, she started visibly.

"When we talk, we don't make any money."

Her eyes were still on the black T-shirt man, who had increased his pace and was clearly homing in on Nina and the girls. The girl with the ponytail stepped back and deliberately turned away from Nina.

"Tomorrow," she said softly, not looking Nina's way at all. "After I sleep. Twelve o'clock. Do you know the church?"

Nina shook her head. There had to be thousands of churches in Copenhagen, and she didn't know any of them.

T-shirt man had almost reached them. He wasn't much older than the ponytail girl, thought Nina. He wouldn't have looked out of place, she thought, as a carpenter's or plumber's apprentice. Not so tall, but muscular, with short fair hair and a tattooed black snake winding its way up his well-defined biceps.

The girl's lips were moving silently, as though

204

she was practicing the name before she said it out loud.

"Sacred Heart," she finally said.

T-shirt man stopped. He seized the girl's upper arm in a no-nonsense grip, and jerked her along the sidewalk, not even glancing at Nina. A few paces further on, the sound of the first slap rang across the street. The ponytail leaped and fell as the girl's head snapped back. He hit her three times, all of them hard, flat blows. Then he let go of her.

Nina snatched the boy onto her arm and stalked off in the direction of Istedgade. Anger pounded through her body in a hot red pulse, but there was nothing she could do now. Not while she had the boy with her. Hell, she probably couldn't have done much even if she had been alone. The thought did not lessen her fury.

Just before she turned the corner, she looked down Helgolandsgade again. The man was already gone, possibly lost somewhere in the shadow of a doorway or a service entrance. The ponytail girl was heading back towards the black motor scooter. She was hunched forward as she walked, her long gangling arms wrapped around her upper body.

One of the other girls touched her shoulder briefly as she rejoined the group, and as Nina turned away, she could hear their high clear voices behind her, already laughing again in a flat, harsh, defiant way. They had another bet going, and the girl with the ponytail was laughing louder than any of them.

Nina carried the boy all the way back to the car. He was awake, but the small firm will that she had noticed when they were getting out of the car in Reventlowsgade had left him again. His legs dangled in a ragdoll fashion against her thighs and belly with every step she took. When she reached the car, he wouldn't even stand on his own while she unlocked the car. She covered the dark, sour-smelling stain on the backseat with the checkered blanket, and let the boy slide out of her grasp and onto the seat. Then she got into the back beside him and simply sat there, staring into the neon dark. She was exhausted. It was exactly 11:00, she noted. For some reason, it pleased her when she caught the hour on the hour; perhaps it was the flat precision of the double zeros.

Traffic up on Tietgensgade had become more scattered. In the old Vesterbro apartment buildings on the other side of the street, she could see into the still-lit kitchens. On the ground floor, a young man was making coffee in a bistro coffeepot, calling back his half of a conversation to someone behind him. He put the coffeepot on a tray with a collection of cups and turned away from the window with a smile on his face. Nina couldn't help wondering if the lives of other people were really as simple as they looked. As simple, and as happy.

Probably not, she thought drily. It was a distortion of a kind she was an expert at providing for herself, or so her therapist had informed her. She was always busy telling herself that she was the only one who didn't fit in, while everyone else was one big happy community. And she was also an expert at making herself believe that she was the only one who could save the world and put things right, while others were too busy buying flat-screen televisions and redecorating their kitchens and making bistro coffee and being happy. It was this distorted view that had sent her on several panicked flights from Morten and Ida, back before Anton was born, and for some years now, she had actually believed Olav when he told her that she was mistaken, and that such distortions were bad for her and the people around her.

Now, with the boy next to her, it didn't seem so easy and clear-cut.

Nina leaned her head back against the upholstery and felt her own tiredness beating against the inside of her eyelids.

She wished she could call Morten. Not to talk to him, because that would do no good. But just so that she could hear his voice, and the television news in the background, and remind herself that there was a normal world out there. She touched her pocket where the mobile ought to be, and was no longer.

She locked the doors and turned on the car radio. There might be something on the news about a missing child. Something that proved that the boy existed, that someone was looking for him. She got the bread out of its bag and offered a slice to the boy. He accepted it and took a careful bite, without looking at her. They sat like that, silently eating, the boy with his eyes lowered in quiet reserve, she with her hand cradling the back of his pale, downy neck. When he had finished, he curled up next to her, and Nina carefully folded one end of the blanket over him like a duvet. She let herself slide a little lower, drawing up her knees until they rested against the seat in front of her, and closed her eyes again. Instantly, a flickering wave of sleep threatened to sweep her away. Sleep. God. She really had to, sometime soon. Tomorrow she could find a phone somewhere and call Morten. Perhaps his voice would not be so cold and hostile, then. His mood was always better in the mornings, and she might even be able to tell him about the boy.

She forced her eyes open once more to look at the child. He had fallen asleep with his eyes still slightly open, a soft glitter of wariness beneath the lowered lids, but his breathing was soft and regular, his lips slightly parted. Like Anton's, when he lay with his head resting limply against the Spiderman web of his pillow.

Nina's own eyes closed.

Finally, peace reigned in the flat. Anton had refused to go to sleep, and had sulked and peeved until nine o'clock so that Morten had missed the news, and Ida had played her music defiantly loud instead of using her headphones the way the house rules dictated. He hadn't had the energy to call her on it. Apparently, she was now done with that particular outburst of teenage rebellion, and the weird, irregular clop-clop pata-pow sounds from her computer game were muffled enough that he could ignore them.

He had opened both the kitchen and the living room windows in the vain hope of catching a breeze, but the air seemed to have congealed, and the long day still stuck to him like the damp back of his shirt. He considered taking a shower, but this was the first time since he had picked Anton up from daycare that he had been able to sit down quietly with a cup of coffee and the news-paper. He would save the shower for later; it might make it easier to fall asleep.

There were days. There were days when he just wanted to pack all this in a time capsule and come back and open it in, say, four years' time. Imagine being able to *do* something; God, how he longed to go prospecting for minerals in the tundra, or go to Greenland again, or Svalbard, and return only when he had had his fill of mosquitoes and polar bears, and quite ready to take up family life exactly as it was, with all the pieces in the same positions on the board. Or nearly the same—there were one or two moves he would like to rethink.

It wasn't that he didn't want all of this, the children and the flat and the mortgages and the securely salaried job he had. He just wished he could have the other things as well. Once he had imagined that he would be able to do both—go to Greenland for three months, perhaps, while Nina held down the fort at home. But that was before she had run away the first time. Running away was exactly what it was, he had never had any doubts about that. And it had happened just as abruptly as if she had simply left him for good. He would never forget that day. It remained under his skin like a poison capsule, and every once in a while, something would prick a hole in it so some of the poison leaked out.

It had happened five months after Ida was born. They lived in Aarhus then, in an uninspiring but cheap two-bedroom flat near Ringgaden. Nina had just graduated from nursing school, and he was doing a Ph.D. at the Department of Geology. Coming home from the department one day, he had heard Ida crying—no, *screaming*—the minute he came into the stairwell. He took the terazzo steps three at a time and practically took the door off its hinges. Ida was strapped into her baby chair on the kitchen table, her chubby face swollen and scarlet from prolonged sobbing. She had no clothes on, not even a diaper, and the pale green plastic kiddy tub on the kitchen floor was still full of bathwater. Nina was standing with her whole body pushed up against the door to the back stairs, looking as if something had her cornered. With one look at her he understood talking to her in that state would do no good; expecting any kind of answers or assistance or action from her was futile. He had no idea how long she had been standing like that. Long enough for Ida to have wet herself and the baby chair rather thoroughly, certainly.

The day after, she had called him from a phone booth in Copenhagen Airport. She was on her way to London, and from there to Liberia, as a volunteer nurse for an organization called MercyMedic. This was not a position she had obtained with just a day's notice, of course. But although the decision had been some time coming, and the preparations had to have been made at least some weeks in advance, she hadn't bothered to discuss it with him, or even tell him about it. Now that he thought about it, it had actually been Karin who helped her, back then. Some French surgeon she was acquainted with had been willing to overlook Nina's lack of job

211

experience. And Morten was left alone with a five-month-old little girl.

Only much later had she succeeded in explaining herself to him, at least to some extent. He had noticed that she was finding it harder and harder to sleep, that she was constantly watching Ida, day and night, that she seemed to be afraid of disasters, real or imagined. He had tried to calm her fears, but facts and rationality didn't seem to have much effect on her conviction that something horrible could happen to the child.

"I was bathing her," she had told him, not that day, but nearly a year later. "I was bathing her, and suddenly the water turned red. I knew it wasn't, not really. But every time I looked at her, the water was red all the same." Only the severest form of self-control had made it possible for her to lift Ida from the bathtub and strap her safely into the chair. And the fact that she had not actually fled from the flat but had waited there until he came home . . . he knew now that that had been a miracle of impulse control.

He had spoken occasionally to colleagues of hers who had been stationed with her at various global hotspots. They admired her. They said she was nearly inhumanly cool and competent in the middle of the most horrible crises. When rivers washed away bridges, when a light grenade set fire to the infirmary tents, when patients arrived with arms or legs blown away by landmine explosions . . . then Nina was the one who could always be counted on. She led a remarkably efficient one-woman crusade to save the world. It was only her own family who could reduce her to abject helplessness.

Ida was standing in the doorway before he realized that the pata-pow sounds from her room had died away.

"Is she coming home?" she asked. She was wearing neon-green shorts and a black T-shirt that read *I'm only wearing black until they make something darker.* A small silver sphere in one nostril represented his latest defeat in the teenage wars.

She never says "Mom" anymore, he suddenly thought. It was either "she" or sometimes "Nina."

"Of course she is," he said. "But she may have to work through the night." He was aware that the last statement was a fairly transparent piece of arse-covering, but he wasn't quite sure whose arse. Was it out of some remnant of loyalty to Nina, or was it just that he didn't like to sound clueless?

"Oh."

Ida withdrew, showing neither relief nor disapproval.

"Bedtime," he called after her.

"Yeah, yeah," she drawled, managing to suggest that she *might* be going to bed now, but only because she felt like it.

He put down the paper and stared into space,

unable to focus his mind on the words. Nina had lied to him. He had heard it clearly in the pauses, in the way she was distancing herself from what she said. That, more than the fact that she had entirely forgotten about Anton, had been what got to him. But he hadn't had the energy to confront her, just as he hadn't had the energy to fight Ida over the headphones issue. Lately, he had been in danger of running out of energy altogether.

Things *were* better. Or so he had thought. No, they really were. Olav had helped her. Helped both of them, in fact. During an otherwise fairly routine debriefing after things had become a little rough in Tbilisi, the Norwegian therapist had somehow made Nina realize that she needed help. Not so much because of Tbilisi, Dadaab, or Zambia, but because of the obsessions that drove her to *be* in Tbilisi, Dadaab, or Zambia.

Nina had come home. Her hair almost shaved to the skull, her body reminiscent of a stick insect's, but with a new . . . well, serenity was perhaps not quite the word. Balance, maybe. A cautiously maintained equilibrium that made him believe they might after all be capable of staying together, of loving each other again. They had moved to Copenhagen. A new beginning. She had begun working for the Red Cross Center at the Coal-House Camp, he had become a "mud logger," as other geologists somewhat condescendingly described his job—collecting and analyzing bore samples from the North Sea oil rigs and other none-too-exotic locations. They both agreed that family was now the priority, if the torn ligaments that bound them together were to have a chance of healing.

Well. He was still here. She was still here. Except that she had lied to him this afternoon. And he didn't know, he couldn't be sure, that he would not get a phone call tomorrow or the next day from Zimbabwe or Sierra Leone or some place equally distant and dangerous.

God damn you, Nina. He set down his mug and got up with an unfocused sense of urgency. He wanted to get away from here. Out of the flat. Just for a few hours. Or a few years. If only everything would still be here when he returned.

A little after four in the morning, the door buzzer woke him. It wasn't Nina who had lost her key, as he had half expected. It was the police. One in uniform, one in a suit.

"We would like to talk to Nina Borg," said the suit, presenting his ID with a motion that had become habit many, many years ago.

Morten felt too much coffee turn into acid in his stomach.

"She's not here," he said. "She's staying with a friend. Is anything wrong?"

"May we come in for a moment? I'm afraid this is a murder inquiry."

The Baronas lived in a small wooden house which stood like an island amidst an advancing tide of project developments. The bareness of the grounds between the new apartment buildings made their modest garden seem like a veritable jungle. A small red bicycle was padlocked to the fence with heavy duty chains.

Sigita opened the gate and approached the house. A smell of frying onions greeted her; Julija Baronienė was cooking supper, it appeared. Sigita pressed the bell button on the peeling blue door-frame. Almost at once, a boy of twelve or thirteen answered. He was wearing a white shirt and a tie and looked somehow unnaturally clean and well-groomed.

"Good evening," said Sigita. "May I speak to your mother?"

"Who may I say is calling?" he said cautiously. It sounded as if he had orders not to let just anybody in.

"Tell her it is Mrs. Mažekienė from the school board," said Sigita, so that the door would not be slammed in her face with the same precipitous speed that had severed the telephone connection.

The boy stood still for a long moment, and

Sigita suddenly realized that he was trying to weigh all the possibilities that this might somehow be to do with him. She smiled reassuringly.

"Er, come on in," he said. "Mama is making supper, but she'll be right with you."

"Thank you."

He showed her into the living room and disappeared, presumably to report to the kitchen. Sigita stood in the middle of the room, taking in her surroundings. The sofa was large, soft, and pale brown, clearly a recent purchase, but apart from that, everything had been here for a long time. The floor was dark from innumerable coats of shellac, and in front of the couch was an Afghan rug that glowed in strong red, white, and turquoise hues. Three of the walls had beautifully carved bookshelves from floor to ceiling, which by the style of the carpentry looked to be as old as the house itself. The shelves sagged from the weight of books and sheet music, and by the fourth wall, between the two tall windows, was an upright piano in shiny dark mahogany, with keys so old and worn they were slightly concave, the ivory yellow with age.

The door opened, and a small, compact woman entered, with a girl who must be her daughter physically hanging on to her in a manner that seemed too young for the seven or eight years she looked to be. A waft of kitchen smells entered with her, and when they shook hands, Sigita felt a cool dampness that somehow made her think that Mrs. Baronienė had been peeling potatoes.

"Julija Baronienė," she said. "And this, of course, is my Zita." Zita stared at her feet and showed no inclination to say hello to the stranger. Her hair was parted into braids, the immaculate partition showing like a straight white line against the darkness of her hair. "You'll have to excuse her," said her mother. "Zita is a little shy—and very much her mama's little girl."

She hasn't recognized me, thought Sigita. And why should she? It's all such a long time ago. But Sigita knew at once, the moment she saw the copper hair and the warm, prune-colored eyes. This was *the* Julija.

"I suppose that is only natural," said Sigita. "Considering what's happened to her."

Julija Baronienė stiffened.

"Why do you say that?" she asked.

No point in beating about this particular bush, thought Sigita.

"I'm not from the school board," she said. "I've come to ask you how you got Zita back. You see —the same people have taken my little boy." Her voice broke on the last few syllables.

With a small mewling sound that made Sigita think of drowning kittens, Zita turned completely into her mother's embrace and hid her face against her belly.

For a moment, Julija Baronienė looked as if

Sigita had jabbed a knife into her body. Then she made an obvious effort and forced a smile.

"Oh, that silly story," she said. "No, no, that was all a big misunderstanding. It turned out Zita had been picked up by the mother of one of her friends, right, Zita?" Zita did not reply, nor did she let go of her mother. Her anxiety made her seem far younger than she was.

"It was awfully embarrassing to have wasted police time like that. But . . . but of course I'm sorry for you and your little boy. Are you sure it's not a misunderstanding too? He could be with a friend. Or perhaps he may have wandered off somehow?"

"He's only three. And my neighbor saw them take him. Besides. . . ." She hesitated, then ploughed on. "There *has* to be a connection. Don't you remember me at all?"

Julija's gaze fluttered around the room before it finally came to rest on Sigita. This time, Sigita saw recognition flare in the prune-colored eyes.

"Oh," was all she said.

Sigita nodded. "Yes," she said. "I'm sorry I lied to you. But after you cut me off on the phone I was afraid you wouldn't even talk to me if you knew . . . if you knew who I was."

Julija Baronienė stood perfectly still, as if the revelation had completely robbed her of the ability to speak or move. In the background, Sigita heard the sound of a door slamming, and voices talking, but she kept her eyes squarely on Julija.

"Just tell me what you had to do," she said. "I won't tell the police, I promise. I just want my Mikas back."

Julija Baronienė still said nothing. The door to the sitting room opened.

"Hello," said the man entering. "Aleksas Baronas. Marius tells me you are with the school board?" He held out his hand politely. He was somewhat older than Julija, a kind, balding man in a grayish-brown suit that hung a little loosely on his frame. It took a moment before he realized something was wrong.

"What is it?" he asked abruptly, when he noticed how fiercely Zita clung to her mother.

Julija apparently had no idea how to answer him. It was Sigita who had to explain.

"My little son has been abducted by the same people who took Zita," she said. "I just want to know what I should do to get him back."

He recovered more quickly than his wife.

"Such stupid nonsense," he said. "Can't you see you're scaring the child? Zita has never been abducted, and she won't be, ever. Isn't that right, sweetheart? Give Papa a kiss. Julija, I'm sorry to rush you, but we need to have dinner now, or we'll be late for Marius's concert."

Zita was persuaded to release her leechlike grip on Julija. Her father caught her up and held her on his left arm, and she threw her arms around his neck.

"I don't wish to be rude," he said. "But my son is playing in a concert tonight, and it's quite important to us."

Sigita shook her head in disbelief.

"How can you . . . how can you pretend like this? How can you refuse to help me? When you know what it's like?" She pressed her hand against her lower face as if that might hold back the sobs, but it was no good.

The man's friendly manner was showing cracks.

"I must ask you to leave," he said. "Now."

Sigita shook her head once more. Tears were streaming down her face, and there was nothing she could do to hinder them. Her throat felt thick and tender. She tore a ballpoint pen from her handbag and seized a random sheet of music from the piano. Ignoring Baronas's involuntary squawk of protest, she wrote her name, address, and phone number in large jagged letters across the page.

"Here," she said. "I beg you. You have to help me."

Now it was Julija Baronienė's turn to cry. With a half-choked sob she turned and fled the room. Zita wriggled free of her father's embrace to follow, but he stopped her.

"Not now, sweetheart. Mama is busy."

Zita looked up at her father. Then she suddenly turned and walked with swift steps to the piano

221

seat. She sat, back completely straight, eyes closed. Then she began to play the scales, slowly, methodically, with metronomical precision. Up and down. Da-da-da-da-da-da-da-dah, di-da-di-da-di-da-di-dah. Da-da-da-da-da-da-da-dah. . . .

A look of pain flashed across Baronas's face. Then he, too, went to the piano, and gently stopped the jabbing fingers by grasping the girl's wrist. He looked at Sigita.

"Otherwise she goes on for hours," he said, looking completely lost. They had smashed up his family, thought Sigita, smashed it and broken it, and he had no idea how to put it back together.

She looked down at Zita's hands, still resting on the worn ebony, as if she would go on playing the instant he released her. Sigita shuddered, and in her mind, the unbearable picture show came back, Mikas in a basement, Mikas alone in the dark, Mikas surrounded by threatening figures who wanted to harm him.

"Please," said Zita's father. "Please go. Can't you see we could not help you even if we wanted to?"

All the way home Sigita thought about Zita's hands. Eight-year-old fingers, bent like claws against the yellowed piano keys. All except for the little finger of her left hand, which wasn't bent like the others, but stuck out from the rest. On that finger, Zita had lost the entire nail.

Jan had been prepared for steel tables and strip-lit ceilings, cold, white tiles or possibly even refrigerated drawers. But the lights in the chapel of the Institute of Forensic Medicine were soft and unglaring, and the still body lay on a simple bier, covered by a white cotton sheet, with a pair of candles lending an unexpected note of grace.

"Thank you for coming," said the officer who had led him in. Jan had already forgotten her name. "Her parents live in Jutland, so it's good to have a preliminary identification before we ask them to make the journey."

"Of course," said Jan. "It's the least I can do."

He felt acid burn at the back of his throat even before they lowered the sheet to show him her face.

She was a thing. That was what caught him most off guard—the degree to which humanity had vanished along with her life. Her skin was wax-like and unliving, and it was in no way possible to imagine that she was merely sleeping.

"It's Karin," he said, though it felt like a lie. This was not Karin anymore.

The shock went far beyond anything he had imagined. He felt like one of those cartoon characters hanging in the air above the abyss, foundations shot to hell, kept up only by the lack of the proper realization: that it was time to fall.

"How well did you know Karin Kongsted?" asked the woman officer, covering Karin's face once more.

"She had become a good friend," he said. "For the past two years, just about, she had a flat above our garage, and although it is completely separate from the rest of the house, still . . . it's different from the way it would have been if she had been merely a nine-to-five employee."

"I understand you hired her as a private nurse. How come you need someone like that?"

"I had to undergo renal surgery a little over two years ago. That was how we met Karin. And since then . . . well, we came to appreciate both her professional and her personal qualities. It was a major operation, and there are still medical issues. Complications sometimes arise. It's been very reassuring to have her nearby. She is . . . she was a very competent person."

It felt completely absurd to stand here next to Karin's dead body and talk about her like this. But the woman wasn't letting him off the hook just yet.

"I hope you understand that I have to ask you where you were tonight? You weren't at home when we called."

"No, I was home only briefly, then I had to go to

the office. The company I run is not a small one."

"So we understand."

"I was probably at the office until seven. Then I went to a flat we keep—the company, that is—and worked from there for a little while. I had intended to spend the night there."

"Where is this flat?"

"In Laksegade."

"Can we call on you there later? It will be necessary to hold a formal interview."

He thought quickly. The Nokia was still in his briefcase. And the briefcase was still in Laksegade.

"I probably should go home to my wife," he said. "She must be very distraught. If you like, I can come to the local station tomorrow. Perhaps tomorrow morning?" Show cooperation, he counseled himself. It might be important later.

"We would appreciate that," she said politely. "Although the case is now being handled by the homicide department of the North-Zealand Regional Police." From her own briefcase, she drew a small leaflet with the stirring title "Regional Police Reform: This Is Where to Find Us." She circled an address in ballpoint pen. "Can you come to this office tomorrow at 11 a.m.?"

He wondered if they were watching him. The taxi slid through the midnight traffic like a shark through a herring shoal, and he couldn't tell whether any specific car stayed behind them.

Don't be paranoid, he told himself. They could barely have established cause of death yet, and they surely hadn't the manpower to follow everyone connected to Karin. Yet he couldn't help glancing around as he alighted on the sidewalk outside the Laksegade flat. The taxi drove off, leaving the street empty and deserted. There was a certain time-bubble quality to the place—the cobbled stones, the square-lantern-shaped street-lights, even the fortress-like headquarters of the Danske Bank, which from this angle looked more like a medieval stronghold than a modern corporation domicile.

He let himself in and snatched up the briefcase. There had been no calls to the Nokia while he'd been gone.

Twenty minutes later, he had fetched the car and was on his way home. Now he felt reasonably certain that he wasn't being followed—the motorway was sparsely trafficked at this hour, and when he turned off at a picnic area between Roskilde and Holbæk, his Audi was the only car in the parking lot.

He got out the Nokia and made the call. It was a long wait before the Lithuanian answered.

"Yes?"

"Our agreement is terminated," said Jan, as calmly as he was able.

"No," said the man. Just that: the bare negative.

"You heard me!"

"The money was not there," said the Lithuanian. "She said she gave it back to you."

"Don't lie to me," said Jan. "She took it." He had seen the empty case in her bedroom. Empty, that is, except for that nasty little note: I QUIT. "She took it, and now she is dead. Did you kill her?"

"No."

Jan didn't believe him.

"Stay away from me and my family," he said. "I don't want anything more to do with you. It's over."

A brief pause.

"Not until you pay," said the Lithuanian, and then hung up.

Jan stood for a moment, trying to breathe normally. Then he banged the phone against the pavement a couple of times until he was confident it was thoroughly broken. He went into the foul-smelling bathroom, picked the SIM card from the wreckage of the phone, and flushed it down one of the toilets. He then wiped the phone itself thoroughly with wet paper towels and dumped it into the large garbage bin outside, stirring the contents with a twig until the phone had sunk from sight into the malodorous mix of apple cores, pizza cartons, ashtray contents and other road-trip debris.

What else?

He had to. He absolutely had to.

First the little plastic box. No more than two by two centimeters square, and a few millimeters thick. No larger, really, than the SIM card, but the few drops of blood trapped within contained coded information a thousand times more complex than the electronic DNA of the mobile phone. He ground it beneath his heel and dropped the remains into the garbage bin.

Then the photo. He took it from his wallet and looked at it one last time. Tried to come to terms with losing it, and everything it meant. Clicked his Ronson and let the tiny flame catch one corner and flare, before he let that, too, vanish into the bin, still smouldering.

He got back into the Audi and waited for his hands to stop shaking, at least enough so that it would be safe to drive on.

Sigita's mobile gave a muffled ring inside her purse the minute she opened her own front door. The sound went through her like a shockwave, and she emptied the purse onto the coffee table. Anything less drastic just wouldn't let her get to it quickly enough.

"Yes?"

But it wasn't Julija Baronienė, a change of heart. Nor was it an unfamiliar voice telling her what she should do to get Mikas back.

"LTV may be willing to broadcast a Missing Person alert on Mikas," said Evaldas Gužas. "Particularly if you will come to the studio and make a direct appeal to the kidnappers."

Sigita stood stock still. A few hours ago, she would have agreed without hesitation. But now . . . she thought of Julija Baronienė and her family, of their obvious fear. And of Zita, one nail missing.

"Wouldn't that be dangerous for Mikas?" she asked.

She sensed his deliberation and almost thought she heard the clicking of his ballpoint pen accenting his thoughts.

"Have you heard from his abductors?"

"No."

"This means that more than forty-eight hours have gone by without a single attempt at contact," said Gužas. "Is this not so?"

"Yes."

"This is most unusual. Instructions usually arrive promptly, to prevent the parents from calling the police."

"Julija Baronienė did call."

"Yes. Within hours of the girl's disappearance. But less than twenty-four hours later, she withdrew her allegations."

229

"And you think this was because she had been threatened."

"Yes."

"But that means it *is* dangerous."

"It's a question of weighing the options," he said. "We have reported Mikas missing and sent out the description of his presumed kidnappers to every police station in Lithuania. We've contacted the police in Germany, where the boy's father now lives. We have even approached Interpol, although there is no indication that Mikas has left Lithuania; on the contrary, the link to Mrs. Baronienė's case gives us reason to believe that it is a local crime. All of this to no avail. We are no closer to locating your son, or his abductors. And this is why I'm considering asking the public for help."

The public. The mere word sent tremors of unease through Sigita's body.

"I'm really not sure. . . ."

"LTV would broadcast your appeal in connection with their late-night news show. We know that this usually causes a great many people to call in, and some of these calls have been helpful in the past. As we are able to show a photo of one of the presumed kidnappers this time, we are very hopeful that it will be beneficial to the investigation at this point."

He always talks as if he has swallowed one of his own reports, thought Sigita. I wonder what he sounds like when he is off duty? She was temporarily distracted by a mental image of Gužas up to his waist in cold water, dressed as the complete angler and sporting a newly caught fish. "The direction of the current gave reason to suspect that trout might be active in the upper left quadrant of the search area," commented off-duty Gužas in her head.

I'm very, very tired, Sigita told herself. Or else it's the concussion. It was as if the imagination she normally kept effortlessly locked down was suddenly bubbling up from the nether reaches of her mind like marsh gas. It made her uncomfortable.

"We have asked your husband, and he has agreed that the broadcast should be made. But we would really like for you to make that direct appeal in front of the cameras. In our experience, this has an effect even on people who would not normally contact the police. Especially when children are involved."

She rubbed her whole face with her good hand. She was exhausted. Too little to eat and drink all day, she thought. Her headache had become so constant she was almost getting used to it.

"I don't know. . . . Will it really help?"

"I wouldn't suggest this to you if there had been any communication from the abductors. Any opening for negotiation or coercion. In those circumstances, public uproar might serve only to increase the pressure on the kidnappers and might endanger the life of the child. But there has been no such communication. Is that not so?"

He is testing me, thought Sigita. He still doesn't believe me.

"No," she said. "But if it's dangerous for Mikas, I won't do it."

"It's a question of weighing the options," he repeated. "I am not saying it is completely without risk, but in our estimation, it is our best chance of finding Mikas right now."

Sigita could hear her own pulse. How could one decide something so vital when it felt as if one's head belonged to someone else?

"We can of course make the broadcast without your consent," he finally said, when the silence had gone on for too long.

Was that a threat? Suddenly, anger roared through her.

"No," she said. "I won't do it. And if you go ahead without me, I'll. . . ." But there was no way to finish. What threats could she make? He had all the weapons.

She sensed a sigh somewhere at the other end of the connection.

"Mrs. Ramoškienė, I am not the enemy," he said.

Anger left her as suddenly as it had arrived.

"No," she said. "I know that."

But once she had disconnected, she couldn't

help but wonder. What was more important to an ambitious young officer like Gužas? Arresting the criminals, or saving the victims?

Her blouse was sticking to her back, and she decided to wrap a plastic bag around the cast and attempt a shower. She had to squirt the shampoo onto her scalp directly from the bottle, instead of measuring a suitable dollop into her palm, and it was equally impossible to wrap the towel around her head in the usual turban-style afterwards. When it was time for the late news, she turned on the television with a fresh attack of nerves. Despite Gužas's words there was no dramatic report on three-year-old Mikas Ramoska, missing since Saturday. And then of course all her doubts came rushing back. Should she have done it? Was there someone out there who had seen her little boy? Someone who might help?

When the phone rang, she snatched at it with such clumsy haste that it clattered to the floor. She retrieved it with another snatch and pressed "Accept Call" even though she didn't recognize the number.

"Hello?"

"It's me."

"Er . . . who?"

"Tomas."

She nearly said "Who?" once more before she realized that the caller was her little brother. She had never heard his grown-up voice, only the first hoarse cracks of puberty. He had been twelve when she fled from Tauragė, and they had not spoken since.

"Tomas!"

"Yes."

A pause. Sigita had no idea what to say. What does one say to a brother one hasn't talked to in eight years?

"We heard from Darius's mother that Mikas is . . . that he has disappeared," Tomas eventually said.

"Yes." Her throat tightened, and only that one word escaped.

"I'm sorry," he said. "And . . . er . . . I was just thinking. If there's anything I can do . . . ?"

An unexpected wave of tenderness washed through her. It stole what little strength she had in her arms and legs, so that she slumped down onto the couch with the phone in her lap, while tears burned their way down the side of her nose yet again. Normally, she never cried. Today, she had long since lost count.

"Sigita?"

"Yes," she managed. "Thank you. Thank you so much. I am so glad you called."

"Er, you're welcome. I hope they find him."

She couldn't say another word, and maybe he realized. There was a soft click as he hung up. But he had called. She had only ever had sporadic news from home, and since she and Darius had separated, her most reliable source of Tauragė information had dried to a trickle. And right now there were a thousand things she wanted to know. What Tomas had been doing since leaving school. If he was still living at home. If he had a girlfriend. How he was.

If he had ever forgiven her.

But perhaps he had. He did call her, after all.

Sigita went to bed, but sleep was a hopeless enterprise. The hideous sense of imagination she had suddenly developed kept tossing images up inside her eyelids, and she didn't know how to turn it off.

If you hurt my boy, she thought, I will kill you.

It was not an outburst of anger, as when two drunks yell at each other—"I'll fucking kill you!" or the like. It was not like that.

It was a decision.

Somehow, it made her calmer. She could almost believe that the kidnappers would be able to sense her decision and realize what the price of harming Mikas would be. Just because she had determined that it should be so. This was of course hopeless nonsense, as the rational part of her well knew. Nonetheless, it helped: *If you hurt him, I will kill you.*

In the end, she went out on the balcony and sat in the white plastic chair she kept there. The heat absorbed by the concrete during the day was being released now that the air was cooler, and there was no need to put anything on over her night dress. She thought of Julija Baronienė, who had her child back. She thought of Gužas, and of Valionis. Had they gone home, or were they still at work? Was Mikas important enough? Or were there so many missing children that no one would work twenty-four-hour shifts just because another one had disappeared?

They wanted me to go on television, she thought. That must mean that he is important. She remembered the little English girl who had disappeared, but couldn't recall her name. It had been all over the news for months, and even the Pope had become involved. And still the girl had not been found.

But Mikas will come back, she told herself firmly. If I believe anything else, I won't be able to stand it.

A taxi drew up in the parking lot in front of the building. Sigita automatically looked at her watch. It was past 2 a.m.—an unusual time to arrive. A woman got out and glanced around uncertainly. Clearly a visitor, trying to get her bearings. Then she headed for Sigita's block.

It's her, thought Sigita suddenly. It's Julija!

She leapt to her feet so quickly that she stubbed her toe on the doorframe. It hurt, but that was irrelevant. She hopped to the intercom and pressed the lock button the moment the buzzer sounded. She limped out into the stairwell and followed Julija Baronienė with her eyes, all the way up.

Julija stopped when she caught sight of Sigita.

"I had to come," she said. "Aleksas wouldn't hear of it, and I had to wait until he was asleep. But I had to come."

"Come inside," said Sigita.

How peculiar that one still says things like "Have a seat" and "Would you like some coffee?" even when life and death and heart's blood is at stake, thought Sigita.

"May I call you Sigita?" asked Julija, twisting the coffee cup nervously in her hands. "I still think of you like that, even though you are a grown woman now."

"Yes," said Sigita. She had seated herself in the armchair, or rather, on the edge of it. Her right hand was clenched so hard that the nails bit into her palm, but she knew somehow that trying to rush the woman on the couch would be a bad idea. She suddenly remembered Grandfather's carrier pigeons. How they sometimes landed on the roof of the coop and wouldn't come all the way in, so that their recorded flight time would be minutes slower than it might have been.

"No use trying to hurry things," her grandfather would say. "Sit on the bench beside me, Sigita, they'll come when they come."

Grandfather had died in 1991, in the year of the Independence. Granny Julija didn't care about the races. She sold the best pigeons to a neighbor and left the rest to their own devices until the roof blew off the coop during a winter storm five or six years later.

Sigita looked at Julija and forced herself to sit quietly, waiting.

"You mustn't tell the police," said Julija in the end. "Do you promise?"

Sigita promised. It still didn't seem to be enough.

"He was so angry because we had called them. He said he had had to hurt Zita because we told, and that it was all our fault." The hand that held the cup was trembling.

"I won't say anything," said Sigita.

"Promise."

"Yes. I promise."

Julija stared at her unremittingly. Then she suddenly put the coffee cup down. She raised her hands to the back of her neck and bent her head so that she could take off a necklace she was wearing. No. Not just a necklace. It was a crucifix, thought Sigita. A small golden Jesus on a black wooden cross; despite the miniscule size, the pain in the tiny face was evident.

"Do you believe in God?" asked Julija.

"Yes," said Sigita, because this was not the time to mince the nuances of faith and doubt.

"Then swear on this. Touch it. And promise that you won't go to the police with anything I tell you."

Sigita carefully put her hand on the crucifix and repeated her promise. She wasn't sure that this meant more to her than the assurances she had already given, but it seemed to ease Julija's mind.

"He gave us an envelope. So that we could see what we had made him do, he said. Inside was one of her nails. An entire nail. I knew it was hers, because I had let her play with my nail polish the day before." Julija's voice shook. "He said that if we went to the police later on, he would take Zita again, and this time he would sell her to some men he knew. Men of the kind who enjoy having sex with little girls, he said."

Sigita swallowed.

"But Julija," she said. "If he is in prison, he can't take Zita."

Julija shook her head wildly.

"Do you think I can risk that? People don't stay in jail forever. And besides, I know for a fact that he is not alone."

Sigita thought it a miracle that Julija had come at all.

"I didn't know he would do that," whispered

Julija, almost as if she could hear Sigita's unspoken words. "I didn't know he would take your child."

"But you got Zita back," said Sigita. "How did you do that?"

Julija was silent for so long that Sigita grew afraid she wouldn't answer.

"I gave him you," she whispered, in the end. "He wanted to know your name, and I told him."

Sigita stared at Julija in utter bafflement.

"He wanted to know my *name* . . . ?"

"Yes. You see, we never register the girls. At the clinic, I mean. Their names aren't recorded anywhere, because the parents—that is, the new parents—all get a birth certificate that makes it appear that the child is their own."

A deep pain burned somewhere in Sigita's abdomen. I was right, she thought blindly. This is God's punishment. This is all my fault because I sold my firstborn child. There was a kind of black logic to it that had nothing to do with reason and the light of day.

"But why . . . what did he want with me?"

Julija shook her head. "It's not really him. He is just the one who actually does things. It has to be the other one. The Dane."

"What do you mean?"

"He came to the clinic some months ago. He wanted to know who you were, and he was willing to pay a fortune to find out, but Mrs. Jurkiene couldn't tell him because nothing was written down. But he recognized me because I had been the one to hand over the baby, back then. Yours, that is. And he asked me if I didn't remember something, anything, about who you were and where you came from. And of course I did remember, because you nearly died, and I looked after you for so many days. But I told him I didn't."

Julija was crying as she spoke, in a strange noiseless fashion, as if her eyes were merely watering.

"He didn't want to believe me, and he kept offering me all this money if only I would tell him something. And all the while the other man stood there in the background with his arms across his chest, and it was so obvious that he was there to look after the Dane and all his money. You know, like a bodyguard. I didn't understand why he wanted to find you after so many years. And in the end, he went away, and I thought that was the end of it. But it wasn't."

"The Dane." Sigita tried to bring her wildly straying thoughts into some sort of order. "Was he the one who. . . ."

"Yes. He was the one who got your child. The first one, that is." Julija looked at her with bright, dark eyes. "We thought we were doing a good thing, you understand? For the girls, and for the babies. They were always rich people, because getting a child that way is very expensive. We thought they would be good to them and treat them like they were their own. Why else was it so important that no one should think they were adopted? And the women were always so very happy. They would cry and cry, and hug the babies tight. But with the Dane, it was just the man who picked up the baby, and I never saw the wife. I've thought about that afterwards."

"You said you *thought* they would be good to them. . . . Don't you think so anymore?"

"Yes. In most cases, anyway. But I've given the clinic my notice. I don't want to work there anymore. It won't be easy, because the salary was good, and Aleksas is a schoolteacher and doesn't make very much. But I don't want to work there anymore."

"But I don't understand. Was it the Dane who took Zita?"

"Not directly. It was that bodyguard. I don't know his name. And it was more than a month later, when I had almost forgotten about the Dane. But the bodyguard didn't believe I couldn't remember about you. And he had Zita. So I told him your name was Sigita, but that wasn't enough. He wanted to know your last name, too, and where you lived. I didn't know anything about that. That was too bad for Zita, he said, because she really, really wanted to come home to her mama again. So in the end, I searched the files until I found it. The receipt for your money. It wasn't your name on it, it was your auntie's. But it must have been enough, because he let Zita come home."

Ass. herbs for the production of natural remedies: 14.426 litai.

Oh yes, Sigita remembered the receipt. But she couldn't make head or tails of the rest.

"If you do as they say," said Julija, "don't you think they'll let you have your little boy back? Like Zita?"

"But I don't know what they want me to do," wailed Sigita desperately. "They've told me nothing!"

"Maybe something has gone wrong," said Julija. "Maybe the bodyguard can't get hold of the Dane, or something."

Sigita just shook her head. "It still makes no sense." Then she suddenly raised her head. "You said you don't register the girls. But what about the people who get the babies—does it say anything about them?"

"Yes, of course. Otherwise we wouldn't be able to register the births."

"Good. Then get me his name."

"The Dane?"

"Yes. Julija, you owe me that. And his address, if you can."

Julija looked terrified. "I can't."

"Yes, you can. You did it to save Zita. Now

243

you must help me save *my* son. Otherwise. . . ."
Sigita swallowed, not liking it at all. But this
was for Mikas. "Otherwise, I may have to go to
the police after all. Then *they* can come and
search your files."

"You promised! You swore on the body of
Christ!"

"Yes. And I really don't want to break that
promise."

Julija sat there, frozen like a trapped animal. It
hurt to look at her.

"I'll try tomorrow morning," she finally said,
"before the secretary gets there. But what if I
can't find it?"

"You can," said Sigita. "You have to."

The phone rang a little before nine the next
morning.

"His name is Jan Marquart," said Julija. "And
this is his address."

Nina woke because someone was beating on
the car window, a series of hard rhythmic
blows. She opened her eyes in time to see a
stooping figure reel across the street and continue
in the direction of the Central Station. Above

Reventlowsgade's numerous streetlights the sky was brightening to pale gray.

The back of her neck was sore, and the ache called back a vague memory of struggling with the weight of her own head during the night. It had not been a good way to sleep, but even this lack of comfort had not been enough to keep her awake. Cautiously, she released her knees from their braced position against the back of the seat. Tendons and muscles protested sharply as she opened the door and stretched her legs onto the pavement.

The boy was still asleep. He had rolled over during the night and his outflung arms rested on the seat, palms upward. He had forgotten where he was, thought Nina with a degree of envy. Even in sleep that mercy had eluded her, and she felt no less tired than the night before.

She rose slowly and walked a few steps beside the car, trying to ease the pins and needles in her legs. It was still more than six hours before she could meet the girl from Helgolandsgade, and in a little while, the sun would begin the process of turning Vesterbro into a diesel-stinking oven. She had to find some temporary refuge for herself and the boy, preferably somewhere that included the possibility of a shower. She could smell her own body—the sour odor of old sweat assaulted her nostrils every time she moved. She felt sticky and exhausted.

The boy stirred in the back seat, still half asleep, but surfacing slowly. He stretched, and then lay there for a long moment, eyes open and staring into the gray upholstery of the seat in front of him. Then he turned his head and looked at her. The smooth, soft look given to him by sleep vanished in an instant and was replaced by recognition and disappointment. But there was a change. The sulky resignation was still there, but the hostility had gone. Perhaps there was even a hint of familiarity, a sense of belonging inspired by everything they had been through together the day before. Karin's empty gaze, the nauseating pool of congealing blood beneath her head. The chaotic escape from the cottage, the hookers in Helgolandsgade, and the slices of untoasted white bread.

He knew whom to stick with right now. He just didn't know why.

Nina produced a faint smile. That was all she could manage. It was still only 5:43, and the thought of yet another long and lonely day with the boy on her hands seemed to leech her of all strength. Completely unsurmountable.

She might go home.

The idea felt heretical after yesterday's long flight, but the cold and stilted conversation with Morten seemed so distant now, floating only somewhere at the very back of her mind. Had he really been as angry as she thought? Maybe not.

He might even be capable of understanding why she and the boy had had to disappear. If she could only find the right way to tell him. She might say that the story about Karin was only an excuse she had made up, that it had been the network that had called her, and that the boy would only be with them for a few days before being sent on to relatives in . . . in England, maybe. That might seem sufficiently safe and manageable even for Morten.

Morten didn't like that she worked with the illegal residents. In principle, he agreed that something must be done. He was unwavering in his opposition to the government's policy when it came to refugees and other immigrants, and when yet another story about grotesque deportations and broken families hit the news stream, he would be genuinely upset and outraged. The problem he had with the network and her commitment to it was purely personal. Morten didn't think it was good for her. He thought she was using it as a form of escape from herself and her own children, from what was supposed to be their family life. When he was in a good mood, he called her his little adrenalin junkie. When he was angry, he didn't say very much, but his antipathy to the network rose in direct ratio to the number of nights and evenings she spent away from their Østerbro flat.

Right now, there was nowhere else in the world

she would rather be. God, how she wanted it. She wanted to sneak up the stairs with the boy in her arms, put on the kettle to make coffee. Leave the boy in front of the television, perhaps, while she herself slipped into their tiny bathroom and pulled the octopus-patterned shower curtain in front of the door. She would stand under the hot shower for a long luxurious moment with her own bottle of eco-friendly shampoo, without perfume and smelling only of simple cleanliness. Afterwards she might pad out into the kitchen on bare feet and set the table for breakfast with oatmeal, raisins, sugar, and milk. The children would have to leave for school, of course, and the boy might then sleep another few hours in Anton's bed before they had to head back to Vesterbro to find the girl from Helgolandsgade.

She would do it. Yes. She would go home. The relief was deep and physical, as if someone had quite literally lifted a weight off her shoulders. She raised her eyes to the mirror and gave the boy a genuine smile as she eased the car away from the curb and headed for Åboulevarden. Everything looked so different in the morning, even on such a morning as this. Morten would help her. Of course he would. Why had she ever doubted it?

Morten made coffee for the detective sergeant and for himself. The uniformed officer had declined, but accepted a cola instead.

His hands moved mechanically in a set of practiced routines that needed little guidance from his brain: fill kettle, click switch, rinse pot, open coffee can.

You don't know whether she is dead or alive, a cynical voice inside him whispered. And you're making coffee.

"Milk or sugar?"

"Milk, please."

He opened the refrigerator and looked vaguely at flat plastic packages of cured ham, mustard bottles, cucumbers, jars of pickled beets. Half past four in the morning. He could smell the bed-sweat on his own body and felt dysfunctional and unhygienic.

"She said that Karin was ill, or wasn't feeling very well, I don't quite recall her exact words. But she had to help her."

"And when was this?"

"Yesterday afternoon. A little past five. She was supposed to pick up Anton. Er, that's our youngest. She should have picked him up from daycare. But she had forgotten."

"Was that unusual?"

He shook his head vaguely, not exactly in denial; it was more a gesture of uncertainty.

"She used to be . . . a little absent sometimes. But not anymore. No. She . . . I think she was distracted, perhaps because she was worried about Karin. They were at nursing school together, and they used to be close. But it's been awhile. Since they saw each other last, I mean."

He put the bistro pot on the table. Then cups. Milk, in the little Stelton creamer that had been a present to them from his mother and father.

She could be dead. As dead as Karin.

"You haven't seen her at all?" he asked.

"No. A neighbor heard someone scream, and found the body."

"Scream? Karin?"

"We don't think so. We think she had already been dead some time by then. We don't know where the scream came from, but our witness was definite he had heard it. He didn't see anyone, but he heard a car drive off. We don't know what kind of car. We don't know whether it may have been your wife leaving the scene, or someone else. We still have searchers combing the area with dogs. That was how we found your wife's mobile."

Uncertainty was nothing new. He had suffered days and even weeks of it before, when the gaps between her calls had grown too long, and one heard disquieting things on the news. This was worse. More specific. Closer to home. He felt a strange brooding anger. This wasn't Darfur, dammit. It wasn't supposed to happen here, not now that she was home again.

The sergeant drank his coffee.

"How tall is your wife?" he asked.

"One meter sixty-nine," answered Morten automatically. And then froze with the cup halfway to his mouth because he didn't know whether this was something they needed to know in order to identify her, or her body.

Then he realized there might be a third purpose behind the question.

"You don't think that . . . that she . . . that she might have anything to do with the murder?"

"We are still waiting for the autopsy results. But it would seem that the blows were struck with overwhelming force. We tend to think that the assailant must have been male."

The reply did not provide any relief.

Suddenly, Anton was in the doorway. His hair was damp with sweat, and the too large Spiderman pajama top had slipped off one shoulder.

"Is Mummy home yet?" he asked, rubbing his face with the back of his hand.

"Not yet," said Morten.

Anton frowned, and it seemed that it was only now that he registered the presence of two strangers in the room. The uniform made his eyes pop still wider. His mouth opened, but he didn't say anything. Morten felt paralyzed, completely unable to come up with an explanation that would make sense in a seven-year-old's universe.

"Go on back to bed," he said, trying to sound casual and everyday normal. Anton gave a brief nod. The sound of his bare feet beat a rapid retreat along the corridor.

"Will you please ask your wife to contact us immediately if she comes back?" said the sergeant. "She is an important witness."

"Of course," said Morten with a growing feeling of complete helplessness.

If she comes back.

Traffic on Jagtvejen was warming up in the gray dawn, but the smaller streets around Fejøgade were still quiet and uncrowded. Perhaps that was why she saw the police car right away. With no blinking blue lights, it looked like a white taxi at first glance, but it was parked in an off-hand, slanted manner, as if the driver could not be bothered to do a proper curbside parallel parking. Nina had time to think that this was the kind of sloppy parking Morten hated, and that he would be irritated if the car was still here when he came down to take the children to school. Then she realized that the bump on the car's roof were cop lights, not taxi lights. And that someone was up and about and had the lights on, up there in their third-floor flat.

Morten would not normally be up this early. He had flexible working hours when he wasn't out on the rigs, and even though he was alone with the kids today, as long as he had them up and ready for breakfast at 7:30, he would be fine. It was now 5:58. Much too early for normality.

Nina continued past her own front door at an even speed. It was of course possible that the cops had merely needed somewhere quiet to park while they enjoyed their morning coffee. But why, then, was Morten up? Were they looking for her? And was it because of Karin, or because of the boy?

She didn't want to believe it. The thought of having to give up her fantasy of a hot shower and a normal family breakfast caused a wave of exhaustion that dug into her already depleted reserves. She slipped the Fiat into an empty slot further up the street and sat there with her hands on the wheel and her foot on the clutch, trying to make up her mind.

There was a part of her that wanted it over and done with.

There would be no need for drama. She could

hand over the boy to professional, caring adults in a quiet and orderly manner, without causing him undue anxiety. And if she really put her mind to it, she might even convince herself that she was doing the right thing. That the boy would be safe and cared for at some institution on Amager, and that the man from the railway station from now on would be a single bad memory in an otherwise happy and safe childhood. Immigration had proper interpreters available to them, they didn't need to chase after Lithuanian hookers with ponytails and coltish legs. If the boy did have a good and loving mother somewhere, surely they would find her.

God only knew how she wanted to believe it. Every single day, she practiced her detachment skills, trying not to care about everything that was wrong with the world. Or rather . . . to care, but in a suitably civilized manner, with an admirable commitment that might still be set aside when she came home to Morten and her family, complete with well-reasoned and coherent opinions of the humanist persuasion. Right now she felt more like one of those manic women from the animal protection societies, with wild hair and even wilder eyes. Desperate. She had her good days, fortunately, but every time she dared to think that this serenity might be permanent, there would be a Natasha and a Rina, or a Zaide or a Li Hua, and her defenses would be blown to shreds, so that once more, reality grated on her naked skin like sandpaper.

Nina turned off the engine. She got out, closing the car door gently, and looked back at her own solid-seeming brown front door, and at the windows up there. She could make the choice. She could do like everyone else would do—take the boy gently by the hand, and go up there to meet the police, safe in the knowledge that she had done everything that could reasonably be expected from a responsible adult. Then she could come clean with Morten, telling him everything in one of those hot confessional rushes that would lead to a familiar, reassuring row about her priorities and his anxiety about her, and finally, finally, to tears and intimacy. Her hands on his face, sliding from his forehead to his cheek-bones, then round to the back of his neck, damp under his short brown hair. Infinite relief.

All of that could be hers if only she would let herself believe what no one else seemed to have any trouble believing: that Denmark was a safe haven for the broken human lives that washed up on its shores.

Up there behind the windows, someone was moving, back and forth, jerkily, like a predator in an inadequate cage. Her conscience winced as she recognized Morten's tall, near-athletic form. Then another man appeared, shorter, rounder, gesturing slowly and soothingly.

A pro, thought Nina, feeling her antagonism increase. Morten was in the hands of one of those policemen who had attended courses in how best to talk to civilians under pressure.

He would be saying things like "We are doing everything possible, and we are very good at what we do" and "We are highly trained professionals, and the best thing you can do for Nina now is to trust us."

He would be telling her much the same thing as he took the boy away from her. "We will do everything in our power to find out what has happened here."

Morten suddenly stepped up to the window, looking out. Inadvertently, she backed a couple of paces. Had he seen her? The last softness had gone from the dawn, and daylight exposed her fully to anyone who cared to see. But she was some distance away, and the Fiat was shielded by other cars. She stood still, conscious that move-ment attracted attention. But she couldn't make herself look away. Finally, he turned away from the window, and she dared move again. She leapt into the car, slammed the door, and hurriedly revved the engine. The Fiat practically leapt into the street, and then stalled. She had forgotten about the parking brake. Cursing, she got the engine started once more and engaged the clutch. Flight responses had taken over, coursing through her body, and turning back was no longer an option.

Had Morten seen her? And if he had, would he tell the police?

A sudden flashback washed through her tired mind. About a thousand years ago, when they had made love for the first time, he had raised her face to his and stared into her eyes, and there had been a startling moment of utter intimacy, utter trust. Now, she wasn't even sure he would let her drive off without setting the cops on her. She could only hope.

A glance at the mirror reassured her that at least the cop car was still unmanned, parked with its lights off by the curb. Then a clumsy gray SUV, complete with tacky roof box, pulled out behind her, blocking her view. Well, at least she was getting away for now, she thought, with the boy safely in the back seat. Then she felt a treacherous little hope that Morten had in fact seen her, but was letting her drive off on purpose. Had he perhaps even given her a discrete, acknowledging wave? Was he even now quietly rooting for her, hoping she would succeed in what she was doing? Trusting her this time, and willing to wait patiently until she returned to him and the flat, to Anton's crappy little drawings stuck to the refrigerator door, to the bathroom shelves that Ida had begun to fill with styling gels and cheap, glittery lipsticks. And when all this was over, the flat and everything it contained would be enough for her. It would. It had to be.

Nina turned onto Jagtvej just as the lights turned amber. Morning traffic was not yet closely packed in the two-lane part of the road, but behind her, she heard beeping horns and a squeal of brakes. The gray SUV behind her had followed her into the intersection much too late and was stuck untidily crosswise, fender to fender with a similar monster that was now blocking all traffic in the direction of Nørrebro.

Nina couldn't help feeling a certain unholy glee as she shifted easily into fourth gear and continued unhindered in her small and rather unremarkable vehicle. She hoped those two CO_2-offenders had a fun time exchanging insults and phone numbers and moaning about the dents in their ridiculously large fenders. A sort of cosmic justice, she thought—the bigger you get, the more you bump into things.

The driver of the Land Rover was yelling at Jučas and jabbing an aggressive forefinger at him. Jučas didn't understand a single word the idiot was saying, nor did he care. He held up both hands disarmingly, and only the acute awareness that there was a police car parked no more than two hundred meters away kept him from punching the guy's lights out instead. It wasn't even rage, just frustration. But God, it would have felt good to plant a fist in that self-righteous, arrogant face and feel the cartilage crunch.

He forced himself to smile.

"No damage," he said, pointing to the Land Rover's intact front. "No damage to you. My car, not so good, but okay. Have nice day." Milky white shards from the Mitsubishi's headlights decorated the pavement, but nothing could be done about that now. What he needed was to get away, as quickly as possible, before the boy-bitch managed to disappear again. He ignored the continued protests of the Land Rover-man, in English now, got back into the Mitsubishi, reversed, and managed to get free of the other vehicle.

". . . driving like an idiot, what do you think the red lights are for, Christmas decorations?"

Jučas just waved, and drove off. Hadn't she turned right at the next intersection?

"Did you see where she went?" he asked Barbara.

It was some time before she answered.

"No," she said. Nothing else.

He threw a quick glance at her. She looked oddly distant, as if the whole thing was no longer any of her business. But perhaps the fender-bender had left her a little shocked.

"No harm done," he said. "It's just a broken

headlight. I can fix it myself, if we can find a garage."

She didn't answer. Right now he had no time to coax and cajole and work out what was wrong with her. He signaled a right turn, but of course he had to wait interminably while about a hundred bicycles went past. What the hell was wrong with people in this city? Couldn't they afford cars? It seemed as if half the population insisted on teetering along on two wheels, endangering the traffic.

Next intersection. He hesitated, causing a chorus of horns behind him. He could see no Fiat. Decided on a left turn, and ended up in a one-way hell full of "enclosed areas" and fucking flower beds that apparently had to be placed in the middle of the street. Reversing aggressively, he tried to get back to the main street, but it was hopeless. Three or four one-way streets later, he had to realize that the battle was lost.

"Fucking hell!"

He hammered both hands against the steering wheel and braked abruptly. Sat there for a moment, fighting his temper.

"She had the boy with her," said Barbara suddenly.

"Did she?" Jučas glanced at her sharply. "Are you sure?"

"Yes. He was in the back seat. I could see his hair."

Right now, he would have preferred the money. But the kid was currency in his own way, and better than nothing.

"You said they were going to adopt him," said Barbara.

"What? Yes. So they are."

"Then what was he doing in that car? I thought his new parents were picking him up?"

"Yeah, so did I. But this Nina Borg person got in the way."

"And why was it that you took his clothes off?" she asked. "For the picture?"

He inhaled a mouthful of air and blew it slowly back out. Easy now.

"To make it harder for them to trace him," he said. "And stop this. You're only making it worse, asking so many questions."

He hated the way she was looking at him now. As if she didn't trust him anymore.

"Hell," he hissed. "I'm not one of those filthy perverts. And if you think that for a moment, then. . . ."

"No," she said, very quickly. "I don't think that."

"Good. 'Cause I'm not."

He drove around for a bit, on the off chance. But the Fiat stayed gone. Finally he went back and parked near her house again.

"Stay in the car," he told Barbara. "She'll be

back. Call me when the cops leave, or if you see her and the boy."

"Where are you going?" she asked, looking at him once more, but this time in a different way. He smiled. It was okay. She still wanted him to look after her, and that was just what he planned on doing.

"I have a couple of things to do," he said. "It won't take long."

It was 7:07, and the public swimming pool in Helgasgade had been open for exactly seven minutes. Nina laid down the deposit for two towels at the ticket booth and continued up the wide brown stairs to the women's changing rooms on the first floor.

They were almost alone among the many empty lockers, and the three women there were silent and introverted, folding their clothes with their backs to one another, guarding their privacy in a very public space. One was young, Nina noticed, the two others middle aged in the determinedly well-trained way. None of them looked at Nina and the boy, who stood beside her on the damp, smooth tiles, hunched and slightly shivering in the early morning chill.

Nina took the boy to the bathroom, and he peed obediently, with his pelvis thrust forward and his hands folded behind his neck. Anton had done the same thing, remembered Nina, because he could then claim that there was no need for him to wash his hands afterwards. Perhaps that was a brand of logic universal to little boys. Nina smiled at the thought.

When they returned to the changing rooms, the three women had all gone out into the echoing cavern of the swimming pool area, and Nina proceeded to undress, her movements awkward and heavy. There was a stiffness in her muscles, joints and tendons, like the aftermath of the flu, and she took her time. There was no hurry. She parked the boy on one of the wooden benches fixed to the wall with solid-looking brackets, turned on the water, and let the hot spray hit her chest and stomach.

She hadn't been eating enough lately. She could see it in the way her ribs protruded under the skin. She had always been skinny, too skinny, but since the birth of her children it seemed nothing stuck to her. Her face had become narrow and somewhat hollow-cheeked, and she had lost whatever softness she had once possessed around her collarbones, shoulders, and hips. Forgetting to eat was not a smart move. But it happened whenever she worked too much, or when Morten went off to Esbjerg and the rigs. She simply lost her appetite, and fed the children mechanically without bothering to feed herself.

"We'll get something to eat later," she promised the boy. "A big English breakfast, how about that?"

He didn't react to her voice except to sit and watch her, eyes huge and curious, legs dangling. Nina turned her back again and began to lather her body with the liquid soap from the automat on the wall. It had a sweet and perfumed smell that felt almost too extravagant for the gray shower room, and Nina was caught up in a moment's pleasure, enjoying the heat and the scent of it. Her skin felt warm, soft, and alive, and the steam rose about her and obscured mirrors and glass partitions. She worked up a new helping of frothy lather and washed her hair rather roughly. She had had it cut quite short again not so long ago. Morten didn't understand why, but he wasn't the one who had to struggle with the heavy, frizzy burden of it. It had curled nearly to her shoulders before she had it cut, and the relief had been enormous. Not least in her job, where she no longer had to wonder what would be the politically correct way of wearing it today. Many of the male inhabitants of the Coal-House Camp saw the female staff as a com-bination of prison wardens and service functions. They felt superior and humiliated at the same time, one of the center's psychologists had once explained.

Possibly it was true. Whatever the cause, conflict always lurked just beneath the surface, and Nina had tried to appear as sexless and neutral as possible. When she had her hair cut so short, it was an oddly mutual relief. Some of her provocative femininity seemed to have disappeared along with the hair, and Nina didn't miss it. Morten did, but she had long ago stopped regulating her appearance in accordance with his opinions.

Nina slid a wet hand down across her navel and the rigidly defined muscles of her abdomen. Despite her two pregnancies, there was nothing much that was ripe and womanly about her body now. Poor Morten.

The boy moved impatiently on the bench. Collecting her drifting thoughts, she turned off the shower and began instead to fill one of the white plastic kiddy bathtubs that were scattered about the shower room. The boy did not resist as she pulled off his new clothes and sat him down in the tub. Crouching next to him, she carefully began to wash his shoulders, chest, back, and feet. Deliberately, she did not touch him elsewhere, but just let him sit in the tub as she used the shower to rinse away the soap. The boy took all this with surprising calm. His fingers trustingly followed the little currents of hot water trickling down his chest and belly, and when a frothy bubble almost miraculously released itself from the edge of the tub and fell with a wet pop against the tiles of the floor, he sent Nina a gleeful smile of delight and surprise—the first she had ever seen on his face since their common journey had begun yesterday afternoon.

Nina felt a new warm sense of relief spreading in her abdomen. She couldn't positively *know,* and she was no expert on responses to pedophilia and child abuse, but it seemed to her that the boy was free of such hideousness. If something like that had happened to him, surely he would have acted differently? More frightened, less trustful?

The relief was almost painful in its ferocity. The boy was still whole. Rescue, in its most complete sense, was still possible.

She turned off the water and dried him gently with one of the towels. Then, silently, they began to dress, and Nina combed his hair with her fingers.

Who was he?

She watched patiently as he insisted on pulling the T-shirt over his head himself. He might have been a child smuggled into Denmark for the purpose of some sort of prostitution or abuse, but would he then be stored like luggage in a central station locker? Nina didn't know very much about that type of crime. She certainly saw her share of human degradation and brutality in her job, but the motives there were usually unsubtle, and the methods simple enough that even the most moronic of criminals could join in. It didn't take a brain surgeon to batter the last few pennies out of an Iraqi father who had already paid almost everything he possessed to the traffickers who had arranged his journey to the border. Nor was it especially difficult to lure Eastern European girls into the country and sell them by the hour in places like Skelbækgade. A few beatings, a gang rape or two, and a note bearing the address of her family in some Estonian village—that was usually enough to break even the most obstinate spirit. And the real beauty of it all for the cynical exploiters was that ordinary people didn't care. Not really. No one had asked the refugees, the prostitutes, the fortune hunters, and the orphans to come knocking on Denmark's door. No one had invited them, and no one knew how many there were. Crimes committed against them had nothing to do with ordinary people and the usual workings of law and order. It was only dimwit fools like Nina who were unable to achieve the proper sense of detachment.

She felt too much, and she knew it. Especially where the children were concerned, her skin felt tender and brittle, like the thin, pink, parchment-like new growth that spread to cover healing wounds. It had been bad after Ida's birth, but when Anton arrived, her sensitivity to the children of the Coal-House Camp had taken on monstrous proportions. It was her imagination, of course, but sometimes it felt as if their gazes clung to her, spotting her vulnerability, tearing through her pitiful defenses and into her soul.

Unaccompanied children would usually be older than the boy from the suitcase, thought Nina, from about ten years of age and up. Often, the staff would have time to form only the most fleeting of impressions. Some of them, particularly the Eastern European ones, had been sold by their parents and trained by backers to beg and steal, and they were instructed to escape the refugee centers at the first opportunity if they were picked up on the streets. The moment their mobiles rang, they were off on the next suburban train, dis-appearing back into the metropolitan underworld they had come from. Other children might con-tinue on to Sweden or England, where relatives awaited. Still others were obviously alone in the world, brought to Denmark for the sole purpose of making money for their owners. All in all, more than seventy percent would disappear from the camps without anyone ever really knowing what became of them.

But the suitcase boy was surely too young to be of use to even the most cynical gang of thieves. Might he be some kind of hostage? Or was he meant to be part of a social security scam? That had happened before, particularly in the UK, she had heard.

He was beautiful, thought Nina suddenly. She didn't know how much that meant among pedophiles, but somehow it made him seem more vulnerable. It was all too easy to imagine that some pervert bastard somewhere had ordered a small European boy for a night's pleasure. Or several nights. She looked at the boy standing in front of her with his T-shirt back to front and the new sandals carefully strapped to his small, narrow feet, and the thought of him sharing a bed with some unknown adult man was sickening and utterly unbearable.

Nina forced herself to smile at him.

Where would he end up if she delivered him to the police? Some orphanage in Lithuania? Or perhaps with a relative who would merely sell him again to the highest bidder? Perhaps with a crewcut, bear-shouldered stepfather, whose huge hands had beaten Karin to death? Nina felt a shudder deep in her abdomen. She had to know more. She had to know.

She pushed open the changing-room door and took the boy's hand in a firm grip. She must find them some breakfast, and then work out which church might be the one the girl from Helgolandsgade had meant when she talked about the Sacred Heart.

The address was in Denmark. Naturally. Sigita didn't know why she had assumed that the Dane lived in Lithuania. She stared down at the carefully penned block capitals and wondered what to do.

Gužas had called half an hour before Julija did. He wanted to know whether she had changed her mind about the TV appeal, and whether there had been any attempt at contact from the abductors. She had told him no. And she had said nothing about Julija and the Dane.

I'll have to go to Denmark, she thought. I have to find that man and ask him what I must do to get Mikas back.

But a sickening little thought kept worming its way into her mind. What if there was nothing he wanted her to do? What if he already had what he wanted, and didn't give a damn about her?

He collects my children, she thought, with a chill of horror. Now he has two.

The other child had come into her dreams during the few hours when sleep had finally claimed her. It had come out of the darkness, large as an adult, but with the face of a fetus, blind and hairless, and a naked, sexless body. It held out its arms to her and opened a toothless, unfinished mouth.

"Mama . . . ," it whispered. "Mammaaaaaaah. . . ." And she drew back from it in horror. But suddenly she saw that it was holding something in its arms. Mikas. The long bluish limbs glistened wetly with embryonic fluid, and Mikas struggled in its grasp like a fish in the tentacles of a sea anemone.

"Mikas!" she screamed, but the fetus child was already distant. It retreated further and further into the dark, taking Mikas with it.

She woke up with her nightgown twisted about her, sticking damply like an extra layer of skin.

Sigita called the airport. There was a flight leaving for Copenhagen at 1:20, and a single ticket would cost her 840 litu. Sigita tried to recall the state of her bank balance. There would be enough for the ticket, just, but what about the rest? It would be difficult to manage in a foreign country with little or no money. And everything cost more abroad, or so she had heard.

Might Algirdas give her an advance on her salary?

Perhaps. But not without asking questions. Sigita bit her lip. I have to go, she thought. With or without money. Unless I call Gužas now and leave it all to him. And if I do that, they may harm Zita. She thought about the small, shattered family, of Zita's clawlike hands on the piano keys, and Julija's terror and despair. She couldn't

271

do anything to make it worse. She mustn't. And it might not be just Zita, either. It could be Mikas too. She couldn't stop thinking about the torn-off nail Julija had received in an envelope. And that was nothing. *Nothing* compared to what people like that were really capable of.

1:20. It would be hours before she could leave for the airport.

She decided to visit her Aunt Jolita for the first time in eight years.

Bang, bang, bang, bang. The big yellow pile driver was pounding the foundations of the new building into the earth with resounding thumps, and a little further off, a huge crane was raising yet another prefabricated concrete element into its place. It appeared that someone had decided that there was room for a new apartment building on the green square of grass framed by the old gray and white Soviet-era blocks. Dust and diesel fumes permeated the air, and the pavement was being ground into the mud under the weight of caterpillar vehicles. Sigita felt a pang of pity for the original inhabitants. Pašilaičiai, where she lived, had barely existed ten years ago, and she often felt it was not so much a neighbor-hood as a constant building site. Only recently had such luxuries as streetlights and sidewalks been re-established after the latest round of construction mayhem.

Once she was through the door, the appalling noise receded a little. She walked slowly up the stairs to the third floor and rang the bell.

A thin, gray-haired woman answered. It actually took a few moments before Sigita recognized her aunt. Jolita stared at her for several seconds, too.

"What do you want?" she asked.

"I need to ask you some questions."

"Ask away."

"Can't we do this inside?"

Jolita considered it for a moment. Then she stepped aside, letting Sigita into the narrow hallway.

"But be quiet," she said. "I have a tenant who is a bartender. He works until four or five in the morning, and he gets furious if you wake him up before noon."

The bartender lived in what used to be the sitting room, it turned out. Jolita preceded her into the small, elongated kitchen instead. At the tiny table, an elderly woman was seated, having coffee. A further two unused cups were set on the table in constant readiness, upturned on their saucers to protect them from dust and flies, just like Sigita's mother always did. The aroma of percolating coffee rose from a brand-new coffee machine, still sitting next to the box it had come in. On the table, too, were a bottle of sherry and a platter full of marzipan-covered cupcakes.

"This is Mrs. Orlovienė," said Jolita. "Greta, this is my niece, Sigita."

Mrs. Orlovienė nodded, with a certain degree of reserve.

"Mrs. Orlovienė rents the back bedroom," Jolita continued her introduction. "So you can't just move back in, if that's what you are thinking."

"No," said Sigita, somewhat taken aback. "That's not why I'm here." Whatever had happened to the Aunt Jolita she remembered? The coal-black hair, the colorful makeup, the jazz music and the professor's cigarettes? About the only remnant of that Jolita were the golden pirate-style hoops that still dangled against her wrinkled neck. They now looked absurd rather than exotic. How on earth could a person age so much in eight years? It was frightening.

"Perhaps you've come to apologize, then?" suggested Jolita.

"What?"

"Oh well, I was just thinking. It wasn't completely inconceivable that you should finally feel a little guilty about the way you have spat in the face of a family that only ever tried to love you and help you."

Sigita was so stunned that at first she couldn't even defend herself.

"You . . . you . . . I. . . ." she sputtered. "I never spat in anyone's face!"

274

"Eight years without a single word—if that's not spitting, what is?"

"But. . . ."

"At first I felt sorry for you. In trouble like that, at such a young age. I wanted to help you. But you did to me exactly what you did to your parents. Disappearing like that, without ever looking back, without so much as a thank-you."

Sigita stood there with her mouth open. She suddenly noticed how bright-eyed the little Mrs. Orlovienė had become, watching the drama with parted lips as if it were a soap opera.

"Your Granny Julija died, did you know that?" said Jolita.

"Yes," Sigita managed. "Mama . . . Mama sent a letter." Two weeks after the funeral. That had hurt, badly, but she had no intention of letting her aunt know that.

"Coffee?" offered Mrs. Orlovienė, holding out one of the unused cups. "Is it broken?" She nodded at the plaster cast.

"Yes," said Sigita automatically. "And no, thanks. Jolita, did someone come here asking about me?"

"Yes," said Jolita without blinking. "There was a man here, some weeks ago. He wanted to know your last name, and where you lived."

"And what did you do?"

"I told him," said Jolita calmly. "Why shouldn't I?"

"He was quite polite," nodded Mrs. Orlovienė. "Not entirely what I would call a nice young man, but quite polite."

"What did he look like?" asked Sigita, although she was fairly certain she already knew.

"Big," said Mrs. Orlovienė. "Like one of those—what are they called now?" She raised both skinny arms to mime a bodybuilder pose. "And hardly any hair. But quite polite."

At long last, Sigita's thoughts began to line up in an orderly fashion instead of tumbling over each other in random chaos. She knew that Aunt Jolita would never have taken in tenants unless she had been forced to. There was obviously no longer any Professor on Mondays and Thursdays. Probably no job, either. And yet here were sherry and cakes and a brand new percolator.

"Did he give you money?" she asked Jolita.

"Is that any of your business?"

That meant yes. Sigita spun and seized the old coffee tin Jolita usually kept noodles in. Noodles, and certain other things.

"Sigita!" Jolita tried to prevent her, but Sigita had moved too quickly. She hugged the tin against her chest with the plaster cast and wrested the lid off with her right hand. When Jolita tried to tear the tin away from her, it clattered to the floor, sending little macaroni stars shooting off in all directions across the worn linoleum. Sigita instantly put her foot down on top of the brown envelope that had also been in the tin.

"What the hell were you thinking?" she screamed, suddenly beside herself with fury.

"Shhhh!" hissed Jolita. "You'll wake him."

"A complete stranger wants to give you money to tell him where I am. He looks like a gorilla. What the hell were you thinking? Don't you realize that he has taken Mikas?"

"That's hardly my fault!"

"You made it easy." Sigita's voice was shaking. "You sold me. Without even warning me. And then they took Mikas!"

Mrs. Orlovienė sat with her mouth open, on the point of dropping her coffee cup. At that moment, the door flew back on its hinges. In the doorway stood a young man, dressed only in black boxers and a foul temper. His hair had been dyed blue and stuck out in odd directions, still coated with several layers of gummy styling gel.

"Stop that fucking racket," he snarled. The two older women were instantly silenced. Mrs. Orlovienė slid a little lower in her chair, as if being smaller would help. Jolita stood her ground, but her hands had begun the nervous rubbing movement Sigita knew so well. The young man transferred his furious glare to Sigita.

"Who the fuck are you?" he asked.

"This is my niece," said Jolita. "She came for a visit. But she's leaving now."

"I fucking hope so," said the bartender. "Some of us are trying to sleep."

He withdrew, slamming the door as he went. A few seconds later, the living room door was slammed with even greater force. The walls trembled slightly.

Sigita bent to retrieve the envelope. It contained eight five-hundred-litu bills and a few lesser bills Sigita couldn't be bothered to count.

"Four thousand litu," she said. "Was that the price?"

"No," said Mrs. Orlovienė. "At first he only wanted to pay three thousand, but in the end he agreed to five."

Jolita made a violent shushing gesture in Mrs. Orlovienė's direction.

"I don't quite see the reason for all this high-minded outrage," she told Sigita. "If some idiot is willing to pay five thousand litu for something you can look up in the phone book, why should I turn down good money?"

"He didn't know my last name till you told him," said Sigita, fishing three thousand litu from the envelope.

"What are you *doing?*"

"This is your contribution," answered Sigita. "I need it in order to get Mikas back." She let the envelope with the rest of the money fall to the floor. Mrs. Orlovienė was the one who snatched it up, ferret quick. Jolita remained where she was, staring at Sigita. Then she shook her head.

"You feel so put-upon, don't you?" she said. "Poor little Sigita who has had such a hard life. But did you ever pause to think what it's been like for your mother? You taking off like that, not even leaving a note? She lost a daughter. Did you ever think about that?"

The accusation hit Sigita like a hardball to the stomach.

"She knew where I was," said Sigita. "The entire time. They were the ones who turned their backs on me, not the other way around."

"Did you ever ask?"

"What do you mean?"

"You sit there in your fancy apartment, waiting for them to come to you, isn't that right? But you were the one who ran away. Perhaps you should be the one to make the first move if you want to come home again."

Not now, thought Sigita. I can't deal with this now. She glanced at her watch. Her plane would be leaving in two hours.

"Goodbye," she said. And stood there, waiting, even though she wasn't sure what she was waiting for.

Jolita sighed.

"Take the damn money," she said. "I hope you get your little boy back."

Jesu Hjerte Kirke, it was called in Danish. The Church of the Sacred Heart lay in Stenogade, squeezed in between a fashion shop and a private school.

Nina had asked an elderly lady in the Istedgade cornershop where she had bought fresh rolls for herself and the boy. They had struggled a bit over the translation; Nina had guessed herself that it might be Catholic, and the old lady's local knowledge did the rest.

Afterwards, Nina had called Magnus from a small, seedy bar on Halmtorvet. The bartender at The Grotto had let her use both phone and bathroom at no charge, but her conversation with her boss had been brief and unsatisfying.

"*Fan i helvete*, where are you? The duty roster is shot to hell, and Morten has been ringing us since seven o'clock. The police want to speak to you. Is this anything to do with Natasha?"

Magnus's tone had become very Swedish, and the words came pouring over her so quickly that she had no time to answer before he interrupted both himself and her.

"No. Don't. I don't even want to know. Only . . . are you okay? Morten wants to know if you're okay."

Nina took a deep breath.

"Yeah. I'm fine," she told him. "Although I won't be in today. Will you please tell Morten there is no need to worry."

It was a while before Magnus answered. She could hear him exhale and inhale, big, deep barrel-chested breaths.

"Well, as long as you're not dead, I was to tell you. . . ." Magnus hesitated again, and softened his voice so much that Nina could barely hear him.

"I was to tell you that this is the last time. If you come back alive, this is the last time."

Nina felt a sharp little snap in her chest and held the receiver at some distance, battling to control her voice.

"Alive," she laughed, too thinly. "How dramatic. There's really no need for such melodrama. Why shouldn't I be alive? I'm perfectly fine. It's just that there is something I need to do."

Magnus gave a brief grunt, and when his voice came back on the line, for the first time he had begun to sound angry.

"Well, fine. If you don't want anybody's help, Nina, you won't get it. But Morten sounded shit scared, I tell you. He says the police have found your mobile phone."

Nina felt a clammy chill along her backbone as he said it. She slammed the receiver down so abruptly that The Grotto's barman raised his eyebrows and grinned knowingly at the two regular patrons ensconced at the far end of the bar. Nina didn't care. Impatiently, she collected the boy, pulling him away from the old table soccer game he had become engrossed in. He yipped in protest as she half carried, half dragged him back to the car, but at that moment, she was too stressed to care. She started the car, turned the corner at Halmorvet and continued down Stenosgade while she followed the second hand on the dashboard clock: 13, 14, 15. . . .

Annoyingly, she caught herself moving her lips. She was counting the seconds under her breath. Sweet Jesus. How crazy was that?

Crazy. Insane. Mentally challenged. (Perhaps even so crazy that you did it on purpose?)

She managed to insert the Fiat into the row of cars parked by the curb in front of the church, in a slot too small for most cars. The boy in the back seat was staring out the window, steadfastly refusing to look at her. The sense of trust and familiarity from their morning bath had vanished, and it was clear that he had not forgiven her for the rough and hasty way she had bundled him into the car.

Sunlight made the digits on the dashboard clock blur in front of her. She leaned back, fumbling for the water bottle and a breakfast roll. She wasn't hungry, but she recognized this particular kind of lethargy from long hot days without appetite in the camps of Dadaab. If she didn't eat something now, she would soon be unable to form coherent thought.

She took tiny bites, chewing carefully and washing down the bland starchy meal with gulps of lukewarm water from the bottle. The she opened the car door and stepped onto the sizzling sidewalk.

Jesu Hjerte Kirke, Sacred Heart, Sacre Coeur. The English and French translations were posted helpfully below the Danish name of the church in slightly smaller letters. A very Catholic name, she thought to herself, full of dramatic beauty and signifying very little. The Lithuanian girl must be a Catholic, or she wouldn't have known about this church.

Mass was announced at 17:00 hours, she noted, but right now the doors were closed, and the huge cast-iron gate to the grounds proved unremittingly locked.

Nina got back in the car again, looking at the church with a vague feeling of unease. It looked like many other city churches in Copenhagen. Red-brick solidity and a couple of striving towers, squeezed in among tenement buildings. It looked cramped compared to the Cathedral grounds in Viborg (where they had buried him) and the small whitewashed village churches of the country parishes around it.

(*Goest thou thither, and dig my grave.*)

283

She blinked a couple of times, then scanned the street for any sign of the girl. Would she actually show? If she did, Nina was going to try to buy a few hours of her time. She turned her head, but the boy was still refusing to meet her eyes. Sunlight ricocheted off a window somewhere, forcing him to squint.

(*Alas, this world is cold, and all its light is only shadow.*)

Nina shuddered, and without thinking drew the blanket up to cover the boy's legs, despite the heat of the day. At that moment, she saw her. The girl from Helgolandsgade was peering into the car through the rear window, her face a pale outline. Nina jerked in her seat, then nodded, and leaned across to open the passenger door.

"I will pay you," she said, hastily. "You just tell me how much you need, and where we can go."

It was 12:06.

The girl jackknifed herself into the passenger seat, looking quickly up and down Stenogade before closing the door. She smelled strongly of perfume and something sweet and rather chemical, possibly rinse aid. She fumbled in her bag and produced a stick of gum.

"It is five hundred kroner an hour, and three thousand for eight hours. How long will it take?" she answered, throwing a calculating look at the boy in the back.

Then she suddenly smiled at Nina, a crooked and unexpectedly genuine smile.

"He is so little," she said. "So cute."

She held out her hand, and Nina shook it, somewhat taken aback.

"Marija," said the girl slowly and clearly, and Nina nodded.

"I will pay for the eight hours," she said, offering up a quiet prayer to the bank. She had been uncomfortably close to the overdraft limit the last time she had checked, but she was uncertain whether this was before or after her latest paycheck had registered. She had never been very good at the money thing.

Nina turned the key in the ignition, and then sat in indecision, hands locked around the wheel. Where could they go? MacDonald's? A café?

No. Suddenly resolute, she turned left onto Vesterbrogade and headed for Amager. They could all do with a bit of fresh air.

Through the yellowed blinds, there was a view of the road, the parking lot, and the grimy concrete walls of some industrial warehouse or other. Every twenty minutes, a bus went past. Jan knew this because he had been sitting there staring out the window for nearly four hours now.

He hadn't considered that boredom would be a factor. But this was like sitting an exam at which one had offered what little one had to say on the subject inside the first ten minutes, and now had to repeat oneself ad infinitum. Even though the context was hideous, and he really shouldn't be *able* to be bored when talking about the brutal murder of someone who had been close to him, this was what had begun to happen. It felt as if his lips were growing thicker with each repetition, his mouth drier. The words wore thin. Concentration faltered. All pretense at naturalness had long since vanished.

"I met Karin Kongsted two and a half years ago, in Bern; she was employed by the clinic that performed my renal surgery. We probably grew more familiar than might otherwise have been the case, due to the fact that we were both Danes on foreign soil; it often works that way. After the operation, I needed fairly frequent check-ups and medical attention, but it was crucial that I didn't neglect my business any more than I had to. Karin agreed to return to Denmark and work for me in a private capacity, and this proved an excellent solution."

At the moment he was telling his story to an older detective, a calm, almost phlegmatic man whose Jutland roots could still be heard in his intonation. His name was Anders Kvistgård, and he was more rigidly polite than the others, punctiliously addressing Jan as "Mr. Marquart." In his white shirt, black tie and slightly threadbare navy blue pullover, he looked like a railroad clerk, thought Jan.

Mr. Kvistgård was the third detective to interview him. First there had been a younger man who had approached Jan with an air of comradery, as if they both played for the same soccer team. Then a woman, who to Jan seemed far too young and feminine for her job. Each time it had been back to square one, excuse-me-but-would-you-mind-repeating, how-exactly-was-it, could-you-please-tell-us, how-would-you-describe. . . .

"A private nurse. Isn't that a little . . . extravagant?"

"My time is the most precious commodity I possess. I simply can't be stuck in a waiting room for hours every time I need to have a blood sample taken. Believe me, Karin's paycheck has been a worthwhile investment."

"I see. And apart from this, how was your relationship with Ms. Kongsted?"

"Excellent. She was a very warm and friendly person."

"How warm?"

Jan was jerked from his near-somnolent repetition. This question was new.

"What do you mean?"

"Were the two of you having it on? Playing doctor when the missus wasn't around? I understand you lived under the same roof?"

Jan could feel his jaw drop. He stared at this sixty-year-old Danish Rails ticket puncher look-alike with a feeling of complete unreality. This was bizarre. The man's expression of benign interest hadn't shifted a millimeter.

"I . . . no. Bloody hell. I'm married!"

"Quite a few people are. This doesn't stop around seventy percent of them from having a bit on the side. But not you and Ms. Kongsted, then?"

"No, I tell you!"

"Are you quite certain of that?"

Jan felt fresh sweat break out on his palms and forehead. Did they know anything? Would it be better to come clean and be casual about it, rather than be caught in a lie? Did they *know,* or were they just bluffing?

He realized that his hesitation had already given him away.

"It was very brief," he said. "I think I was taken by surprise at. . . . Oh, I don't know. Have you ever been through a serious operation?"

"No," said the railway clerk.

"The relief at still being alive can cause a certain . . . exuberance."

"And in this rush of exuberance you began a relationship with Karin Kongsted?"

"No, I wouldn't call it that. Not a relationship. I think we both realized that it was a mistake. And neither of us wanted to hurt Anne."

"So your wife was ignorant of the affair?"

"Stop it. It wasn't an affair. At the most, it was . . . oh, it sounds so sordid to call it a one-night stand, and it wasn't, but I think you know what I mean."

"Do I, Mr. Marquart? I'm not so sure. What are we talking about? One night? A week? A couple of months? How long did it take you to realize that it was a mistake? And are you certain that Ms. Kongsted understood that just because she was having sex with you, she had better not think this constituted an *affair?*"

Jan tried to remain calm, but the man was subjecting him to verbal acupuncture, sticking in his needles with impeccable precision, and observing him blandly all the while.

"You're twisting everything," he said. "Karin is . . . like I said, Karin was a very warm person, very . . . womanly. But I am perfectly sure she understood how much my marriage means to me."

"How fortunate. Is your wife equally certain?"

"Of course! Or . . . no, I didn't tell Anne about the . . . episode with Karin. And I would appreciate it if you didn't either. Anne is easily hurt."

"We will just have to hope it doesn't become necessary, then. Can you tell me why Karin Kongsted left the house so suddenly yester-day?"

"No. I . . . I wasn't there myself. But seeing that

she went to the summer cottage, she must have decided to take a few days off."

"Am I to believe you haven't seen this?" Kvistgård fished out a vinyl sleeve and placed it on the table in front of Jan. Inside was Karin's note, with the brief, bald phrase clearly visible through the plastic: I QUIT.

"I didn't take it seriously. I think it was meant as a joke. She had been complaining that it was too hot to work . . . like I said, I think she was simply taking a few days off and had a slightly . . . untraditional way of announcing it."

"According to your wife, Karin Kongsted appeared upset and off balance when she drove off."

"Did she? Well, I can't really say. I told you, I wasn't there."

"No. But you did make a call to SecuriTrack in order to locate the car she was driving. Why did you do that, Mr. Marquart?"

There was a high-pitched whine of pressure in his ears. He was aware that he was still sitting there with a stiff smile glued to his face, but he also knew that any illusion of casual innocence had long since evaporated. There was no way he could make light of this, no way he could pretend it didn't mean anything, that it was just a routine precaution when a company car went missing. He couldn't do it. That bloody railway clerk had unbalanced him completely and nailed him in

290

free fall, with no life lines left to clutch.

"I can see this needs a bit of mature consideration," said Anders Kvistgård. "Perhaps you wish to call an attorney? I'm afraid that I have to caution you that charges may be brought against you."

The mile-long, surprisingly natural-looking beach of the Amager Strandpark was only sparsely populated by bathers, despite the dragging heat. Weeks of drought and sunshine had apparently satisfied the city's hunger for beach life and first-degree burns, thought Nina. For most people, the holidays were over. In the spot Nina had chosen for them, they were alone except for a couple of students lying on too-small bath towels with open textbooks in front of them, and their only other human encounter had been with a sweat-soaked young man on rollerblades who had narrowly missed ploughing into the boy on the cement path.

Now here they were, sitting side by side on their brand-new soft towels, staring out across the mirror-smooth sea. Not a breath of wind rippled the surface, and the waves merely lapped the sand in soft, flat, nearly soundless surges. The silence among the three of them was equally noticeable, thought Nina. The boy sat still, with his head lowered, only moving his hand now and then to let the dry sand sift through his fingers in a steady stream. Marija reclined on her towel with half-closed eyes behind new shades bought at a local convenience store. She had taken off her tight jeans, revealing a pair of long, pale legs, as slender as the rest of her T-shirt-clad body. She hadn't said much in the car. A trip to the seaside would be okay, she agreed, as long as towels, sunscreen, sunglasses and a new bikini were part of the deal. Nina had had a brief flashback to negotiations with her own sulky teenage daughter, and had in the end secured a compromise that left out the bikini. For the boy, she had found a small dusty set of bucket, sieve, rake, and spade in red and yellow, languishing on a rack at the back of the store. Later, she had also bought them all ice cream from the kiosk. Marija had taken the boy by the hand and pointed to the faded pictures of cones and popsicles, and to Nina's relief the boy had answered her, opting for the biggest of the lot. After that encouraging breakthrough, silence had unfortunately descended, even though Marija had tried to encourage the child with soft, careful questions. Demonstratively, the boy sat with his back to them, working his fingers through the hot, white sand.

Glancing at Marija, Nina decided to break the

silence. She and the girl, at least, could have a conversation. But what did one ask someone like Marija? Her work in Helgolandsgade? Her life before Copenhagen? Her hopes and dreams, if any had survived? The fact that Nina had bought her time and her presence here lay like a vague discomfort between them—it was a little too much like the selling and buying that went on between Marija and the men that sought her out at night.

"How long have you been in Denmark?"

Nina had meant to ask how she liked it here, but caught herself in time.

Raising her head, Marija looked at Nina with a faint smile that was at the same time amiable and distant.

"Seven weeks," she said, jerking her head at the city behind them. "It is a beautiful city."

Nina looked at Marija's long slender legs and feet, half buried in the sand. Two small round scars gleamed pinkly on her thigh, just above the knee. Cigarette burns, thought Nina mechanically, and the image of the small muscular man with the serpent tattoo flashed before her eyes. But it might not be him. Marija had, after all, only been here for seven weeks, and the scars had healed as much as such scars ever do.

Noticing her glance, Marija discretely slid a hand down her thigh, covering the scars. Then she suddenly leapt to her feet in a shower of loose sand.

"I go swim," she announced, indicating the mirror sea. "Just a quick one."

Nina smiled and nodded agreement, while Marija pulled off her T-shirt to reveal a soft, white cotton bra with wide straps. Another unwelcome image presented itself, this time of Ida and the way she had been standing in front of the mirror in her cramped little room last week.

She had bought herself a bra. One of the tight, elastic sport models that prevented abrasion and over-bouncing, which of course was quite sensible. It had to happen sometime, and Ida was way ahead of Nina in the bosom department. Nina and Morten had actually joked that Ida now, at thirteen, had bigger breasts than Nina would ever have, barring implants. Yet there was still something overwhelming about the sight of her, standing there with her narrow back turned, her shoulder blades sharply outlined under this new bra that she had to have bought with her own money and without consultation. Without asking Nina's permission, even.

Nina shook her head quickly. And just exactly what was it that Ida was supposed to ask permission *for?* Growing up?

Marija ran into the water wearing bra and panties, and dived in when it was up to her thighs, her arms describing a perfect curve over her head. She surfaced several meters away and swam back and forth at a practiced crawl for a while before flipping over onto her back. She kicked up a furious cascade with her legs.

"You come too," she called, with a grin that reached her eyes for the first time. "*Ateik čia!*"

The boy had left off his sand-sifting to look at her, and something was released in his expression, an eagerness, a yearning. He looked questioningly at Nina, causing a melting hot sensation some-where behind her midriff. He was asking her for permission.

She nodded briefly and drew him close, so that she could help him out of his T-shirt and underpants. As soon as she let him go, he scurried across the firm damp part of the beach until the first ripples reached his bare feet. When a deeper surge lapped his ankles, he gave an enthusiastic shriek and continued a few steps forward, then stumbled and pitched onto his bottom, a mixture of elation and anxiety visible on his face. Marija reached him in a few long steps and helped him to his feet again, and Nina could hear them talking. Marija said something, and the boy answered her in the characteristic whine children employed when they were in need of help. Marija smiled, ruffling his short white-blond hair so that it stuck wetly in all directions. Then she said something else, taking his hands and towing him gently through the water. The boy was giggling and shrieking so that all his white milk teeth showed, and Marija was laughing too, now, a high-pitched girly laugh. She waved a hand at Nina.

"Come," she said. "Very nice."

Nina returned the wave but shook her head. She wanted the boy and Marija to be alone together in this. The boy had clearly missed having someone around who could understand him. The same might be true of Marija, thought Nina, watching the tall, skinny girl leaping joyfully about in the water. Hearing her own language spoken might not be an everyday occurrence, certainly not from someone as friendly and unthreatening as this. There was no reason Nina should butt in now. Marija knew what she was supposed to do —win the boy's confidence and try to find out where he came from. Anything would be useful, thought Nina. His name, the name of a town or a city, or of a street. Anything at all, as long as it helped pull him from the void he was floating in and anchor him somewhere, *with* someone.

Marija hadn't asked why, and Nina guessed that not asking questions had become a survival mechanism. That she had agreed to help, despite the man with the serpent tattoo, was little short of a miracle.

And another small miracle was taking place before her very eyes.

Marija said something to the boy, and he struggled free of her embrace with a scream of laughter. He splashed her with water, and then replied to her question, feet firmly planted in the wet sand. Instinctively, Nina understood what it was, even before the boy repeated his answer in a louder voice.

"Mikas!"

It was his name.

Marija and the boy whose name was Mikas stayed in the water until Mikas's lips were blue from cold and his teeth chattering like little castanets. Marija's long, dark hair hugged her shoulders wetly, and there was still laughter in her eyes as she let herself drop down onto the towel next to Nina, stretching so that she caught as much as possible of the hot afternoon sun.

Nina wrapped Mikas in the other towel, rubbing dry the narrow white shoulders, his chest and back, his legs. Then she helped him put on the T-shirt and the pants and liberated the spade-and-bucket set from their net bag for him. At once, he ran the few feet to the wet part of the beach and set to with an eager enthusiasm that made Marija and Nina smile at each other tolerantly, as if they were a married couple sharing a moment of pride in their offspring. Then Marija crouched forward, looking at Nina with a small sharp worry-wrinkle between her eyebrows.

"I know his name now," she said, in her heavy English. "He is Mikas, and his mother's last name is Ramoškienė. He remembered that when I asked him what the daycare staff calls his mama."

"Preschool?" said Nina, taken aback by the apparent normality of it. She knew precious little about Lithuania, she realized, and her ideas had run along the lines of Soviet concrete ghettos, TB-infected prisons, and a callous mafia. Somehow, preschools had not been part of the picture. "Anything else?"

Marija asked Mikas another question. He answered readily, without pausing or looking up from his work with the spade and bucket even for a second.

"He is from Vilnius. I am sure," said Marija. "I asked him if he liked riding on the trolley busses, and he does. But not in the winter when the floor is all slushy."

Marija smiled in triumph at her own invention.

"He said he is sometimes allowed to press the STOP button. But he has to wait until the driver says, 'Žemynos gatvė.' "

Nina rummaged in her bag and came up with a ballpoint and a scruffy-looking notepad from some company of medical supplies.

"Will you write it out for me?"

Marija willingly took the pen and paper and wrote down both the name of Mikas's mother and that of the street near which she must live. Nina took it with a feeling of having brought home the gold. Then she realized that knowing his name and roughly where he came from was not actually enough. There was something else she desperately needed to know.

298

"Ask about his mother," she said. "Does he live with her? And why isn't he there now? What happened—does he know?"

Marija frowned, and Nina guessed that she was searching for the right words, comforting and unthreatening enough that she wouldn't upset the boy too much. A stab of outrage at Marija's own capsized life went straight through Nina's chest. She felt such rage at the thought of the Danish, Dutch, and German men who felt it was their perfect right to serially screw a young girl month after month until not the least remnant of the girly sweetness and the coltish awkwardness would remain. What do such men tell each other? That it is quite okay because it is her own choice? That they are offering her a way to make a little money and start a new life? How very grand of them.

With so many men, and such fine generosity, a national collection aimed at young Eastern European and African girls ought to raise millions. Why didn't Marija's customers keep their flies zipped and organize a fundraiser instead?

Marija had moved closer to the boy and was helping him turn the sand-filled bucket upside down. She ran her finger round the edge of the resulting cupcake shape, saying something with a reassuring smile.

Mikas was obviously uncomfortable with the question. He twisted, and began to fill the bucket with fresh sand, but the purposefulness had gone out of him, and after a few spadefuls, he dropped the little red spade and looked around, as if searching for something to hide behind. Then he looked directly at Marija, and answered her with a few soft words.

She nodded and put her hand against his cheek to keep his attention a little while longer. But at her next question, he struggled as if overwhelmed by a cold wave. His face closed, and with a thin frightened exclamation, barely audible, he tore himself free of her gentle grasp and ran towards the water.

Marija shot an accusing glance at Nina, blaming her, or, at least, her questions.

Nina got up quickly and caught up with Mikas in a few long strides. She swung him onto her hip and held him as gently as she could. At first he fought her, kicking against her shins and thighs with bare feet. Then he curled limply against her shoulder, not in trust but in resignation. Marija had risen too, and was pulling on her clothes with angry jerks.

"His mother?"

The question hung in the air between them while Marija buttoned her jeans, not looking up.

"Marija."

Nina put her free hand on Marija's arm, and finally the girl gave up her button battle and met Nina's eyes.

"Sorry." Marija took a deep breath. "It is just that he was so upset. I do not like it."

Nina shook her head slightly, but she had to know. "What did he say about his mother?"

"I don't understand all. Children say what they like, no more," said Marija apologetically. "But he said he lives with his mama, she is nice, but he couldn't wake her."

Nina frowned. Couldn't wake her? She looked at Marija doubtfully.

Had Mikas's mama been ill? Or unconscious? And did it have anything at all to do with his involuntary trip to Denmark? As Nina recalled it, a three-year-old's grasp of the concept of time left something to be desired. She cursed her own linguistic inadequacies.

She needed to know if his own mother had sold him. Such things did happen. She knew that very well.

"What happened to take him away from his mother? Did he say?"

Marija raised her carefully plucked and penciled eyebrows.

"He said the chocolate lady took him. I do not know what that means."

"Does he miss his mother? Does he want to go back to her?"

Marija froze, and the look she gave Nina was completely naked.

"Of course he misses his mama. He is just a baby!"

301

Sunny Beach Solarium and Wellness, said the glass door leading down to the basement floor, with the added legend *New lamps!* Inside was a reception area with a dark-haired woman behind a desk. She was talking to someone on the phone, and Jučas could not make out which language she was speaking. Not Lithuanian, at any rate, but then that was hardly surprising. She was dressed in a white uniform as though she were a nurse or some kind of clinic assistant, and in Jučas's estimation, she was too old to be a whore. Perhaps it was actually possible to acquire a tan in this place.

The woman lowered the receiver for a moment and asked him something he didn't understand.

"Bukovski," he said, and then continued in English. "I have to see Bukovski."

"Wait," she said. "Name?"

He just gave her a look. Suddenly her gestures took on a nervous quickness that had not been there before. She rose and disappeared into the regions behind the reception, to emerge a few minutes later with the expected permission.

"You go in," she said.

It was surprisingly spacious, thought Jučas.

There weren't any windows, but heavy-duty ventilation ensured that the air was cool and almost fresh. There were a couple of exercise bikes and two treadmills, but for the most part, the floor space was given over to numerous well-worn TechnoGym machines and a large free-weight area. This was no pastel-colored wellness center for fat-fearing forty-year-old women or middle-aged men with aspirations to a "healthier lifestyle." This was a T-zone. The worn gray carpeting was practically impregnated with testosterone and sweat, and Jučas felt at home immediately.

Dimitri Bukovski approached him with open arms.

"My friend," he said. "Long time no see."

They embraced in the masculine back-patting way, and Jučas endured the two smacking kisses Dimitri planted, Russian style, one on each cheek. Dimitri was an Eastern European melting pot product, a little Polish, a little Russian, a little German and a touch of Lithuanian. He must be over fifty by now, and balding, but he looked as if bench-pressing two hundred kilos was still no great challenge. Pecs and biceps bulked under his black T-shirt. Years ago, in a similar basement in Vilnius, it had been Dimitri who taught Jučas about serious training. Now Dimitri lived here in Copenhagen, and out of three possible Danish contacts, he was the only one who would not go squealing to Klimka the minute Jučas left.

"Nice place," said Jučas.

"Not bad," allowed Dimitri. "We're running it as a club, so we have some say in who gets admitted. Some people here do serious work. You want a workout?"

"God, yes. But I don't have the time," said Jučas with genuine regret.

"No," said Dimitri, "I understand this isn't just a courtesy call. Still working for Klimka?"

"Yes and no," said Jučas vaguely.

"Oh? Well, it's none of my business. Step into the office, then."

Dimitri's office was little more than a cubby-hole. A desk and two brown leather armchairs were squeezed into the narrow space, and the walls were covered with photographs, many of which were of Dimitri standing next to some celebrity or other, mostly singers or actors, but also a few politicians. Pride of place had gone to a picture of Dimitri, grinning from ear to ear, shaking hands with Arnold Schwarzenegger.

"Home Sweet Home," said Dimitri, with a vague gesture at his mementos.

Jučas merely nodded. "Did you find me anything?" he asked.

"Yeah." Dimitri opened a small safe bolted to the wall beneath the Schwarzenegger photo. "You can have your pick of a Glock and a Desert

Eagle." He put the two weapons on the desk in front of Jučas.

Both were used, but in good condition. The Glock was a 9mm, the classic black Glock 17. The Desert Eagle was a .44, bright silver and monstrously heavy, and appeared to be somewhat newer than the Glock. Jučas picked them up one by one. Ejected the clip, checked that the chamber was empty. Worked the safety. Aimed at one of the pictures on the wall, and dry-fired. The pull on the .44 was somewhat stiffer than the Glock.

"How much?" he asked. "And are they clean?" He had no wish to acquire a weapon that could be traced to someone else's crimes.

"My friend. What do you take me for? Would I sell you a dirty gun? Two thousand for the Glock, three for the Eagle. Dollars, that is. For an added five hundred, I throw in extra ammo."

"Which one would you choose?"

Dimitri shrugged his massive shoulders.

"Depends. A Desert Eagle is kind of hard to ignore. Very effective as a frightener. But if you actually want to shoot someone, I'd go for the Glock."

He bought the Glock. It was cheaper, too.

Nina dropped Marija off in Vesterbrogade at 4:47.

She noted the time specifically because the time on her own watch didn't match that of the clock on the arch by Axeltorv. Hers was two minutes ahead, and she couldn't help trying to calculate which of the two was correct.

The girl stood by the curb, hunched and uncertain, as if she wasn't sure where to go. There was sand in her damp hair, Nina noticed, but apart from that, not much was left of the girl from the beach. She was no longer smiling.

Nina watched her in the rearview mirror until the girl turned to walk in the direction of Steno-gade, narrow shoulders tensed and raised as though she were cold. An acidic, heavy puff of exhaust and hot pavement reached Nina through the open car window, and for a moment she had to struggle with a burning compulsion to turn around and drag the girl back into the car. But Marija hadn't asked for her help, and Nina hadn't offered. Nina had written her name and phone number on a piece of paper, and afterwards got the money to pay Marija from an ATM in Amagerbrogade. That was all she could do at the moment.

She thought it was probable the police were monitoring her accounts and would make a note of the withdrawal, but she told herself it didn't matter. Not now.

She had sensed it at the moment she had heard the boy call for his mama at the summer cottage. Now she knew for certain. Mikas did not come from some orphanage in Ukraine or Moscow. He was not an orphan, he was not alone in the world. He had a mother, and from what little information Marija had gained from him, it seemed most likely that he had been abducted. Not sold, borrowed, or given away, but taken. And somehow he had ended up in the clutches of the man who had killed Karin. How and why, the gods only knew, but this was not Nina's concern.

If the boy's mother was still alive, she would probably have reported him missing to the Lithuanian police, and it should be a small matter to have the boy returned to Mama Ramoškienė, the daycare, and the trolley busses of Vilnius. Even the Danish police ought to be able to handle that, she thought. They were usually surprisingly effective at getting people *out* of the country. They might even make an effort to investigate who was behind the abduction. If for no other reason, then because of Karin's death. No one could murder proper Danish citizens with impunity.

So. It really was that simple.

A smooth, warm feeling of serenity flowed

from her diaphragm into the rest of her body.

She could take Mikas home to Fejøgade, and call the police from there. She might be allowed to remain with him while the police checked up on the information Marija had garnered from him. Nina knew that her perseverance could be quite convincing, and no one could claim it was better for Mikas to be in the care of some burned-out social worker he didn't know. She wanted to stay with him so that he wouldn't be left in the hands of strangers, until his mother could be flown in from Vilnius and he would finally be in her arms again.

Nina imagined how the boy's mother would arrive in a storm of smiles and tears, how she would take Nina's hands in wordless gratitude. Suddenly, Nina felt tears well up in some soft, dark place inside her. She didn't cry often, and certainly not in moments of success. Tears of joy were for old women.

But you don't see all that many happy endings, do you? a small cynical voice commented inside her. Nothing ever really comes out the way you want it to.

"This time, it will," muttered Nina stubbornly.

Large houses made Sigita uncomfortable. Somehow, she felt that the people living in them had the authority and the power to decide, to denigrate, and to condemn. No matter how many times she told herself that she was just as good as they were, there was always some little part of her that didn't listen.

The house in front of her now was huge. So enormous that one couldn't take it all in at once. It was completely isolated, perched at the top of a cliff overlooking the sea, and buttressed by white walls on all sides. Sigita thought it looked like a fortress, and she was surprised to find the gate open, so that anyone could just walk in. What was the point, then, of building a fortress?

The taxi left. She was still shocked by the cost of it. How could she have imagined that the hundred kilometer ride would be more expensive than the flight from Lithuania to Demark? Now there was almost nothing left of the money she had taken from Jolita. I should have taken all of it, she thought. But taking only some had felt a bit less like stealing. And in the end, Jolita had, after all, consented.

Now she was here. She had no idea what she

would do afterwards, and she wasn't even sure this was the end of her journey. The name on the brass plaque fixed to the white wall was the right one: MARQUART. This was where he lived, the man who collected her children. But she didn't know if this was where Mikas was.

Trying to make a stealthy approach was pointless—discrete surveillance cameras had already noted her arrival. She began to walk up the drive to the white fortress.

When she pushed the doorbell, a ripple of cheerful notes sounded on the other side of the door, a cocky little tune somehow out of sync with the tall white walls, the endless lawns, the heavy teak door. She heard footsteps inside, and the door opened.

A boy stood in the doorway. She knew at once who he must be, because of his likeness to Mikas.

"Hi," he said, and added something, of which she didn't understand a single word.

She couldn't answer. Just stood there looking at him. He was dressed in blue jeans and T-shirt, with a pair of shiny racing red Ferrari shoes on his feet, and a matching red Ferrari cap on his head, back to front, of course. He was slender and small for his age; no, more than slender, he was bonily thin. In spite of that, his face looked oddly bloated, and his tan couldn't conceal a deeper pallor, particularly around his eyes. One arm sported a gauze bandage under which she detected the contours of an IV needle that had been taped to his skin. He was ill, she thought. My son is very, very ill. What has happened to him in this alien country?

Again, he spoke, and from his intonation she thought it might be a question.

"Is your mother or father home?" she asked in Lithuanian, unable to absorb the sudden knowledge that of course he wouldn't be able to understand. He looked so much like Mikas, and she could see a lot of Darius, too, in his eyes and in his smile. It seemed absurd that she wasn't able to talk to him.

"Is your father at home? Or your mother?" she tried again, this time in English, though she thought he would be too young to understand any foreign language. But he actually nodded.

"Mother," he said. "Wait."

And then he disappeared back into the house.

He returned a little later with a delicately built woman who looked to be in her mid-forties. Sigita looked at the person who had become her son's mother. A pale pink shirt and white jeans underlined her pastel delicacy, and there was something tentative in her manner, as if she were uncertain of her bearings, even here in her own house. Like the boy, she was fair-haired and quite tanned; the superficial likeness was such that no one would ever question their relationship.

"Anne Marquart," she said, offering her hand. "How may I help you?"

But the moment she saw Sigita's face properly, she froze. There was clearly the same jolt of recognition Sigita had felt on seeing the boy. The genetic clues could not be erased. This woman saw her son's traits in Sigita's face, and was terrified.

"No," she said. "Go away!" And she began to close the door

Sigita advanced a step. "Please," she said. "I just want to talk. Please. . . ."

"Talk . . . ?" said the woman. And then she reluctantly opened the door. "Yes, perhaps we'd better."

The window stretched the whole length of the living room, from floor to ceiling. The sea and the sky flooded into the room. Too much, thought Sigita, especially now that the wind was stronger, and the waves showed teeth. Had they never heard of curtains, here? Houses, after all, had been invented to keep nature out.

The space was huge and cavernous. At one end was an open fireplace, with a fire that Anne Marquart turned on with a remote control, like a television. The floor was some kind of blue-gray stone unfamiliar to Sigita. In the middle of the room, with several meters of empty space on all sides of it, was a horseshoe shaped sofa upholstered in scarlet leather. Sigita knew that this was the kind of interior that magazines begged to photograph, but it surfeited even her need for order and clean lines, and she felt ill at ease, sitting here in the middle of this stone and glass cathedral.

"His name is Aleksander," said Anne Marquart, in her neat British accent that sounded so much more correct than Sigita's. "And he is a wonderful boy—loving and smart and brave. I love him to pieces."

Something uncoiled itself inside Sigita. Ancient knots of guilt and grief came undone, and an instinctive prayer sprang to her lips. Holy Mary, Mother of God. Thank you for this moment. Whatever else happened now, at least she knew this much: that her firstborn child was not drifting in the dark, alone and bereft, like the naked fetus-child of her nightmare. His name was Aleksander. He had a mother, who loved him.

Aleksander himself had disappeared again, she knew not where to. Anne Marquart had said something to him in Danish; his face had lit up in a pleased grin, and an enthusiastic "Yesssss!" had hopped out of his mouth. Sigita had the feeling he was being allowed something that was otherwise strictly regulated. Video games? Computer? It was obvious that they were wealthy enough to provide him with anything he wished for. Sigita felt a peculiar pain. If Mikas ever found out what kind of life his brother was living, would he be envious?

The thought brought back all her fear for him.

"I am not here because of Aleksander," she said. "But because of Mikas. My own little boy. Is he here? Have you seen him?"

Anne Marquart seemed taken aback.

"A little boy? No. I. . . . You have another child, then?"

"Yes. Mikas. He is three, now."

Something was going on inside Anne Marquart. She was staring into her teacup, as if any moment now a profound and essential truth would be revealed there. Then she suddenly raised her head.

"Same father?" she asked.

"Yes," said Sigita, not understanding the intensity with which Anne Marquart endowed the question.

"Oh God," said Anne Marquart softly. "But he is only three. . . ."

Amazed, Sigita saw silent tears on Mrs. Marquart's face.

"It's not fair," whispered Aleksander's mother. "How are we expected to bear this?"

"I don't understand," said Sigita hesitantly.

"You have seen that he is ill?"

"Yes." One could hardly avoid it.

"He suffers from something called nephrotic syndrome. He has hardly any kidney function left now. He needs dialysis twice a week. We have a small clinic in the basement so that he doesn't have to travel all the way to Copenhagen for treatment, but still . . . he hardly ever complains, but it's tough on him. And . . . and eventually, it will stop working."

"Can't he get a transplant?" asked Sigita.

"We tried. My husband gave him a kidney, but . . . but we are not . . . biologically related, of course. And Aleksander rejected it, despite all the medication, and now he is worse than before. . . ."

At that moment, Sigita finally realized why Jan Marquart had come looking for her. And why her son had disappeared.

The boy was sitting with his eyes half closed and showed no reaction when Nina parked the car in Fejøgade. The police car had gone, and the windows of the third floor flat were empty and closed. Morten might not be home yet, thought Nina distractedly, or he could have taken the children to stay with his sister in Greve. He liked to get them out of the way when a crisis was brewing. He didn't want them to see that there was anything wrong, didn't want them to see him losing control. And at the moment, he was probably half out of his mind.

Nina closed her eyes and felt the worm of

conscience gnawing at the back of her mind. Tonight, she would have to put everything right. Rest her head against his shoulder and run her hands over his face while she told him why there was nothing more to be afraid of now. They could let the children stay overnight with Hanne and Peter and pick them up in the morning.

She lifted Mikas from the car and carried him up the stairs. He was awake, but tired and limp, as if he had spent everything he had on the beach. He didn't stir as she eased the keys out of her pocket. She could hear the muted roar of a video game the Jensen children were playing, and the rattle of pots and dinner preparations behind the Jensen door. But she didn't feel like answering her neighbor's curious questions—which would, no doubt, be endless—and so she unlocked her own front door soundlessly and slipped inside.

The flat was quiet and cool, and for the first time since she had picked up the suitcase yesterday, Nina felt a genuine pang of hunger. She kicked off her sandals in the hall and walked barefoot into the living room. Mikas slid willingly from her hip onto the couch and subsided there in a small heap of three-year-old exhaustion.

The remains of breakfast were still scattered across the little coffee table in front of the television. Two bowls of souring milk and soggy cornflakes. An unopened, unread newspaper. A meal on the run, diagnosed Nina, taking the bowls

316

into the kitchen where she pitched the contents into the bin and loaded the dishes into the dishwasher. She put fresh cereal into a new bowl for Mikas, adding an extra spoonful of sugar. The boy had eaten only a couple of ice cream cones, a breakfast roll, and a few slices of untoasted bread in the time he had been with her. He had to be just as weak at the knees as she was. And she was acutely aware, now, of the lightheaded feeling that came from not having eaten for too long.

She cut herself two slices of dark rye and sandwiched a thick wedge of salami between them. Cornflakes bowl in one hand, glass of milk in the other, and her solid sandwich clenched between her teeth, she returned to the living room. A strange flickering feeling of happiness settled in her stomach. Home. It felt fantastic. Now all that was missing was Morten and the children.

But there was no rush, just as there was no need to hurry the necessary call to the police. She placed the cereal bowl in front of Mikas and dropped into the armchair next to the couch with a muted thud. Slowly, she chewed her way through the soft rye and the sharp spiciness of the salami, eyes closed, mind gently drifting. When she was done, she climbed to her feet and went into the bedroom, where she pulled off the damp, dirty T-shirt and put on a crisp, clean shirt instead. From the living room, she could hear the rattle of Mikas's spoon against the bowl.

• • •

The doorbell rang.

It wasn't the muted scale of the door phone, but the insistent ring of the old-fashioned push-button on the door frame itself. Anton used it when he wanted to announce his presence, though his usual noisy progress up the stairs generally made any other signal redundant. No, it was probably Birgit next door, who must have noticed her arrival after all.

She might even know that the police were looking for Nina. Birgit was nice enough, really, but her curiosity was boundless, and sometimes Nina wished the walls between the flats were just a little thicker. Particularly now, when she could have done with a few more minutes on her own with Mikas.

Resignedly, she reached for the lock catch, but something made her hesitate. It was too quiet out there, she thought. Anton would have been bouncing off the floor, if not the walls, and Birgit usually had the door to her own flat open, yelling over her shoulder at her own children. It was silent out there. No scrabbling feet, no throat-clearing or nose-blowing. It was not a natural silence.

Automatically, she put the security chain on the door before opening it enough so that she could see whoever it was. A slender, fair-haired woman stood there on the landing, smiling politely, yet somehow reticently.

"Please," she said, bending forward slightly. "I think you know my son. I am Mikas's mother. May I come in?"

Instantly, Nina's mind was flooded with the fantasies she had entertained earlier, in the car. Mikas's mother, holding her hand and thanking her, as only one mother could thank another. Her happy ending. It was here, now.

But even as she slid the chain off the lock, she knew something wasn't right. The woman pushed open the door herself, with a smile that had grown oddly apologetic. As if she didn't really want to come in, thought Nina. And then she saw that Mikas had come into the hallway behind her. He stood there, still wearing his nice new sandals and holding the breakfast bowl, while a pool of dark yellow pee formed around his feet.

Smiling still, the woman held out her hand to him. He jerked from head to foot, and the bowl slid from his hands and hit the pine floor with a sharp clack.

There was a man behind the fair-haired woman. He must have been standing against the wall on the landing, out of sight until now. His massive shoulders in the too-hot leather jacket filled the doorframe, and she recognized him at once. The neo-Nazi haircut, the fury in his eyes, the huge, closed fists. In one hand he held a smooth black gun. There was no haste in the way he moved, noted Nina; it was all very calculated and precise, the routine actions of a man who had done this dozens of times. A single powerful stride brought him into the flat. He took the time to close the door behind him, and Nina heard the click of the latch with a peculiar lack of fear. She backed a couple of steps, and felt her foot slip in the puddle of warm urine, milk and cornflakes.

Idiot, she told herself, in the long stretched second that followed. Of course she's not his mother. You didn't have time to call anyone. Then the blow fell, and turned the world dark red and swirling. Then black.

Barbara was clinging to his arm.
"Don't hit her anymore," she said. "Jučas. Don't do it!"

Jučas.

Not Andrius.

He lowered the gun. The boy-bitch lay in a heap at his feet, one side of her face completely covered in blood.

"Don't kill her!"

Barbara was as pale as a sheet. She didn't look young anymore, and for the first time he considered what the difference in their ages would mean in ten years, or twenty. When she turned fifty, he would be only just past his fortieth birthday. Did he really want to come home to a fifty-year-old woman then?

"Don't be silly. I'm not going to kill her," he said, wondering what the hell he was supposed to do with her if he didn't. He shook off Barbara's hand and stepped across the crumbled form. Where had the kid gone?

Barbara found him crouched next to the toilet, squeezed into the corner as if he was trying to push himself through the wall. A sound was coming from him now, a sort of squeaky whine, with every breath he took.

"But baby," said Barbara, kneeling down in front of him. "We're not going to hurt you!"

The child didn't buy that particular lie anymore. He screwed his eyes shut and whined even more loudly.

"Make him be quiet," said Jučas.

Barbara glanced at him.

"He's just scared," she said.

"Then give him some of that damn chocolate. Do you have any eyedrops left?"

"No," she said. But he thought she might be lying.

"Stay here," he said. "And keep the damn kid quiet!"

The boy-bitch hadn't stirred. He grabbed her shoulder bag, the only thing she had had with

321

her apart from the child, and emptied it into the kitchen sink. Wallet, Kleenex, a fuzzy old roll of mints, car keys, two other sets of keys, and a dog-eared diary. No mobile. He took all the keys with him, and went quietly down the stairs to look for the red Fiat. He found it half a block away, hidden behind a big green-plastic container meant for recycling glass. On the backseat was a smelly blanket and two shopping bags, one containing kid's clothes, the other full of apple cores and bread and beach toys. That was all. The boot proved equally uninteresting; there was a plastic crate full of starter cables, sprinkler fluid, an aerosol can of puncture-repair foam, and other first-aid items for unreliable cars, a bin liner that turned out to contain empty bottles, a pair of gumboots, and a flashlight.

He took the blanket and left the rest, and locked up the Fiat once more.

She didn't have the money. He felt the certainty of it in his gut. And the other one, the blond one with the boobs, she hadn't had it either. She would have told him. In the end, she would have told him.

Which meant only one thing.

He was now completely sure that the Dane had lied to him.

There were still a number of things he didn't understand—what the boy-bitch was doing with the kid, for instance. And how and why the blond one was mixed up in it at all. But he knew enough. And he knew how he was going to make the Dane pay what was owed.

He drove the Mitsubishi onto the pavement and parked it right by the front door. Upstairs, Barbara had at least managed to extract the boy from the toilet. She was crouched next to him and had her arms around him, gently rocking him back and forth. It seemed to be working; he was quiet again.

The boy-bitch was still lying where he had dropped her. But she was breathing, he noticed.

"She's fine," he told Barbara. "I'm taking her down to the car."

Barbara didn't answer. She just looked at him, and her eyes were almost as wide and frightened as the boy's.

"I'm doing this for you," he said.

She nodded obediently.

He rolled up the bitch's limp body in the disgusting blanket and eased open the door with his hip. The stairwell was still deserted. What would he say if he met someone—she's had a fall, we're taking her to the hospital? But no one came. He maneuvered her into the back of the Mitsubishi and covered her completely with the blanket, then parked the car in a more legal and less noticeable spot. So far, so good.

When he got back to the flat, he could hear

Barbara murmuring to the boy. In Polish, not Lithuanian.

"Stop that," he said. "He doesn't understand a word you're saying."

Jučas didn't either, and he didn't like it when Barbara spoke in her native language. It gave him a feeling that there was a part of her he couldn't access.

When they got to Krakow, she would be speaking Polish with everyone, he suddenly realized. Everyone except him. Why hadn't he thought of that before? But he hadn't. He had only been thinking about the house, about Barbara, and the life he imagined them having together.

The Dane would make it all possible. The Dane and his money. He could still recall the fizzy feeling of triumph when he had realized how easy it would be.

It had been Klimka who had told him to look after the Dane, and had emphasized that there would be no funny business. This man was a good client, with businesses not only in Vilnius but also a couple of places in Latvia, and he paid Klimka good money—very good money—to keep the other sharks at a distance. Now he was in Vilnius himself and wanted only a single bodyguard to follow him around. Discretion was essential.

And so Jučas had played the nanny from the moment the man got off the plane with his ridiculous little trolley that turned out to contain an unreasonable number of U.S. dollars. They had gone directly to some kind of private clinic, where the Dane tried to buy information about some Lithuanian girl or other who had apparently given birth to a baby. When Jučas had seen the sum he had offered the head of the clinic, he had begun to feel jumpy. It was as if the Dane had no idea what it was he was waving in the woman's face. A tenth would have sufficed; would, actually, have been too much. People had been murdered for less.

He called Klimka to ask for backup. Klimka refused—the Dane had specified one bodyguard. Jučas would just have to handle it for now, but if things looked tricky, he could call, of course.

Yeah right, thought Jučas. If the shit really hit the fan, he needed his backup with him, not a couple of phone calls away. He walked around with his senses tuned to max all day, paying precious little attention to whatever the Dane was saying and doing, because he was too busy scanning the surroundings. When the nurse more or less slammed the door in their faces and they had to return to the hotel, Jučas heaved a sigh of relief.

Premature, as it turned out. In a bout of depression, the man downed most of the contents of the minibar, then went for the hotel bar, already so inebriated that the bartender refused to serve him. After which performance the idiot staggered out the door, without the dollar trolley, thank God, but still with enough of a wad in his wallet to get into every kind of trouble. There was nothing Jučas could do except curse and follow.

That proved only the beginning of a very long night. But as the booze went in, the story came out, little by little, mixed with the drinks. And Jučas listened, at first indifferently, but then with growing interest. Fledgling plans formed in his mind. And the next morning, when he poured a sizeable but unbruised hangover onto the small private Danish plane, it was with almost tender feelings that he buckled the guy's seatbelt for him and made sure a good supply of puke bags were in reach.

It had taken a little while to make the nurse tell him what she knew, but he had, after all, had some experience in making people do things they didn't really want to do. And when he discovered that Sigita Ramoškienė actually had a second child, everything had fallen brilliantly into place.

He had sent his first package to the Dane, and made him an offer. The price was easy to remember, and non-negotiable: one million U.S. dollars.

He still didn't understand why things had come apart the way they had. But one thing, at least, was very clear. The Dane was not going to put one over on him now.

"I'll take him," he said to Barbara, reaching for the boy.

She hugged the child even closer.

"Can't we take him with us?" she said. "He is so small. He could easily become ours."

"Are you insane?"

"He'll forget all the old stuff quickly. In a year, he will think he has always been with us."

"Barbara. Let him go."

"No," she said. "Andrius. It's enough now. We can take him and leave for Poland right now. You don't have to hit anyone anymore. No more violence."

He shook his head. The woman had gone completely insane. He should never have brought her here. But he thought she might get them into the flat without any fuss, and so she had. Now he wished he had just kicked in the door.

"The money," he said.

"We don't need it," she said. "We can live with my mother, at least to begin with. And then you'll find a job, and we can get a place of our own."

He had to breathe very calmly and carefully to keep the rage at bay.

"You may want to live like a sewer rat for the rest of your life," he said. "But I don't."

Resolutely, he seized the boy's arm and tore him from Barbara's grasp. Luckily, the kid didn't scream. He simply went limp, as though he had suddenly lost consciousness. Barbara was the one doing the whining.

"For God's sake shut up," he said. "Not all the neighbors are deaf."

"Andrius," she begged. She looked as if she were dissolving. Tears and mucus made her look swollen, damp and unattractive. Yet some of the old tenderness returned.

"Hush," he said. "Stop crying, can't you? Go back to the hotel, and I will pick you up later. Once we get the money, Dimitri has a new car ready for us. And then we leave for Krakow."

She nodded, but he couldn't tell whether she believed him or not.

When he got back to the car, he saw that the boy-bitch had moved. The blanket had slipped, so that one could see a little of her face and shoulder. Damn it. But it was best just to get out of here, now. He could always stop later and cover her up again. He put the boy into the kid's car seat still fitted between the driver's seat and the passenger seat. Just as well he hadn't removed it yet. He fumbled with the straps and buckles— this had been Barbara's department until now— but luckily the child made no move to resist him. He turned his head away and wouldn't look at Jučas, but apart from that he was a life-sized doll, limp arms, limp legs, no more screaming defiance.

Barbara came out just as he was finishing, but he merely slid into his own seat and drove off, steadfastly ignoring her. He couldn't bring her.

He knew that he would probably have to kill someone. The boy-bitch at the very least, but perhaps also the Dane. And he didn't want Barbara to see.

Jučas drove past the house twice just to get his bearings. There was a wall, but the wrought-iron gates were wide open, so there was really nothing to prevent him from driving straight up to the front door. Was it really that simple? It was hard to believe. In Lithuania, rich people had to guard their money better.

The third time, he turned into the gate and continued up the driveway. He let the car coast to minimize the noise of the engine and didn't stop in front of the main entrance. Instead, he followed the driveway around the house and into a huge garage at the basement level. Here, too, the doors were wide open. There was space enough for five or six cars, but right now the only occupants were a dark blue Audi station wagon and a low sports car silhouette shrouded by dust sheets. He parked next to the station wagon and turned off his engine.

The kid had stayed quiet during the ride, never looking at Jučas. Every once in a while he cried softly, with barely a sound. No screaming and sobbing, just this timid, hopeless crying, which was worse, in its way. Jučas felt like assuring the boy that he meant him no harm, but he knew it couldn't be helped. He knew that from now on the monster in that little tyke's nightmares would be him. And what about Barbara? The look she had given him back in the flat . . . as though she, too, were becoming scared of him. Hell. I'm not the kind of bastard who would hit a woman or a child, he told himself.

Completely unwelcome, the memory of the other one came back to him. The blonde. Crouched on the bed, with wide unfocused eyes that no longer understood he was in the room. The uncertain, labored voice, calling. "Ni-na. Ni-na."

He sat motionless for a moment, still with his hands on the wheel. What's the bloody use, he thought. What's the use of running from Klimka and his world, where fear is a bludgeon you use to batter people into compliance. What's the use of dreaming about Krakow and a house with a lawn and Barbara sunbathing on a quilt, when all this shit stays with you.

He got out of the car. Reached for the rage because it was the only thing that might get him through the next bit. He opened the rear door and looked down at the boy-bitch, still huddled in a boneless pile without any spark of consciousness. It was all her fault, he told himself. Her and the filthy swine who was trying to do him out of his money. It was them. They did it, and he was not going to let them get away with it. You don't fuck with me.

And the rage came. Like a wave of heat, it washed through his body, made hands and feet prickle and shake a little, but in a good way. It was best done now, while she was still just an object. He took the plastic shopping bag and emptied out all the stuff that Barbara had brought —bananas, lukewarm cola, some kind of soap she had liked because it smelled of roses and lily of the valley. Even though he didn't really feel like touching her, he climbed into the back of the car to the bitch. He grabbed her shoulders and rolled her limp body into his lap. She weighed nothing at all, he thought. No more than a child. He pulled the bag over her head and then realized he had nothing to tie it with. Instead, he tied the handles themselves into a knot under her chin, which would have to do. When he saw the plastic cling closer to her face with each breath she took, he knew it was enough. By the time he came back, it would be over.

He pushed her away with disgust and wiped his hands on his trousers, as if touching her had somehow contaminated him. The bitch got what she deserved, he told himself carefully, clinging to the strength the rage gave him. And as he went to pull down the garage doors, it wasn't her face that swam before his eyes. In the sudden darkness, other images forced themselves on him, the Pig, the Pig from the orphanage who pushed little boys up against rough, damp basement walls, down in the dim semi-darkness that smelled of pee and petrol and unwashed old man.

Filthy bastard swine, he thought, they were all filthy swine, and he was going to show them that nobody did such things to him. Hell, no. Not to him. He found a light switch and turned on the fluorescent overheads until he had found what he was looking for—the automated gate system that such a filthy rich bastard had to have. He yanked the wiring right out of the box with hardly any effort, leaving the bared copper threads bristling and exposed. So far, so good.

There was a door that had to lead into the house, but it was locked. He considered kicking it down, but decided that it was much simpler to ring the bell and wait for someone to let him in. He glanced back at the car. The boy sat there, still strapped to his little seat, staring at him through the windshield. Jučas slammed his palm against the light switch so that both boy and car disappeared in the garage darkness.

Sigita was shaking all over.

"You can't!" she screamed, and for a few moments didn't register that she was screaming in Lithuanian. She searched desperately for the English words this woman would understand.

"You can't take a kidney from a three-year-old child! He is too small!"

Anne Marquart looked at her in astonishment.

"But Mrs. Ramoškienė. Of course not. We . . . we're not going to."

"Why did you take him, then? Why did people come to Vilnius and steal him from me, and take him to Denmark?" She didn't know for certain, but it had to be that way. Didn't it?

"I don't know where your little boy is, or why he is gone. But I assure you, we could never ever harm. . . ." She broke off in the middle of the sentence and stared blankly out at the ocean for a while. Then she said, in a completely different tone of voice: "Would you excuse me? I have to call my husband."

These people are rich enough to buy anything, thought Sigita. They bought my first child. And now they have paid someone to steal the second.

"He's only three," she said helplessly.

333

Di-di-da-da-di-di-diiih. . . . The unsuitably gay little tune from a different doorbell made them both freeze. There was the sound of child-light running feet from the hallway, and Aleksander's voice called out something in Danish.

"He always wants to get the door," said Anne Marquart absently. "With him in the house, there's no need for a butler."

Then, too quickly for natural speed, the door to the living room slammed back against the wall, and a man stood there, in the middle of the floor. He took up all the space, thought Sigita, and left no room for anybody else. It wasn't just that he was big. It was his rage that made everything around him shrink. He held on to Aleksander with one hand. In the other was a gun.

"Get down on the floor," he said. "Now!"

Sigita knew at once who he was, even though she had never seen him before. It was the man who had taken Mikas.

Aleksander struggled and tried to twist free of the man's grip. The man grabbed a handful of his hair and jerked the boy's head back, so the child emitted a thin sound of pain and fright and outrage.

"Don't hurt him," begged Anne Marquart. "Please." She said something in rapid Danish to the boy, and he stopped struggling. Then she lay down on the floor, obediently.

Sigita didn't. She couldn't. She stood there, stiff

as a pillar, with the noise of her own blood crackling in her ears like a bad phone connection.

"Where is he?" she asked.

The man didn't like that she wouldn't do as she was told. He took a step forward, then raised the barrel of the gun against Aleksander's cheek.

"Who?" he said.

"You know damn well. My Mikas!"

"Don't you care about this one?" he said. "Is the little one the only one that matters?"

No. No, it was no longer only about Mikas. It had never been only about Mikas, she knew that now.

"Lie down, bitch," he said. "It will be better for all of us if I don't lose my temper."

He didn't say it in any menacing tone of voice, he was just offering information. Like the little signs by the predator pits in Vilnius Zoo: *Please don't climb the fence.*

Sigita lay down.

"What are you saying?" asked Anne Marquart in English. "Why are you doing this?"

The man didn't answer. He merely forced Aleksander down onto the floor next to them, then slid his hands over Anne's body, not in any sexual way, just professionally. He found a mobile phone in her pocket and bashed it against the stone floor till it broke. He then upended Sigita's bag, fished her mobile from the wreckage, and treated it to a similar destructive bang.

"He took Mikas," explained Sigita. "My son Mikas. I think your husband paid him to do it."

The man looked up.

"No," he said. "Not yet. But he will."

It was nearly half past eight in the evening before they let him go. Jan felt as if he had been run through a cement mixer.

"Go home and try not to think too much about it," said his lawyer, as they shook hands in the parking lot.

Jan nodded silently. He knew it would be impossible not to think. Think about Anne, and about Inger and Keld. Think about Aleksander, and about an organ cooler box somewhere, with a kidney inside that had a maximum of twelve useful hours left before it became just so much butcher's waste. Think about the Lithuanian and Karin, who was dead whether he could get his head around it or not.

They had shown him pictures. They had meant to shock him, he knew, and it had worked. Even though he had seen her at the Institute of Forensics, it was somehow worse to see her in the place where she had died, crouched on a bed, blood in her hair. Crime scene photos. It made the violence of what had been done to her too real and unclinical. You could *see* the power behind those blows, the force that had killed her. He thought of the Lithuanian and his huge hands, and the words on the phone when he had tried to end it. *Not until you pay.* Fear tore at his stomach.

Nor had the police lost interest in him. He hadn't told them about the Lithuanian or about Aleksander and the kidney he so desperately needed. Even though Jan had rid himself of the stolen Nokia, the photo of the boy, and the blood sample with the perfect DNA match, he still clung to hope, irrationally and beyond all realism.

Perhaps they sensed the lie and all the things he left unsaid. Perhaps that was why they kept coming at him for such a long time, even after he had sacrificed his self-respect and told them about Inger's visit. And of course, they had sent someone to the villa in Tårbæk to check the usefulness of this alibi. Thinking about it was almost unbearable. He imagined Keld frowning and putting down his pipe. Getting up to perform polite handshakes with the cop. Hearing about Karin and the fact that Jan was a suspect. For a wild moment, he even thought that Keld might get into his old black Mercedes and drive directly to the house by the bay to take Anne away from him.

But of course, he wouldn't do such a thing. They were married, and Keld had a lot of respect for that institution. Which didn't mean he also had to respect the man his daughter had consented to marry, and Jan knew that that respect would now have evaporated. If it had ever really been there. In the midst of his general misery, that knowledge hurt with its own specific pain.

"You'll be all right," said the lawyer, patting him on the shoulder. "You have at least a partial alibi, and they have no physical evidence linking you to the scene. Almost the opposite, I believe. And the other thing . . . well, it will be very difficult for them to lift the burden of proof on that one."

Jan nodded, and got quickly into his car.

"See you tomorrow," he said, slamming the car door shut before the man had time to say anything else.

The other thing. . . .

It was the man in the blue pullover who had said it. The one that looked like a railway clerk. "People like you, Mr. Marquart. People like you don't have to kill anyone themselves. After all, it's so much easier to pay someone else to do it."

That was an accusation that clung worse than a direct murder charge. Not least because it was much too close to the truth. He *had* tracked Karin. And he had offered the man money to go and get her. That he had never meant for the man to kill her—how does one prove that when she did in fact die?

The way home felt long, even though he didn't actually want to get there. After several weeks of clear skies and sunshine, clouds had begun to roll in from the west, darkening the twilight. A strong wind made the pine trees sway so that it looked as if they were trying to fall on top of the house. The automated garage door failed to work, again. He was too tired to get annoyed and merely left the car on the gravel outside. He could smell the sea even though he had smoked three cigarettes during the drive. The sea, and something else— the ozone-heavy damp smell of rain that hadn't quite arrived.

He had barely inserted his key in the lock when the door slammed open, so abruptly that it tore the bunched keys from his hand. Something hit him in the face, and he was knocked backwards, ending up on his back in the gravel at the foot of the stone steps.

The Lithuanian stood there on the threshold, with the light at his back so that he looked barely human, a giant form towering above him, filling Jan's entire field of vision. He had a gun in one hand. The other clutched the back of Aleksander's head like the timber grab on a bulldozer. An involuntary sound shot up from the depth of his diaphragm. Please no. Not Aleksander.

. "For God's sake," he whispered, not realizing that he was speaking Danish and that the giant would not be able to understand. "Let him go."

The Lithuanian was looking down at him.

"Now," he said, in a voice that made Jan think of rusting iron. "*Now* you pay."

Anton was tired and surly. "Peepy" was Morten's mother's idiosyncratic term for it—possibly an amalgam of peevish and sleepy, and in any case a word that admirably covered the fit-for-nothing-yet-unready-to-sleep state with which his son struggled on a regular basis.

If only Nina hadn't taken the damn car, thought Morten. Today of all days he could have done without the trek from the daycare to the Fejøgade flat, dragging along an uncooperative seven-year-old. Anton considered it beneath his dignity to hold hands like a toddler, but he kept lagging behind if Morten didn't chivvy him along.

She had called her boss, but not him. Magnus had relayed her assurances, almost apologetically.

"She's okay," he said. "She said you shouldn't worry."

Of course it was nice to know she wasn't lying dead in a thicket somewhere in Northern Zealand, but apart from that, it wasn't very helpful. She was still out there somewhere, in that alternate reality to which he had no access, where violence and disaster always lurked just around the corner. He knew it was irrational, but he couldn't shake the feeling that Nina had somehow single-handedly managed to drag that world back with her to Denmark, disturbing the coffee-and-open-sandwiches tranquility of the family picnic he would have liked his life to be.

"I'm hungry," whined Anton.

"I'll make you a sandwich when we get home."

"On white bread?"

"No. On rye."

"I don't like rye," said Anton.

"Yes, you do."

"I don't! It's got *seeds* in it."

Morten heaved a sigh. Anton's pickiness came and went. When he was rested and happy and secure, he cheerfully wolfed down fairly advanced foods such as olives and broccoli and chicken liver. At other times, his repertoire shrunk alarmingly, and he would balk at anything more challenging than cereal and milk.

"We'll fix something," he said vaguely.

"But I'm hungry *now*."

Morten surrendered and bought him a popsicle.

There was a smell in the hallway that warned him the second he was about to cross the threshold. He stopped. Two floors below, Anton was making his way up the stairs by a method

341

that involved taking two steps up and hopping one step down. Apparently, it was essential to perform the hops with maximum noise.

Morten switched on the lights. The semi-twilight of the hallway fled, and dark huddled silhouettes became coats, scarves, shoes, boots, and a lonely-looking skateboard. But on the worn wooden floor, there was an alarming pool of congealing blood. And a little further on, a cereal bowl lay on its side in a puddle of spilled milk and cornflakes. And something else—the something that caused most of the smell: urine.

"Anton," he said sharply.

Anton looked up at him from the landing below without answering.

"Go and see if Birgit is in. Perhaps you can play with Mathias."

"But I'm hungry."

"Do as I say!"

Anton's eyes widened in alarm. Morten wanted to comfort and reassure, but at the moment he simply couldn't. The fear that rose inside him left room for little else. He closed the door to the flat and rang the doorbell on his neighbor's side of the landing. Mathias opened, but Birgit was hot on his heels.

"Hi," she said. "Have you been burgled?"

"Why do you ask that?" said Morten, his fear still crouched right behind his teeth.

"I saw a police car parked outside this morning."

"Oh. I see. Er, could Anton stay with you for an hour or so? It's quite a long story, but I'll tell you all about it later." He deliberately dangled the tale in front of her like a steak in front of a hungry dog, because he knew that curiosity was one of the more powerful driving forces in Birgit's life.

She wasn't thrilled that she would have to wait for her titbit, but perhaps she sensed his curbed tension.

"Okay," she said. "Mathias, you can show Anton that new game of yours."

"Yessss!" said Mathias, and Anton brightened too. They scurried along the corridor to Mathias's room.

"Thanks," said Morten.

Birgit remained in her doorway, discretely trying to look past him and into the flat as he opened the door again, but he didn't think she saw much before he closed it behind him.

He avoided the bloodstain and stepped across the milk and pee puddle. Glanced into the kitchen and the living room. No one there. Ida's room was also deserted; she was with her classmate Anna this afternoon, he remembered. But in the bed-room a dirty T-shirt had been tossed across the bed. Nina's T-shirt. She had been here.

He stood very still, trying to collect his chaotic thoughts. What had happened? The bloodstain was ominously large. It could not have come from some trivial injury like a cut finger. And

343

pee—where did that come from? Vague memories of a forensic TV series rose in his mind. Something about traces of urine and feces because all muscles let go at the moment of death.

Moment of death. No.

No.

He fumbled for his mobile. He had to call the police.

Then he heard a faint sound. A heave, or a sobbing breath. He tore open the door to the tiny bathroom.

On the lid of the toilet sat a woman he had never seen before in his life. She looked a wreck. She had obviously been weeping hard, and there was a quality of surrender about her. Her shoulder-length fair hair had slipped from what looked to be an immaculate chignon, but even under these circumstances, there was an unconscious elegance to the slender neck and the long legs.

Morten stood there gaping.

"Where is Nina?" he asked.

The woman looked up at him. Her eyes were swollen with grief.

"*Juz po wszystkim*," she said. And then in uncertain English, "Is over. Everything is all over."

Morten's pulse roared in his ears. *Nina.* What the hell had happened?

She woke because she was drowning. She couldn't breathe. Something wet, black and sticky clung to her mouth, nose, and eyes, and with each breath she tried to take, she drew in only crackling darkness. No air. There was no air.

Panic had already seized her body before she had come completely to her senses again. Her hands clawed purposelessly at the darkness in front of her and encountered something soft and heavy. A blanket, perhaps. She tried to pull it off her body, but it tangled around her shoulders and arms, and she struggled like a trapped diver trying to get back to the surface.

Her chest hurt now. And still the darkness clung to her face. She gasped for breath in hard short heaves, and some part of her brain registered a perfumed smell of roses. An omen of death, it seemed. The smell of roses and lilies always reminded her of burials. Finally, she freed one hand from the blanket and raised it to her face.

A plastic bag.

First she tried to rip it. Then to claw holes in the plastic with her fingers, so that she might breathe. Air. Everything in her was screaming for oxygen, and her lungs cramped painfully. Again, she clawed at the bag, and this time, something gave. The bag loosened enough so that she felt a touch of air.

Easy. Breathe slowly.

Her thoughts slipped and wandered, and she had to struggle to get a grip on them in the curious black and milky gray place that was her brain.

Someone had pulled a bag over her head. All she needed to do to be able to breathe again was pull it off. She reached above her head and yanked the bag all the way off, and finally, she could breathe freely, in long noisy gasps.

The darkness around her was still deep and black. For the first few dizzy seconds she was unsure whether she actually had her eyes open, and an absurd impulse led her to feel her eyelids, just to check.

"You're not dead, Nina. Take a breath, and get a grip."

It helped.

The words sounded real in the darkness, and Nina raised herself up on one elbow and turned her head a little. It hurt to move. Particularly one side of her face and head, which felt heavy and tender at the same time. Something wet and sticky lay like plastic wrap over her cheekbone and throat. Blood, she thought dispassionately, and recalled how the man from the railway station had stormed into the flat, gun in hand. She felt vaguely surprised that he hadn't killed her then, on the hallway floor. But for some reason, he must have decided to wait.

She turned her head the other way, and for the first time noted a slim crack of light in the middle of all the darkness. That, and a low, persistent whine, like that of a trapped animal.

Mikas.

She knew right away that it was him, but his crying was so muted that it sounded as if it was being transmitted to her from another planet. Where was he?

Nina fumbled with one hand in front of her, and came up against a smooth cool glassy surface. A car window. She was in the back of a van, she thought. The floor beneath her was covered with some kind of felt, prickly and new under her hands. She felt her way along the side of the van until her fingers closed around some kind of wire mesh. A dog barrier? Her eyes were getting used to the darkness, and she could just make out a seam of light around what looked like garage doors. A carpark or a garage, she thought, picking up the oily smell of tires and fuel. She had no sense that the man was here, but the sound of Mikas's crying leaked back to her through the mesh.

He was afraid.

"Mikas!"

Nina listened in the darkness. Waves of nausea rolled over her, and her tongue felt huge and shapeless when she tried to talk.

She called again, shaking the mesh testingly.

"Mikas, don't be scared. I'm right here."

She reminded herself that he wouldn't understand, but she hoped the sound of her voice would at least reassure him that he was not alone. Perhaps he did actually recognize it. He was silent for a few moments, as if listening. Then the faint, toneless weeping continued.

She got onto her knees and felt along the bottom of the car, probing and sliding her fingers into every space and crevice she encountered. A flattened ring caught her interest. She pulled at it, and felt the lining beneath her shift and move. There was a hatch beneath her, and she suddenly realized that this was the kind of car that had a spare wheel embedded in the bottom of the cargo space. She managed to pull back the lining and open the hatch, and there, beside the spare, was the folded plastic package she was hoping for. The car's tool set.

She felt a rush of triumph. If the man from the train station thought she was just going to lie there and die with a badly tied shopping bag over her head, he was much mistaken. And he was also mistaken if he thought locking her in the back of a van would keep her captive much longer. Nina felt a pang of contempt mixing with the fury that was growing in her belly. Weren't they all like that? The vultures that fed on the flesh of the weak. The pedophiles, the rapists, the pimps. All the damned lowlifes of this world. This was what they were really like. Such *stupid* little people.

This man was no exception. He wasn't getting Mikas. And he wasn't getting her.

She drew a wrench from the package and hefted it. She didn't know where the man had gone, but leaving Mikas here presumably meant he was coming back. The boy was what he had come for. The property he had come to reclaim. Smashing the window might be too risky, and too noisy. Instead, she made her way back to the mesh. The screws that fastened it to the car were easy to find even in the dark, and in the tool kit was a screwdriver that was a close-enough match.

Suddenly, light flooded the garage outside the van, and she instinctively cowered to the floor. She thought she heard voices. If help was within reach, she ought to bang and kick the sides of the van; but somehow, she didn't think that whoever was out there had come to rescue her.

If he came back, could she pretend she was still unconscious? She reached for the plastic bag, but couldn't bring herself to pull it over her head again.

Then the lights went out, and darkness descended once more. She crouched, still waiting. But no one came.

Loosening all the screws took a while, and she had to pause twice to fight back nausea. But finally the mesh came free, and she slid it to one side.

"Mikas?"

Silence reigned up there. She wormed her way past the headrest of the driver's seat and tumbled forward into the cabin. She could feel the boy move beside her, in trembling jerks, but she couldn't see him properly. Quickly, she opened the driver's door, and light from the overhead bulb flooded the cabin and revealed Mikas's face, frightened and blinking. Did he even recognize her? She wasn't sure. He had been strapped into a child's car seat, the way one would normally secure a three-year-old child for a trip to visit a grandmother, or an outing in a park. Nothing else was necessary. Mikas's soft short fingers picked at the buckle, which he couldn't undo, and his lips moved in a murmur of weeping.

She undid the buckle for him, with a soft click.

Then she heard the shot.

Anne and some other woman were lying on the stone floor in the living room with their arms raised like the victims of a bank robbery. One of Jan's own toolboxes had been upended on the coffee table so that pliers, bits of wire, screwdrivers and duct tape were scattered over the glass surface. It was only then he realized, in his daze, that Anne's hands and feet had been taped to the floor so that she couldn't move from her odd position. Her face was completely expressionless. She didn't look frightened or angry, just . . . he wasn't quite sure what to call it. "Determined" seemed too weak a word. Her eyes were the color of shadows on snow.

The other woman lay in much the same way, except that one arm was in a cast. That, too, had been forced to one side and stuck down with tape at a different angle. She looked a bit like Aleksander, he thought. And then a pounding shock went through his diaphragm as he realized who she must be. He had no idea how or why, but it had to be his son's biological mother who was lying there.

He felt a trickle of blood from one nostril on his upper lip and wiped it away reflexively. He had to get a grip. He had to get control of this situation, not just let himself be dominated. He turned to the Lithuanian.

"This isn't necessary," he said, slowly and carefully in English, wanting to make sure the man understood. "What is it you want?"

"What you owe me," said the man.

"Okay. But what about your end of the deal?"

The man stood still for a moment. Then he

jerked his gun hand in the direction of the door. "That way," he said.

The other woman, Aleksander's Lithuanian mother, started to shout something incomprehensible. The man snarled at her, and she fell abruptly silent.

For a moment, Jan hesitated. But getting the man out of the room Anne was in had to be a good idea. If only he would also let go of Aleksander. He could see Aleksander was scared to the point of panic. His eyes looked huge in his pale, thin face, and there were tear tracks on his cheeks. Jan attempted a smile, but knew it came out wooden.

"It's okay, Sander," he said. "The man will leave in a minute."

"Shut up," said the Lithuanian. "Speak English. I don't want you to say things I don't understand."

"I just told the boy not to be frightened."

"Don't do it again."

"Okay. Okay." Don't anger him. Or . . . don't anger him *more*. The man's suppressed fury was vivid in every move he made.

They went into the hallway and down the stairs to the back door, which the man made Aleksander open. With his gun hand, he flipped the switch and turned on the light in the garage. There was an unfamiliar car in there, some kind of van. And inside, on the front seat, a child.

It was him—the boy from the photograph. Jan recognized him immediately. But what was he doing here? It wasn't the child Jan had paid for. Just one of his kidneys.

"What is he doing here?" he asked the Lithuanian. And at that moment the truth began to dawn on him, like a series of flashes at the back of his mind. The Lithuanian had never meant to deliver a neat little transplantable organ. How could he? He didn't have access to the doctors or the technology for an operation like that. The suitcase Karin was supposed to pick up at the railway station . . . it had never contained an organ box. It had contained a living child.

Karin.

No wonder she had freaked.

A rush of pain went through him, and a bizarre image invaded his mind. It was as if he had ordered a steak at a restaurant and had been presented with a cow and a meat cleaver instead.

"Not like that," he said to the Lithuanian, hoarsely. "You didn't say it was a living child."

"Perfect match," said the Lithuanian. "Same father, same mother. Now you pay."

"Of course," said Jan, somehow managing to keep any sign of tremor from his voice. "Let's go upstairs again. You'll get your money."

The Lithuanian switched off the light. The child hadn't moved at all, and Jan felt a stab of pity for the poor kid.

• • •

"Dollars," said the man. "Not . . . that." He pointed the gun at Jan's laptop.

"But I can transfer the money to an account only you have access to," tried Jan, but he could see that it was useless. Glowing numbers on a computer display wasn't *money* in the Lithuanian's world. "I don't have that much cash lying around!"

The man came closer, still with Aleksander in his grip. Casually, as though Aleksander were a toy he had almost forgotten about.

"You said you had the money ready."

"And so I did. But Karin took it."

"Karin?"

"The one you—" he stopped himself short of saying "killed." It might not be a good idea to bring that up now. "The one at the cottage. She had it. It's not my fault that you couldn't find it."

Out of the corner of his mind, he saw Anne stir. Don't move, he thought, as if he could reach her telepathically. Don't make him see you, don't make him notice you right now.

The other woman said something in Lithuanian. She wriggled, trying to get free, he supposed. The man snapped something at her, and she stopped struggling. She too had been crying, he could see.

"She didn't know where it was," said the Lithuanian, facing Jan once more. "She would have said." He raised the gun and pointed it at

Aleksander's head. "Last chance. Don't fuck with me."

Jan opened his mouth, but no words came, no sound. Aleksander may die because this idiot doesn't understand about money transfers, he thought, feeling his world shift beneath him. He crouched a little lower and considered a flying tackle; go for the gun, make him let go of Aleksander, something, anything, anything except this suffocating feeling of helplessness.

"I know where the money is," said Anne suddenly, in crystal clear and perfect English.

The Lithuanian looked at her rather than Jan now. Possibly considering whether Anne might be telling the truth.

Dammit, Anne, thought Jan. Can't you see that this is not the kind of man you can bluff?

"It's not true," he said quickly. "She doesn't know anything about any of this."

But the man had taken a box cutter from the tool box wreckage. He cut the duct tape so that Anne could sit up. Blood was trickling down one wrist from an accidental cut, but she didn't even seem to notice it.

"Show me," said the giant.

Anne nodded. "I'll get it," she said. "It won't take a minute."

A few moments later she was back with two heavy yellow manila envelopes. Jan looked on in disbelief as she upended them and let thick green bundles of thousand-dollar notes tumble out onto the floor.

Anne had taken the money. Not Karin. The discovery made the blood pound in his ears.

"Anne . . . what . . . why?"

The Lithuanian was staring down at the money, and for the moment, at least, didn't seem to care that they were speaking Danish.

"It's now been two years since I decided to leave you," said Anne. "Do you know why I couldn't go? Because of that bloody kidney machine in the basement. But when I saw that case on Karin's bed with all that *money* inside, things just fell into place. I had no idea what you needed so much cash for, but I had the feeling you wouldn't call the police if it disappeared. *I* could take it. And then I would be able to look after Aleksander without your help."

"But. . . ."

"And you still don't get it, do you? Right now you're wondering if it is because of your pathetic little affair with Karin. Oh yes, I know. But that's not why. Don't you realize? You nearly killed Aleksander. *You* had to give him the kidney he needed. *You* would take care of everything. Because God forbid anyone should know. You nearly killed Aleksander *because you didn't want my father to know that you couldn't give me a child.* This marriage was always more about my family than about me, wasn't it? My father was the one you really wanted. Well, fine. You can have him. But I'm getting out."

Jan heard the words, but they didn't really register. He saw the Lithuanian let go of Aleksander. The boy gave a sob and ran to Anne, who put her arms around him without noticing that the blood from her wrist smeared his fair hair.

"Pick it up," ordered the Lithuanian. "Put it back into the envelopes."

It took a moment before Jan realized that the order was meant for him. His whole body felt alien to him, as if everything was dissolving, inside and out. He took a step forward, not toward the money but toward Anne. He saw the man raise the gun, but it had ceased to matter. Even when he saw the flash from the barrel and felt the impact to his chest, it still didn't really matter.

The Dane fell heavily, across the money. Jučas turned and raised the gun again, this time to aim at the wife. But she was gone. He could hear her running footsteps somewhere, in the hall perhaps. And, of course, she had taken her son with her.

He glanced down at the man to decide whether he should shoot him a second time, but he looked like a goner, and right now it was more important to get the wife and the kid before they succeeded in calling for help. Shooting the boy would be no fun at all, but he knew it was necessary now. He had to do some house cleaning here, make sure there was no one left who could identify him. The little one he could take with him, seeing that Barbara was so keen on it, but the older boy had to go. He had eyes in his head, he would be able to remember and tell others what he had seen. Jučas didn't want to wake up one morning in Krakow to find the police pounding on his door.

Four or five quick strides brought him to the door. The hallway was empty, the front door still closed and locked. Where had they gone? He opened another door and found a huge kitchen with shiny white cupboards and black marble worktops. But no woman and child. He withdrew to the hall again and wondered whether they had fled down the stairs to the garage. A good thing he had sabotaged the gate; they wouldn't be able to get out in a hurry.

Then he heard a soft bump overhead. Excellent. Now he knew where to look. He headed up the stairs to the second floor.

The first room was a bedroom, probably the parents'. He switched on the light and looked under the bed. Checked the bathroom. Nothing. He continued along the landing to a sort of feminine office, with a blonde-wood desk and a small chintzy sofa by the window. Also empty.

In quick succession, he opened two more doors. A bathroom and a boy's bedroom. He had to spend precious time opening wardrobes and knocking over a playhouse shaped like a medieval castle, but still no sign of the woman or the boy. Then he attempted to open the second to last door along the landing.

It was locked.

He raised the Glock and aimed at the lock. The shot rang in his ears but did less damage to the door than he had expected. Despite his temporary deafness he heard a muted cry, but it sounded as if it came from above. Possibly he was shooting at the door to the attic stairs? He fired one more round, and this time the door began to give way when he put his shoulder against the woodwork. One more shot ought to do it.

At that moment, something hit him from behind. Something heavy, sharp-edged and hard. It drew a line of fire across the back of his neck and made him stagger briefly. He was turning as the second blow came, but he was off-balance, and he didn't even have time to raise his hands. The one shot he did get off went wild, smashing into the banister. Then the bloody toolbox hit him directly in the face.

He was lying on his back staring up at the little one's mother. Her eyes looked completely wild, and a strip of duct tape still dangled from her plaster cast. She could only hold the toolbox with one hand, but she swung it as though it were a handbag.

This time it smashed into his right arm, and he lost all feeling in his fingers and couldn't even feel the gun anymore. The crazy bitch dropped the toolbox and went for the Glock.

She'll bloody kill me, he thought. If she gets hold of it, she'll kill me.

He grabbed a handful of light brown hair with his left hand and pulled her all the way down to the floor. She wasn't screaming, but she fought like a woman possessed. She kneed him in the chest, and he still couldn't use his right hand. Then he felt something punch him in the leg, but it wasn't till the bang registered that he realized that she had shot him. He had no idea how bad it was. He only knew that if he didn't finish her *right now,* anything could happen. He rolled over so that his full weight held her pinned to the floor, and with his left hand—unfortunately more clumsy than his right—reached for her head in order to pull it sharply back and to one side, a swift jerk so that the neck would snap.

He didn't understand why it didn't work. He only felt another punch, this time on the side of the neck. From the wet heat he understood that he was bleeding. And from the manic racing of his heart, he understood that it was a lot. Strange. It felt almost like the throbbing pump he loved to feel in his body when he was training.

But the throbbing grew fainter. More distant. As though he was moving away from himself. Suddenly he saw the dream family quite clearly. The mother, the father, the two children. They were sitting around the dinner table, laughing. He wanted to call out to them, shout at them, but they couldn't hear him. He was outside, and he could not get in.

Even before Nina pushed open the door to the hall, she knew the house was enormous. The stairs winding up through the stairwell would not have been out of place at some corporate domicile built to impress, and yet there were enough domestic details to suggest that this was actually a private home—a collection of outdoor boots, neatly lined up on a rack, winter coats and scarves on pegs in the wide space under the stairs, two footballs in a net.

Everything else was white, including the staircase itself, and Nina stood for a moment, trying to adjust to the glare of a multitude of halogen spotlights.

There was a strange silence, as if the house had swallowed everything living and was now busy digesting. She sensed movement, but the sounds that did reach her were muffled and diffuse. Running footsteps, a door being opened and closed, the muted clicking of heels or toes against floorboards. But there had been a shot. Straining to hear, Nina felt adrenalin invading every single tired cell in her body.

Nothing.

Or, no . . . something. Something closer than the footsteps she had heard. She went up the stairs as quietly as she could, and listened again. A liquid moan reached her through a set of double doors leading off the hallway. She recognized the sound of human pain and felt automatic emergency reflexes kick in, forcing her own pounding headache into the background. Someone was injured. She needed to know whether there was one or more, how critical the injuries were, the priority of treatment.

She checked her watch.

It was 9:37 p.m., later than she would have guessed.

She pushed open the door and entered an enormous living room.

A man and a woman lay on the floor. The woman was immobilized by wide strips of duct tape, but apart from an arm in a cast, which obviously had already been treated and was therefore irrelevant right now, she appeared to be uninjured. Frantic, but unharmed. Nina ignored her and focused on the man instead. He lay partly on his side, limbs outflung, like a fallen skater. Around him, a bizarre number of dollar bills lay scattered across the stone floor. Blood from the sternum area had soaked through his white shirt and run down to mix with the big wet stains of sweat under his arms.

ABC, she thought. Airway, Breathing, Circulation. She knelt next to him, tilting back his head a little to check his mouth. No blood, which was encouraging, and no obstructions. He blinked and gazed at her with eyes that might be unfocused and shocky, but still seemed reasonably present.

"What happened?" she asked, not only because she wanted to know but also to establish contact and to find out whether he could answer.

He didn't even attempt to reply, just closed his eyes again, but it seemed more dispirited than actually comatose. He wasn't unconscious, in her estimation; his breathing was fast and pain-afflicted, but unhindered, and his hands reasonably warm. There seemed to be no catastrophic hemorrhage going on, inside or out. She pulled the bloodied shirt to one side. He had been shot high in the chest, above the heart. The entrance wound was not enormous, but she could see no exit wound, which suggested that the projectile was still somewhere in his body, possibly lodged against the scapula. That, too, was to his advantage right now. Exit wounds were messy.

Cautiously, she pushed back the lips of the wound. She could see splinters of bone in among the bleeding tissue. The man's collarbone had been shattered. The sharp fragments worked like shrapnel inside his shoulder, increasing both the bleeding and the pain, but the shot must have missed all major arteries, and he was not lethally wounded. He was beginning to rock back and forth, probably in an effort to escape what was no doubt a significant level of pain.

"Hold still," she said. "Moving makes it worse."

He heard her. He stopped rocking, even though his eyes stayed firmly closed.

Nina glanced around for anything that might be used as an emergency compress, but this was not the kind of home that had tablecloths and cozy plaids and decorative cushions on the couch. In the end, she took off her own shirt and used it for a makeshift bandage; there was nothing she could cover him with to alleviate the effects of the shock, and the only thing she could use to pillow his head were the blood-spattered dollar bundles.

She had done what could be done for him. She turned her attention on the woman.

She was struggling feverishly against her bonds. Her smooth brown hair stuck damply to her fore-head, and she had obviously been crying. There was something familiar about her, but Nina couldn't quite pinpoint what.

Nina had pushed the cries of the younger

woman from her consciousness while tending to the injured man, and this might have given her the impression that Nina didn't care and wouldn't help her. At any rate, she had stopped shouting. But now her eyes glittered wetly, and she spoke, in slow careful English.

"Please. Help me."

Nina spotted a box cutter in the jumble of tools, wires, and whatnots scattered on the coffee table from an upturned toolbox. She used it to cut the tape that held the woman down. The minute she was free, the woman catapulted off the floor and exploded into motion with a speed that seemed out of sync with her short, square, unathletic figure. She seized the toolbox with her good hand and ran out of the room.

At that moment, shots rang out from above. Two shots, close together.

Nina suffered a brief moment of doubt. She glanced at the injured man. She wasn't sure how stable his condition was, but there was little else she could do for him now. She wiped both hands across her face. They were trembling, she noted, little sharp jitters she couldn't control. She checked her watch again to steady herself, and at that moment her subconscious finally came up with the answer, and she knew who the woman must be.

It was 9:39 p.m. Nina gave the injured man one last look, then she got up and followed Mikas's mother.

Sigita couldn't get clear. The man lay across her, pinning her to the floor, and one hand had closed around a handful of her hair. He was heavy. In a brief flash it reminded her bizarrely of sex with Darius, but this would not end in laughter and release. The gun had slipped from her hand, and she had no idea where it was. The massive body on top of her made it harder and harder to breathe. She knew people died in this way in nightclubs and football stands, but could one be crushed to death by the weight of a single person? It felt like it.

Where was the panicked strength that had driven her a moment ago? She had swung that tool-box at his head as if she meant to knock it clear off his neck. He had taken Mikas. And even though she had pleaded and begged, lying on the stone floor of that absurd ballroom of a living room, he had not told her where her child was. Not even when he took the Dane and returned so quickly that she understood Mikas must be nearby. He had just snarled at her that if she wanted the kid to survive, she had better shut up, and she had dared ask no more questions after that.

Now her head filled with the nightmare visions she had tried to keep at bay these last long days. What if Mikas had been hidden away in a box somewhere, or in the trunk of a car, every breath he took? Or worse. She saw his tiny body in the cargo hold of a refrigerated van, cold and blue and gutted like an animal. Who said he was even still alive? How could she trust anything the man had said? They only needed his kidney, they didn't care about the rest—his dark blue eyes, his bubbly laugh, the eagerness in his face when the words came tumbling out so quick and jumbled even she could not make heads or tails of them.

The man didn't move. Was he dying? She began to struggle again, even though she barely had breath left in her heaving lungs.

Then, suddenly, someone was helping her, rolling the heavy form to one side, so that she could sit up. She gasped and drew blessed air in long, shivery sobs, watching while the skinny short-haired woman who had cut her loose knelt beside the big man's trembling body. She had no shirt on, only a white bra, and it looked as if someone had sprayed her with red paint. No, not paint. Blood. There was blood on the wall, too, a long red arc like graffiti painted with a spray can. The woman was pressing her hands against the man's neck, but Sigita could see how the blood spurted between her fingers. One side of the man's neck had been torn open, and she slowly realized that this was something she had done. She had fired the gun blindly and felt it kick twice in her hand, but she had had no idea if she had hit him, or where. It seemed she had. In the leg, and in the neck. If he died now, she would have killed him.

"Mikas?" she asked, with what little breath she had.

"He is okay," said the dark-haired woman without looking up, and Sigita had no breath to ask what do you mean, okay, where is he, is he hurt, is he scared?

The battered door eased open a fraction, and Anne Marquart poked her head out. It looked almost comical.

"Was anyone else hit?" asked the dark-haired woman sharply.

"No," said Mrs. Marquart, staring at all the blood, and at the massive body on the floor. "We're . . . we're okay."

The dark-haired woman bent even further over the man who had taken Mikas, and said something Sigita didn't hear. He didn't answer. After a while, a sound did come from him, but it was just a sort of hissing sigh. The blood was no longer spurting quite so forcefully. Sigita got up slowly. She realized that she was smeared with blood, too, covered with it, in fact, in her hair, on her neck, down the front of her shirt. *His* blood. It made her skin crawl. Somehow, it was worse than if it had been her own. She felt dirtier. She could hear Anne Marquart saying something in Danish, possibly to Aleksander, who was still somewhere on the other side of that shot-to-pieces door and, Sigita hoped, couldn't see any of this.

"Is there anything we can do?" asked Sigita belatedly. The woman didn't answer right away, just crouched there with both hands pressed against the man's neck. Sigita could count every vertebrae in her curved spine, could see the effort that made the skinny, bare shoulders tremble.

Then the straining shoulders slumped, and the woman straightened.

"He is dead," she said.

Sigita stared at the big, heavy body.

"I shot him," she whispered. She wasn't quite sure how that made her feel. She suddenly remembered what she had promised herself if they harmed Mikas. *If you hurt my boy, I will kill you.* Does an act have to be conceived in the mind before it can happen? And once one had thought of it, did that bring it closer to reality? She had thought it. And now, she had done it. The calm she had felt then seemed very distant now.

"I think you are wrong," said Anne Marquart quietly, bending to pick up the gun. "I think I was the one who shot him."

Sigita stared at her in confusion. What did she mean by that?

Anne looked utterly calm. She raised the gun carefully.

"Watch out," she said. And fired a deliberate shot into the doorframe.

"It might be better that way," said the dark-haired woman thoughtfully. "The police will have no trouble believing *her* statement."

Finally Sigita understood. She was a stranger here, a foreigner without credibility, money, or connections. She remembered how hard it had been to make Gužas believe her at first, and they at least spoke the same language.

"I had to do it," said Anne, nodding at the big motionless body. "It was self-defense."

Sigita swallowed. Then she nodded.

"Of course," she said. "You had to defend your child."

Something happened when they looked at each other. A silent agreement. Not a trade-off, more a sort of covenant.

"Not Mikas," said Sigita. "But me. He can have mine. If it's a good enough match."

"You had better leave now," said Anne. "But I hope you'll come back. Soon."

"I will," said Sigita.

Suddenly, the dark-haired woman smiled, a brief intense smile that made her dark eyes come alive and banished all the jagged seriousness.

"He is downstairs in the garage," she said. "In the gray van."

Mikas was standing in the doorway with the darkened garage behind him. He was holding on to the doorframe with one hand, as if he had only just learned to walk. When he caught sight of her, an expression slid across his face that was neither happiness nor fear, but a mixture of both. She couldn't lift him, the stupid cast was in the way. But she squatted down beside him and pulled him into her embrace with her good arm. His little body was warm, and smelled of fear and pee, but he clung to her like a baby monkey and hid his face against her neck.

"Oh, my baby," she murmured. "Mama's little baby."

She knew there might be bad dreams and difficult times. But as she crouched here, feeling the warmth of Mikas's breath against her skin, she felt that something—life, fate, maybe even God— had at last forgiven her for what she had done.

There wasn't much time, thought Nina. In a little while, it would all begin—police, ambulances, paramedics, all the things that followed in the wake of death and disaster. They had exactly the time it would take for the first cars to reach them from Kalundborg.

Anne Marquart had made the emergency call, from her son's mobile. She had lent her own dark-blue station-wagon to Mikas and Mikas's mother. It would be better if they simply weren't here when the authorities arrived, she had said. Jan Marquart was still lying on the living room floor, but now as comfortable as she could make him, with pillows, blankets and proper bandaging.

Anne Marquart might look as if a rough wind could snap her in half, but there was an unexpected strength beneath the pastel-colored fragility. That she had a dead body in a pool of blood on her upper landing seemed not to shake her, and she stuck to her decision to claim responsibility for his death with no apparent effort. She and Nina had covered the body with a bedspread, mostly out of consideration for Anne's son Aleksander, and Anne had politely offered Nina the loan of a cream-colored shirt to replace the one that had served as emergency bandaging for her husband's gunshot wound. The label said Armani, Nina noticed with a pang of guilt as she stuck her haphazardly washed arms into its expensive sleeves.

Anne took her out of the house, around the corner, to a separate entrance at the back.

"This is it," said Anne, tapping a code into the digital lock. "Up the stairs. Just go in. I'll keep an eye on Jan until the ambulance gets here."

Nina merely nodded. The door to Karin's flat had been sealed with yellow POLICE tape, but Nina opened it anyway, ducking beneath the seal. The light in the small hallway came on automatically as she entered—there had to be a photo sensor somewhere. She located the switch and turned on the light in the living room as well.

This was Karin's home. Her coats and shoes in the hallway, her perfume still in the air. Her specific blend of chaos and tidyness. Piles of papers and books were allowed to grow abundantly, because Karin did not consider such things mess. But Nina knew that if she checked the laundry basket in the bedroom, she would find even the dirty clothes neatly folded.

She recognized Karin's old rocker, an heirloom that had followed her since their dormitory days. But apart from that, it was clear that styles had changed as her bank balance swelled. Conran and Eames rather than Ikea. A genuine Italian espresso maker in the open kitchenette. Original modern art on the walls.

On Karin's desk was a compact little printer, but no laptop. Presumably, the police had taken it away, along with some of the piled papers—you could tell, somehow, that there were gaps in the arrangement, and one drawer had been left slightly ajar.

Nina dropped into the rocking chair. She hadn't come to pry. She was here to say goodbye, as best she could.

Karin's fear. That was what kept coming back to her. It had been obvious that Karin had been terrified during the last hours of her life, even before the Lithuanian found her. Had it been Jan Marquart who scared her? He hadn't seemed particularly terrifying to Nina, but then, that might be because she hadn't met him before a nine-millimeter projectile had made a mess of his shoulder and left him shocked and bleeding on his own living room floor.

Karin knew him better. Well enough for her to be shit scared of going against his orders. And it had even been she who had taken the dollar bundles still lying on the stone floor next to Jan Marquart. What had Karin imagined Jan would do? Why had she fled this lovely flat so precipitously, to hide out in an isolated summer cottage?

She was afraid of people who put little children into suitcases, thought Nina suddenly, and of the people who pay them to do it. She thought I might be able to save Mikas. And I suppose I did. But there was no one around to save Karin.

She heard distant sirens now. Time was running out. She got up to turn off the lights and leave, but as she reached for the switch, she noticed the various postcards, Post-its, and photographs that Karin had stuck to her refrigerator door.

There was an entire Nina-section, she realized. Top left was a picture of her and Karin, an ancient one taken at a concert at the Student Union Hall way back in a former century when they had been at nursing school together. Karin's hair looked huge, teased into a festive post-eighties pile on top of her head; her eye-liner would have done Cleopatra proud, and her earrings almost reached her shoulders. Her eyes were laughing at the camera, with familiar sparkling warmth. Nina, of course, wore black, but for once she had been able to muster a smile for the photographer, albeit somewhat less exuberant.

She has kept this for seventeen years, thought Nina. I wonder how many fridge doors it has been stuck to?

Below it was Nina's wedding picture, somewhat hastily taken in front of the sow-and-piglets sculpture by the Registry Office. Nina had forgotten who had had that particular flash of artistic inspiration, but both she and Morten looked ridiculously young, eyeing each other with an earnest intensity that almost looked like somber premonition. Nina's dress could not quite disguise the four-months bulge that was Ida.

Still further down came the baby pictures of Ida and Anton. She and Morten had sent them out like picture postcards of holiday attractions, post-partum snapshots of rather purplish-looking wrinkled little creatures, supplemented by tiny black fingerprints.

My life is hanging here, thought Nina, and has been stuck to this door year after year, alongside pictures of nephews and nieces, dental appointments and holiday postcards. Here, where she might look at it every day if she wanted to.

A hodgepodge of feelings assaulted her, a sticky dark mixture of loss, grief, self-hatred, and guilt. It would take time to sort it out, more time than she had at the moment. She switched off the lights. Closed the door and heard the electronic lock click. As the sirens came closer, she plopped herself down on the front steps to wait. She really ought to go check on Jan Marquart, but right now she couldn't contemplate looking at him. It wasn't his hands that had beaten Karin to death, but he had paid the man who had done it. Karin's fears had been well-founded.

Her head hurt like hell, and she knew she probably should be hospitalized, but she just wanted to go home. At long last, and if at all possible. She had washed her arms and hands as best she could, short of soaking them in a tub for hours, but despite her scrubbing, she could still feel the Lithuanian's blood as a stickiness between her fingers and under her nails.

She hadn't been scared. Or not of him, at any rate.

He had been lying in a pool of blood that grew bigger and bigger around his head. He hadn't moved of his own volition, but faint spasms went through the big body, as though he were cold, and seeing him like that made it hard to feel anything except pity. That was how he looked—pitiful.

When she rolled him away from the woman,

376

she had seen at once how the blood spurted in rhythmic jets. In that second, she knew he was dying. Yet she still instinctively knelt next to him, sticking two fingers into the messy neck wound. She had been able to feel the rubbery toughness of the torn artery, but although she tried to clamp it, blood still bubbled and spurted around her fingers, in a hot and uncontrollable flow.

The man had looked at her with a gaze already distant and milky. As if someone had drawn a curtain. She knew that look. She had seen it before. Of course she had. Nurses saw people die.

Yet this was different.

The smell of hot blood and the sticky, scarlet flow of it down her arms dizzied her.

(Don't let go of time, Nina. Stay awake. Don't forget time again.)

She'd shaken her head irritably and tried to catch the man's gaze once more. There was something she needed to know.

"Did you kill her?"

The man blinked, and his breath sounded wet and soggy. Perhaps the trachea had also been damaged? He wasn't looking at her, but she couldn't tell whether he had heard her or not.

"Karin. The woman in the summerhouse. Did you kill her?"

His lips parted, but it could be anything from a snarl of pain to an attempt at speech. His eyes were glazed, like dark dry rocks on a beach. He

377

hadn't answered her. And yet she felt completely certain.

I could let him die now, she thought, looking down at her own hands. I could just let go and stop trying. He killed Karin, and he does not deserve any better.

But she didn't.

Instead, she slid her fingers further into the wound. Perhaps, if she got a better grip, if she squeezed harder . . . she was using both hands now, but blood still gushed up her forearms. And when it finally did ease off, it was not because she had succeeded in stemming it. It was because there was nothing left to pump.

The sternum heaved towards her, then fell in a sudden collapse of breath. She stayed as she was for a while, fingers still uselessly clutching, and an ache of ancient grief in her chest.

She would not have been able to save him no matter what she had done, she thought, and as the knowledge hit her, it eased a deeper and older pain inside her.

(He would have died no matter what she had done.)

Nina asked the policewoman who had driven her home to leave her by the front door. She was sore and tired and hurt, and being polite to a stranger in her home was entirely beyond her. Pretty much everything was beyond her right now.

She knew Morten was waiting. The policewoman had told her as much. He had been notified right away and was reportedly "very happy and thrilled to have her back safe and sound."

Nina grimaced at the phrase as she took the first step up the stairs. No doubt Morten was relieved, but "thrilled to have her back" might be overstating it, and "happy" was not really a word that applied to their relationship right now. In fact, he looked anything but happy, confirming her worst fears.

He must have seen her arrive through the window, because he was waiting in the open doorway, arms crossed. Nina slowed her progress involuntarily.

"So there you are."

His voice was toneless and barely more than a whisper.

Not angry, not miserable. Something else she couldn't identify, and the look he gave her made her duck as if he had thrown something at her. She girded her tired loins and continued up the last few steps to the landing.

She was so close that they were nearly touching, and she had to fight back an impulse to put her face against his neck in the little hollow place by his collarbone.

"May I come in?"

She tried to make her voice sound casual and self-assured, but her throat was closing into the tight and tender knot that usually led to tears. She fought them. She didn't want to cry now; she needed to be the one to comfort him. She raised her head to catch his eyes, and in his gaze she saw something huge and dark come unstuck. His chest heaved in a single sob, then he grabbed the back of her head with both hands and drew her close.

Helplessness.

That was what she heard in his voice, and had seen in his eyes. The total and abject feeling of powerlessness that she knew seized him when something took her away from him.

"Don't," he said, holding her so tightly that it hurt, "don't *ever* do this again."

September

There was flour all over the kitchen. Flour on the kitchen table, flour on the floor, greasy doughy flour on one tap, and even a few floury footprints in the hallway.

"What are you *doing?*" asked Morten, putting down his laptop bag.

"Making pasta!" said Anton enthusiastically, holding aloft a yellow-white floury strip of dough.

God help us, he thought. Nina must be having one of her irregular attacks of domesticity. And it was typical of her that she couldn't just buy a package of cake mix and have done with it. He still shuddered to recall the side of organic beef that had appeared in the kitchen one day. The flat had looked like a slaughterhouse for the better part of twenty-four hours while Nina carved, filleted, chopped, packaged, and froze unsightly bits of bullock—or attempted to, because in the end they had to persuade his sister to take most of it. She lived in Greve and had an extra freezer in the shed.

Now here she was, hectic spots in her cheeks,

running ravioli through a pasta machine he had no idea they possessed.

"Good job," he said absently to Anton.

"Hey you," said Nina. "What did they say?"

"Esben does it this time. But I've promised to take his next shift. I have to leave on the twenty-third."

Normally, his job required him to do a two-week stint on the rigs in the North Sea every six weeks, but this time he hadn't wanted to go. What he really wanted was for all of them to go on holiday. He had already managed to swap his way to a week's leave from the mud-logging. But Nina refused.

"What I need is a big dose of normal everyday life," she had said.

He had finally managed to drag her to the clinic so that Magnus could look at her. Magnus had stitched up the cut above her hairline, probed her battered skull with his fingers, and sent her on to the National for further check-ups.

"At the very least, you are concussed," he had said, shining his penlight into her eyes. "And you know as well as I do that we have to make sure it's nothing worse. What the hell were you thinking?" He looked at Morten. "If something like this ever happens again, don't let her fall asleep. People can slip right into a life-threatening coma without anyone noticing."

Dry-mouthed, Morten had nodded. Even

though the doctors at the National later pronounced her skull uncracked, Magnus's words stuck in him, and it was more than a week before he could sleep normally beside her. It felt like the times he had needed to look in on the children when they were tiny, just to make sure they were still breathing.

Less than two weeks later, she was back on the job. And he had a strong feeling that Operation Ravioli had a lot to do with her need to prove that she was on top of it all. Could manage the job *and* her family, could be a Good Mother, could do it all and be *here* again.

He wanted to tell her that it wasn't necessary. That it was okay if she was feeling irritable and tired, that it was okay to resort to easy fixes. If she had anything to prove, it certainly wasn't as a pasta chef.

He had been looking at her for too long. Caught, as he often was, by the sheer vitality and intensity of her eyes. He had once found a chunk of dolorite that reminded him so much of the storm-gray color of her eyes that he had dragged it all the way back from Greenland in his pocket.

"Is anything wrong?" she asked.

"No."

She held his face between her wrists so as not to get flour on his office shirt and gave him a kiss.

"We're making three kinds of ravioli," she said.

"One with spinach and ricotta, one with prosciutto and Emmentaler, and one with scampi and truffle. Doesn't it sound delicious?"

"Yes," he said.

Morten had stayed up long after she had fallen asleep, and Nina woke to find him kneeling on the bed next to her. She reached for him, and drew him down. He let himself fall. Kissed her deeply and with a certain ferocity, pressing his fingers into her mouth, then down the curve of her neck, over her breasts, her arms, and wrists. His fingers meshed with hers, and he let the full weight of his body push her into the mattress.

His eyes were nearly invisible in the darkness. Nina saw only a vague glitter of reflected light, and she sensed something, some sort of melancholy grief, settle between them. Or perhaps it had been there the entire time, and she hadn't noticed.

She turned her head to look at the digital display of the clock radio.

"No." Morten's voice was hoarsely insistent. "Not now."

He tilted the clock so that the numbers were no longer visible. Then he caught her face and turned it towards his in the darkness, drawing her leg slowly but firmly to one side.

She let go. She let herself fall into him, into the feeling, into the warm zone where time meant nothing.

She ran all the way home. She couldn't stop the panic even though she knew she was being hysterical, that he would no doubt be sitting at the kitchen table as usual, with an egg sandwich and a non-alcoholic beer in front of him and coffee brewing on the coffee machine. It was just the way it was—sometimes her father went home even though the school day wasn't over. It didn't happen often, three or four times a year at the most, and he was usually back at work the next day. Usually. But sometimes, when it was bad, two or even three weeks might pass by, and then it was "not too good." That's what her mother always said when people asked. "No, Finn isn't feeling too good at the moment." And then people didn't ask any more questions, not if they knew him.

Eggs and cress, she thought. He'll be sitting at the kitchen table, and he has just cut himself a good helping from the somewhat shapeless cress hedgehog that Martin has made in kindergarten. And he is drinking non-alcoholic beer because he has taken his medication.

She looked at her watch. Twenty past eleven. If she could see him at the table, she wouldn't even need to go in. She could just turn around and make it back to the school in time for her next class.

But he wasn't at the table. And so she had to go in.

His furry green loden coat was on its peg in the hallway. His shoes were left neatly side by side in the shoe rack, with his briefcase next to them. She eased open the door to the bedroom, thinking he might be taking a nap, but he wasn't there. Then she noticed that the door to the basement stairs had been left ajar. And she heard the sound.

She was late both for her Danish class and for Geography, and the teacher took her outside and made her explain. At first she didn't know what to tell him.

"I had to change my clothes," she finally said.

And it wasn't till much later that anyone realized why, and then of course they began to ask different questions. Why had she just gone back to the school?

The school psychologist in particular asked that question, and a whole bunch of other questions, mostly beginning with "What were you feeling when. . . ." or "What were you thinking when. . . ." Those, she couldn't answer. She couldn't remember feeling or thinking anything at all. Or doing anything. It wasn't that she didn't remember being in the basement, and she remembered everything else too: her father, and how he had been lying in the bathtub with his clothes on, and that the water had been scarlet. She remembered seeing his mouth move when he saw her, but it was like a film with the sound off, she couldn't hear what he was saying. She was looking at the red stuff on his arms. And that was when time had disappeared, she thought, but she wasn't sure how. She remembered going over to Mrs. Halvorsen next door and telling her to call an ambulance. What she couldn't understand, what simply didn't make sense, was that more than an hour had passed. That it was now suddenly half past twelve, and that she had changed her clothes. I went over there right away, she kept saying, to herself and to others. I went over there right away.

The telephone drew her from her nightmare. She fumbled for it and managed to take the call before the ring woke Morten. Or so she thought.

At first, there was only a lot of hectic breathing at the other end. She was about to hang up, when finally a thin and panicked voice came on.

"Please come."

"Who is this?"

"Natasha. Please. . . ."

Nina sat up abruptly and turned on the light. Still half asleep, Morten muttered something unintelligible. The word "Hell" could be distinguished, but other than that, she had no idea what he was saying.

"Natasha, what is it?"

For several long seconds she heard only the tear-choked wheeze of the girl's breathing.

"He touched Rina. Touched. . . ."

"Report him," snapped Nina angrily. "Or I will!"

"I think maybe he is dead," said Natasha. "Please come. I think maybe I kill him."

There was a click as the connection severed. Nina slumped in the bed, remnants of her nightmare a blood-like taste in her mouth. Morten rolled over, away from the light, and went back to sleep. He had never really been properly awake. The sheet that covered him slipped to reveal the top of his buttocks.

Call the police, she told herself. Come on. 911. You know the number. God damn it to hell. The wound in her scalp had only just healed, and she still got random headaches.

She closed her eyes for a moment. Then she let herself slide carefully from the bed, put her arms into yesterday's T-shirt, and slipped into the bathroom for a quick splash of water to her face.

She dressed as quickly as she could, and lifted the car keys from their peg by the door in the hallway. It was still the summer that wouldn't die. Outside, the September darkness hugged the city in a close and damp embrace, the night hardly cooler than the day had been.

It was 4:32 a.m., she noted.